Anacostia, Southeast Washington, D.C

Senator Kelsey Ryles had left Trinity and Joshua with a lot to think about. Ryles' had his personal driver drop them off at Joshua's studio per his request. For the past 15 minutes, Joshua and Trinity just sat staring at nothing. Joshua had poured them both double shots of Jack Daniels Single Malt when they first arrived. Finally, Joshua cleared his throat to break the trance. Raising his glass Joshua said, "Here's to saving humanity". Trinity just stared at the glass for several moments before finally saying something.

"Are you crazy Joshua? Humanity? Is that some kind of sick military humor!? Well, I am not amused."

"Trinity please", Joshua implored. "I

wasn't thinking. I'm just as lost as you are. I'm simply defaulting to what I know. If not humanity, then what should I say?"

"What are we going to do Joshua? This is all so unbelievable. How could history get everything so wrong: the lies, the manipulations? How do we move on from here? What are we even fighting for now Joshua? I thought I was revenging the death of my son. Now I find out that we are in some intergalactic war and our existence is one huge lie. Humanity has been a pawn for these aliens and there is no God. We were bred and engineered as part of an alien mutiny to promote their goals. We exist only to help this alien crew get off this fucking planet."

"Trinity, until I have more proof as

promised by Senator Kelsey Ryles, I'm going to maintain my healthy dose of cynicism. I will admit standing in the sanctuary staring at the bodies of several aliens in hibernation chambers went a long way to convince me he's telling the truth, but I still need more proof. Truthfully, I was in shock and did not think to examine the bodies in detail. With today's movie props anything is possible and I'm not trusting what I saw at this point. So far, I can accept we are fighting a global conspiracy, with a group of elitists acting on the mandates dictated by some ancient prophesy, who need to be stopped. Beyond that Trinity, I just need to get to the bottom of this nightmare. I'm a soldier that needs to understand my opponent. Until then, we are fighting in the dark and that's a recipe for failure. Knowledge is power Trinity and right now we have no knowledge. We have no choice, but to engage Ryles and prove one way or another if this alien crap is real."

Joshua poured himself another double shot of Jack Daniels and slid the bottle over to Trinity. Without waiting for Trinity, Joshua immediately chugged down his drink and sat in silence as Trinity slowly grabbed the bottle and poured herself a generous helping.

An hour later, Trinity was softly crying in Joshua's arms. The bottle of Jack Daniels now sat empty. Joshua wished he had another bottle. He was still too sober to allow his subconscious to take over and think about everything that Ryles had said. So, for now, he just focused on comforting Trinity and holding her tight.

Eventually Trinity fell asleep. Gently Joshua cradled Trinity and took her into his back office where he laid her in his twin bed. After checking to ensure the doors were locked and the alarm was set, Joshua crawled into bed next to Trinity. A twin bed didn't allow for a lot of space, so it was a fight for Joshua to fit his frame in bed with Trinity. As Joshua wrapped his arms around Trinity, she snuggled even closer into Joshua's body and moaned. A few minutes later, both were sound asleep and for the moment, all thoughts of the past 24 hours were forgotten.

* * *

Somewhere over the Atlantic Ocean

Three days had passed since Trinity and Joshua had been briefed by Ryles. They were now on Ryles' Learjet 70 private airplane heading to Heathrow Airport. Joshua had just awoken from his hour-long nap. Joshua got out of the spacious seat and stretched his legs. That's when he noticed Trinity staring at him.

"What Trinity?"

"How can you just sleep at a time like this? As soon as the plane started taxiing, you were asleep."

"Trinity, in my old line of work, you have to learn to sleep where you can. Also, the most dangerous part of any flight is takeoff and landing. One of my old team members Preach had a philosophy, if you are relaxed during a crash, you have a better chance of surviving the crash. Ironically, it was Preach, who died during in a helicopter crash during the Blackhawk down incident in Somalia. While I have never put his theory to the test, at least I get a great few hour of sleep during the flight. Come on, let's relax for the remainder of this flight so we have a clear head when we talk with Ryles and see where this shit show is going."

Six hours later, the Learjet landed at Heathrow. As the plane pulled into a private hanger, Ryles' limo pulled up as the jet taxied into the hanger. Immediately after the plane came to a stop and the stairs lowered, Trinity and Joshua got into the limo.

"Ms. Winters and Mr. Palmer welcome

to England. Senator Ryles has been expecting you. First, we must make a brief stop in Basingstoke where we will meet Senator Ryles. From there we will pick up an escort enroute to Stonehenge. It's about a 35-minute drive, so sit back and enjoy the champaign chilling in the bar.

Basingstoke, England

The limo pulled up to The Vyne. It was an elegant castle with a picturesque view of a beautiful pond outlined in a dense wood line. While typically this was a popular tourist attraction, there were no tourists visible today. Instead, there were security patrolling the grounds carrying assault rifles at the ready position. One team of guards was a K-9 unit which immediately started sniffing their vehicle, obviously looking for explosives. Joshua was impressed with the security so far. Typically, security teams utilize mirrors to search for explosives hidden under vehicles. While effective in its day, this method no longer provided the same level of screening as a K-9. Advances in explosive technology, allowing for smaller more powerful explosives and the ability to camouflage bombs to look like car parts, practically made mirror screening obsolete.

After security gave the "all clear", Kelsey made his way out to the limo to meet Trinity and Joshua. "Welcome to England. I hope your flight was enjoyable. Is there anything you would like before we get started?" Trinity responded, "I don't know about Joshua, but I would like to get this started as soon as possible."

"Truthful Senator, I'm struggling right now. While the several aliens in the hibernation chambers were impressive and real looking, I have seen some pretty crazy things coming out of Hollywood, so

I'm giving you one chance to prove your extraterrestrial stories are not the delusions of an insane senator or I will wrap my fingers around your neck and snap it before your impressive array of bodyguards can save you. And yes, I am willing to trade my life for yours. At least, I will die knowing I have killed the so-called architecture behind the mass genocides you stated you have committed in the name of saving our species. Is that understood Senator?"

Kelsey starred at Joshua and Trinity a momentum before finally nodding his head. "I promise you before this day is finished, you will have all the evidence necessary to make an informed decision. Now if you're finished threatening me, can we get into the SUV and get started?"

Without waiting for a response, Kelsey turned and headed for the black armored SUV parked in front of the castle. Trinity and Joshua followed without question.

The drive to Stonehenge took about 47 minutes via A303. The drive was uneventful, and Trinity took the time to think about how she got here as the countryside rolled by. How the death of her son Robby, could lead to a global, now extraterrestrial conspiracy was almost overwhelming to the point she had to fight to keep her mind from shutting down. Killing Daniels might have brought the death of her son to closure under normal circumstances, but now. It just didn't seem like anything would ever be right again. In the face of all the millions that had died over the centuries in this alien mutiny, her son's death almost became a non-event. Like it did not matter in the grand scheme of things. While Kelsey might not view her son's death as significant, she would never forget him. She vowed to herself, as she stared out the window, that the Committee would pay each one of them.

As the driver pulled up, Joshua noticed a virtual army swarming the hillside around Stonehenge. Several other armored SUVs had already parked. Kelsey, Trinity and Joshua were the last group to arrive at Stonehenge. There was a total of nine individuals assembled in the center of Stonehenge. Joshua noted there was an impressive set of guards arrayed around Stonehenge. There were guards standing near each SUV prepared for a quick exit if necessary. In addition to the stationary guards, there were four Stryker vehicles with mounted M2 .50 caliber machine guns supplemented by M60 Coax machine guns. It also appeared that each Stryker had a full complement of dismounted soldiers deployed to support their respective Stryker vehicle.

Once the trio joined the others Kelsey made quick introductions. Once the introductions were completed Kelsey began, "Trinity and Joshua, I'm sure you are wondering why we are here at Stonehenge. You asked for proof to determine if we are worthy of your support. I know you think we are monsters and truthfully from your perspective, I cannot blame you. We have been fighting this civil war amongst my crew for so long, we've closed ourselves off to the fact there might be another way to win. Your actions over the past few months have proven your race has significantly advanced enough to help us in our intergalactic fight that expands eons and countless galaxies. Our war over the millennium has created an unexpected side-effect, a hybrid race. A true hybrid Sanarian race that is more powerful than our pure race. We are your creators. If we had allowed the other crew members to have their way initially, your evolution as a species would not have happened. Without us taking the DNA Matrix Sequencer, you literally would only have been bred as a slave race. Instead, the others in our crew experimented with our combined DNA and it had unexpected side-effects. So again, why are we here at Stonehenge? The crew that is loyal to me, over the millennium designated certain locations that seemed resistant to change. These locations were then programmed into our teleportation system at our headquarters located in the heart of Mount Everest. We built our command center in the most geographically secure areas in the world. In addition, it is in one of the most remote, harsh environments on the planet. Once the command center was built, we sealed the entrance to protect it from all except us. It wasn't until World War II that we realized how important it was for us to make our Headquarters truly inaccessible. Each team member has a device that transmits a signal to the crew member on duty. Once received, the crew member on duty will then transmit one or all of us to the command center. Stonehenge is one of two original sites that remains. Interestingly enough, Stonehenge started off as one stone, we moved into place as a location marker in 3100 BC. Over the years the locals increased that number to 75. Easter Island is the other remaining location. Once again what started out as one marker, which is now called a moai, has now grown to 900 monumental statues."

"The other sites are now located in the middle of thriving metropolitan areas. Our team had no way of knowing earth's population would eventually grow to 7 billion people."

"Now if you are ready, I will transmit the signal and have us transported or to borrow a line from Star Trek, "Beam me up Scottie." With a nod of their heads Kelsey activated a device that resembled a watch on his wrist. A few seconds later, the air around the 12 individuals began to vibrate then hum. The air finally begins to shimmer and sparkle. Trinity stared in wonder at the dazzling effects then her vision turned white. When her vision finally returned, she realized she was no longer standing in the middle of Stonehenge. One moment she was there then the next she was standing in a sealed room. An instant later, she was on her knees throwing up the contents of her lunch and simultaneously losing control of her bowels. When she managed to turn her head, to her relief, she was not alone. After a few minutes, everyone seemed to have recovered. Kelsey's crew moved to what appeared to be changing stations and started to remove their soiled clothing before heading toward a communal shower.

Kelsey stood over Trinity and Joshua. "I probably should have warned you about the unfortunate consequences of teleportation, but you wanted proof, and I couldn't risk you saying no." Joshua was intimately familiar with death up close and personal. He had seen the enemy and his own men lose control of their bodily functions either through fear, serious injuries or death. Having already turned off his sense of smell and disgust, Joshua became analytical. "Kelsey, do you mind explaining what the fuck just happened to us?"

"Wouldn't you like to shower first Joshua?"

"As a matter of fact, no! I want to know why my body decided to lose its ability to control itself."

Sighing, Kelsey began. "This might be hard for you to handle, but the gist is, your body has been slightly altered. The teleportation system was designed to transport supplies and heavy equipment from orbit. Out of necessity, we adapted the technology to transport organic material. The adaptation is not perfect. Each time you use the system your cellular structure is slightly damaged. While not permanent, there is a theoretical limit on how many times you can use the system before your body shuts down from the cumulative damage. Through trial and error, we calculated beyond six uses, your body will lose the ability to heal itself. Since we are clones, we have never been overly concerned about this limitation. Although having witnessed the death of one of our crew members, we keep the use of this technology down to extreme emergencies. Regardless of being a clone, it's a very painful way of dying. So, our protocol is to limit teleportation use to four times per lifetime. Most of our interaction is conducted via the sanctuaries through ALLIE."

Trinity could see Joshua losing it as the words so effortlessly flowed from Kelsey's month. She put a hand on Joshua's chest and faced him until he only looked at her. "Relax please. We came here for answers. If you kill him that will never happen."

Joshua looked back at Kelsey and said between clenched teeth, "You should have given us a choice." With that, he turned away and took a seat and started deep breathing to calm down.

"While I agree with Joshua, we came here for answers. So, I will overlook this lapse in your judgment. But if you aren't completely honest with us going forward, you won't have to worry about Joshua because I will kill you myself." Kelsey nodded. "Now, please explain why there is a limitation to how many times we can use this system."

"Without getting too technical, imagine using a fax machine and you fax the original. Now the receiver writes you a note in the margins of the fax and faxes it back to you. You then respond and send it back. Finally, the receiver sends you their final response. While the notes are legible, the original fax message is now distorted. It's that distortion that the system can't compensate for by the seventh use of the transporter. Even after the first use on a cellular level you feel the difference, which is why you lose bodily control. Now, can we please shower? I would prefer not to linger in my own excrement any longer if that's alright with you.

Directorate Headquarters - Undisclosed Location Outside of Roanoke, Virginia

As soon as the meeting was over, Colonel (Col.) Myers returned to the Directorate and immediately went to work. While he found all this alien stuff hard to believe, at the end of the day, it did not matter. He had long ago learned how to turn off his emotions and do the job at hand. His leadership mentor that taught him so much would frequently quote Alfred Lord Tennyson. "Ours is not to reason why, ours is but to do and die."

This was no different. The leaders might have changed, but the mission is still the same. There are enemies that need to be neutralized and he was one of the best at this job. While the loss of Grimm was something that needed to be addressed now wasn't the time. Trinity Winters would one day pay with her life for killing Grim, but Winters provided the Directorate with two valuable services. Grimm was out of control and eventually would have had to be dealt with. He was a psychopath, and his only impulse was to kill. Lately, it had taken everything in his power to keep Daniels from becoming a serial killer. If Winters hadn't killed Daniels, he would have been forced to retire Daniels permanently. Evidence had also been planted to implicate Staff Sergeant Daniels in the assassination of the President. The ongoing investigation had hampered operations. Even with the new President, a member of the Committee, If the new President had prematurely closed down the investigation, the ensuing unanswered questions would have led to a public outcry that they would not have been able to shut down. Every news agency in the world was flashing pictures of Staff Sergeant Daniels. Everyone asked the same question, what would cause a highly decorated Delta Force operator to assassinate the President of the United States. The military had stepped up to explain how he was captured and tortured. The Army Spokesmen went on to describe some of what was done to him and how it planted seeds of darkness inside of him. He was assessed numerous times by the unit psychologist, and it was ultimately deemed more beneficial to keep Daniels in the field. While he was monitored closely and team members reported the change in his behavior around chasing the kill, bringing him back to the states prematurely would create a potential time bomb. At one point, the psychologist insisted that Daniels take a 2-week leave back home to help him remember why he is over here fighting. When Daniels returned, out of the blue to everyone's surprise, Daniels submitted his retirement paperwork. As part of protocol, Daniels was monitored and asked to attend therapy sessions. For six months, we tracked Daniels then he disappeared off the radar. We put our Criminal Investigative Unit (CID) on the task of locating him. We did not inform law enforcement because technically he had not broken any laws. So many times, soldiers like Daniels will go off and live a life of seclusion."

The talking heads continued to babble

in the background. Col. Myers was confident that their efforts to frame Daniels would not unravel, and his apparent suicide would end the matter. The US Military of course would be tied up in congressional investigations for the next few months, but eventually the news cycle will move on to the next crisis. The Directorate had other pressing matters to consider.

While losses were expected within the Night Stalkers during the normal course of action, they were always expected to win. Their last engagement with Joshua's team exposed a gap in the Night Stalkers' operational protocols. The previous Commander had become complacent. They had grown too arrogant in their abilities and forgot just how dangerous a group of dedicated professionals with a cause could be. The recruitment efforts had already begun. Talent scouts were out in force across the globe, actively recruiting from the ranks of every Special Forces group ever created. According to Major (Maj.) Wayne Carson, the new Night Stalker Leader, it would take six months to rebuild, organize and train the new team members. Using Special Forces trained individuals like SAS, GS9, SEALS, and Delta cut training time down by two years. Modifications to the Night Stalkers' training would be to focus on engaging ex-Special Operators like themselves with slightly less training and less sophisticated equipment.

While losses were a part of normal operations, Trinity on the other hand was a situation that needed to be addressed. It has been a long-standing policy to hold individuals accountable for the intentional targeting of members of Special Operations Groups. Israel's famed Mossad taught the Special Operations community the value of this policy. Once the new teams were trained, Trinity and Joshua's team would be targeted for termination. Wayne had already asked to lead this effort.

Col. Myers had underestimated Trinity and allowed her to live in the hospital. He wasn't about to make the same mistake again. Several members of his Night Stalkers were now dead because of strategic failures at all levels of command. Hubris was always the downfall of teams like the Night Stalkers. The feeling of being invincible, above the law and untouchable. Truthfully, they were untouchable, but that did not mean invincible. The new training program had to be modified to remove the arrogance from the team.

Directorate Headquarters - Undisclosed Location Outside of Roanoke, Virginia

President Sartingson, the newly appointed president of the United States, adjusted his tie to hide his discomfort as he stared at the shadowy faces of the 8 members representing The Committee.

President Sartingson said, "What you're asking me to do is tantamount to political suicide. I will never be able to get away with it."

The representative from Germany responded, "It doesn't matter Bill. Under the 1973 Emergency War Powers Act, you can unilaterally take military action without congressional approval for 90 days before congress withdraws funding or they declare a formal declaration of war. Regardless in 90 days, the balance of power will forever shift into our hands, and we will no longer have to manipulate activities from behind the scenes."

The representative from Africa spoke up next. "Since we recovered the Ark of the Covenant or AI, we've been able to pinpoint the location of the alien spaceship to the Gaza Plateau in Egypt, more specifically beneath the Great Pyramid, Khufu . It's paramount that we secure it before other governments suspect what's going on."

"So once again, I'm going to repeat your orders. You are to secure the Gaza Plateau by any means necessary and hold it until we can reactivate the alien spaceship."

The Asian representative then spoke up. "We are in the process of finalizing the fake intelligence that points to a terrorist plot to use man-pak nuclear weapons to wipe Israel off the face of this planet. The intelligence will point to ISIS using the Great Pyramid to construct their nuclear bombs. It will also say that the Egyptian military is supporting ISIS. This will allow you to justify a large scale military force versus a simple surgical strike with Special Forces . Since the latest uprising and the military overthrow of the Democratically elected president, things have been unstable in Egypt and loyalties are very questionable. We will ensure there is appropriate human and electronic intelligence to support this operation as a clear and present danger."

The President nodded then cleared his throat.

Colonel Myers stood at parade rest during the entire briefing to the newly ascended President of the United States. The Committee member from Russia addressed the Colonel. "Col. Myers, we need your Night Stalkers to track down the other components to the spaceship. Now that we know how to locate them, it is imperative that they be retrieved as soon as possible. According to the tracking software, there are 3 more devices left to acquire. Our manuscript refers to these components as artifacts that have been lost over the centuries. Using the software, you will be able to track these components down to a 10 square mile radius, but after that you will need to use folklore to find them. The artifacts left to find are the Holy Grail, The Spear of Destiny, and Pandora's Box. The Grail is in South America in the Amazon Jungle region. The Holy Grail is the access key to the ship's navigational system. The Spear of Destiny is in the Himalayas. It is the decipher key for the communication's array. Finally, Pandora's Box is in Mexico. It is the matter/anti-matter energy source that powers the star-drive." According to our manuscript, Pandora's box is why the Mayan society disappeared. They activated the Box, and the entire society was disintegrated. Special precautions need to be taken when recovering it. Without the proper shielding the same thing will happen to your team. While we believe it is still shielded, let's not take any chances."

The German Head spoke again.

"Gentlemen, the next 90 days will usher in an unprecedented change in the course of human evolution. It will be a time of enlightenment for some and a time of fear for others. The world will not understand and therefore will try and stop us. We can expect direct opposition from the governments of China, Russia, Germany, and England. Unfortunately, we still have Joshua and Trinity that will need to be dealt with. Bill, we want the Pyramids secured in 30 days and all ship components recovered in 90 days. Good luck gentlemen, the future of all mankind is in your hands."

With that last statement, all eight screens went blank. The President and Col. Myers both stood there for several seconds then turned and went their separate ways. President Sartingson hoping, he wouldn't be responsible for starting World War III. Col. Myers hoping his Night Stalkers were up to the task of recovering the artifacts and handling the likes of Joshua's team.

* * *

Somewhere Inside Mount Everest, Nepal

20 minutes later, showered and changed into nondescript jumpsuits, Trinity and Joshua joined the others in the command center. There was a conference room located off to the right when they entered the command center. Everyone was already seated except Trinity, Joshua, and Kelsey. With only three seats vacant, they took a seat at the end of the table.

"Welcome my friends, it's been a while. Time is short with the cruiser Alpheratz's A.I. being found. The finding of the A.I. or Ark of the Covenant for Trinity and Joshua's sake, will unfortunately start a cascade of events that will lead to the Alpheratz becoming operational again. We have reached a critical point in the conflict with our fellow crew members. Up to this point, I truly believed the only way to stop Xan'lima from achieving his goal was to cull the human population. Based on the advances in human technology influenced by Soa'limae, I no longer believe culling is an effective option. If anything, using the H5N1 avian flu or a coronavirus now will only serve to make it easier for the Committee to gain access to the Alpheratz buried under the great pyramids of Giza. The Committee will simply wait out the effects of the virus in their protected underground complexes then swoop in to activate the Alpheratz with no opposition. I've briefed you on Joshua and Trinity's activities over the past year. I have asked them here to formally join our cause. We are at a crossroads, a nexus point."

Kelsey then turned to address Trinity and Joshua directly. "While we tried to prevent your species from evolving to protect you, I will concede that we should have moved on from that strategy a long time ago. The fact that we're even having this conversation proves the status quo no longer exists. I'm not asking for forgiveness, but the greater good is now about the intergalactic greater good. Not just the greater good for this planet. It's no longer possible to stop my old crew from accomplishing their mission. When their mission is completed, the inhabitants of Earth will discover they are not alone in the universe and just how little your planet matters. The other thing we've been protecting you from is your own destruction when you discover this knowledge."

"Governments will try and possess this technology at all costs. Religious orders will try to suppress and deny the truth. Either way, without our intervention, the knowledge alone will lead to a global war, the likes of which will make World War II look like the little shoot war when The United States invaded Grenada in 1983."

"So, what do we do now?" Trinity said. "I personally think you all are monsters. Your sanctimonious right to play God with our lives. Hitler's atrocities are nothing compared to the genocide that you have committed in the guise of the "Greater Good". On the other hand, if your other crew members have their way, the whole planet will be destroyed. So, I'll ask the question again, "What do you propose to do about this situation and why do you need us?"

Ryles hesitated a moment before he began. "First of all, asking for your forgiveness is something I would never expect to receive. If there is a Hell, I fully expect to be the first person in line. I've been in this battle so long; I figured our stalemate would hold forever. The events of the past year have finally convinced me of the errors of our ways. The bottom-line is that we must negotiate with our fellow crewmates and create a global strategy that will allow Earth to survive the reawakening of our spaceship. The awakening of our ship will trigger a signal that will attract our ancient enemy to this plant. The only way to do that is by securing one of the ship's components before the Committee retrieves all of them."

"Before I proceed any further, Trinity and Joshua, I would like to introduce you to part of my crew. Counterclockwise from me is Ce'limae referred to now Dr. Brenda Calms; Kec'lima now Dr. Susan Aires; Mec'lima now Sal McKinsey; Ja'limae now Michelle Longa; Ped'lima now Lucas Jacquot; Na'limae now Maria Vasquez; Xi'lima now Gabriel Arseneault; Ca'lima now Zane Adebowale; and Va'limae now Anastasia Kuznetsov. While I know you think we are monsters and responsible for the death of millions of your kind, we see things differently. Our perspectives are very different and spans millions of years. Our larger fight for the universe makes those deaths pale in comparison to the hundreds of billions that have died at the hands of the Xandurans. We have witnessed whole galaxies perish at their hands. In trying to protect you, our crew rebellion on planet earth has created something, previously thought impossible, hybrid-Sanarians. Not just hybrids, but a species that is more powerful than us. Brenda, please take over and explain what I am saying."

"Before I give you all of the details of the plan, we first need to educate you on just how much Soa'limae has manipulated the human genome and why you are truly hybrid-Sanarians, more powerful than we would ever hope to become. At this point,

I will let Dr. Brenda Calms take over the briefing."

Brenda stood up and took over the presentation. She activated a view screen that was somehow part of the wall. "Over the years, we have been monitoring the results of Soa'limae experiments, the Chief Science Officer of our crew. His genetic manipulations over the millennium have produced some extraordinary results. Imagine a human with the strength of Samson. Samson was as strong as ten men. Imagine a human with a life span of Methuselah who lived to be 969 years old. Currently humans only use about 10% of their brain capacity. Imagine if you could use 25% or even 100%. Extrasensory perception would no longer be a product of science fiction or quacks. Soa'limae unlocked psychic abilities such as intuition, telepathy, psychometry, clairaudience, and clairvoyance within humans. Just imagine the ability to move objects with your mind. Starting fires with a thought. The ability to heal with a touch. Humankind is on the brink of these things now based on the gene manipulations of Soa'limae. The human genome contains around 20,000 genes, that is, the stretches of DNA that encode proteins. But these genes account for only about 1.2 percent of the total genome. The other 98.8 percent is known as non-coding DNA. Most scientists agree that while some non-coding DNA is essential, most probably does nothing for us at all. The explanation is simple, Soa'limae turned off those genes. Even though most of these genes have been turned off, Mankind on your own have started activating some of these dormant non-coding DNA through practices like meditation, martial arts, and yoga. I believe Arthur C. Clarke said it best, "The only way to discover the limits of the possible is to go beyond them into the impossible." You as a species are evolving in ways that Soa'limae did not predict. "The only reason you don't know about these variants for yourself is through our culling of the more exotic variants of Soa'limae manipulations. Even now, at mankind's current level of evolution, you are almost a new species that we call Homo Superior. There is this misconception about the human brain and how much of its capacity a person uses. There is this myth perpetrated by science fiction movies that humans use between 5 to 10% of their brain capacity. This myth has been repeated so much that it is often referenced as fact. The reality is that there is no part of your brain that is just sitting there not being used. Dr. Ben Carson, who pioneered the use of hemispherectomy in children, helps to illustrate my point. Most adults, who had this procedure performed on them, died because in adults, neural pathways are hardwired. In children, who have developing brains, their neural pathways are flexible. That's why it's so easy for kids to learn new languages at a young age. When Dr. Carson performed hemispherectomies on kids, the other hemisphere adapted and picked up the other functions of the brain. So truthfully, science should be talking about how a person uses their brain more efficiently. Joshua, through your martial practice, you have already increased the efficiency of your brain capacity versus the typical human who just sits on the couch and watches TV. It has been proven that people who train martial arts are more alert and focused than those who have never trained before. The studies also show that the longer a person has trained, the more enhanced his or her cognition becomes. You have the ability to read others via your empathic abilities. Read their intent, predict their martial actions. How do you think you survived so many encounters in the military where so many of your teammates with the same training did not? Your martial training has honed these abilities. Your meditative practices have heightened and increased your Delta Brainwaves. This Delta waves allow you to read your opponent. When you are sparring, it's not that you have faster reflexes, you are reading your opponent's intent before they make it. You have started to learn how to harness your Qi and effect healing, while at the same time use Qi as a weapon to injure your opponent. Have you ever wondered why during the dead of winter when everyone is bundled up, you are only wearing a light jacket? You have learned to use your Qi to heat your body."

"Joshua, when was the last time you were sick?" Joshua hesitated a few seconds as he thought about it before he responded. "Truthfully, I don't remember.

It's been years." "Exactly!" Kelsey said. "That's because your Qi is working for you."

"Now imagine being able to read thoughts at will, telepathy; telekinesis; empathic; clairvoyance; psychokinesis; and precognition. All these abilities are within your grasp now. We can train you to open all your seven chakras and fully harness your Qi's full potential. Without any more genetic manipulations, we can teach you to increase your brain's efficiency by 25%.

"To fight our ancient enemy, your brain will need to operate at the 50% efficiency level. This unfortunately is only achievable through further genetic manipulation through the DNA Matrix Sequencer. We have been following

Soa'limae's genetic manipulations over the millenniums. There have been results that I would not have thought possible. There are DNA strains native to this planet that when mixed with ours created a superior race. Imagine the strength of Samson. The ability to heal in hours vs days or weeks or months."

Joshua finally couldn't take it any longer. "This is all preposterous. What you are saying is simply impossible."

"Joshua, what are the physical attributes that make a vampire in your lore?"

"Are we seriously having this conversation?"

"Please, bear with me and just answer the question."

Clearly frustrated Joshua responded,

"Whatever! A vampire has superhuman strength, supernatural speed, and the ability to transform into other animals, mainly bats. They cannot be killed unless beheaded, a wooden stake driven through their heart or direct exposure to sunlight."

Ryles stepped in at this point. "Remember Joshua and Trinity, behind every legend, there is some basis of truth. Let Brenda strip away the folklore for just a moment."

"As you know, Soa'limae was experimenting with the human genome. He did some remarkable things considering he did not have the DNA Sequencer that we took with us. Because he could not be exactly sure of the effects of his gene splicing, there were a lot of variants to the human genome that had to be culled by us. Soa'limae didn't care about those variants. They were just a stepping stone to achieving their end result, a species capable of helping them repair the ship. We did our best to exterminate the more dangerous variants. Vampires and werewolves were very real, not the horror movie versions though. Vampires had extreme strength, the ability to heal almost instantaneously, and super speed. They could see incredibly well at night, but sunlight wreaked havoc on their vision. It was a choice that they only came out at night versus a necessity. The unfortunate side effect of this variant was a taste for human blood. While vampires could eat regular food after a while, the taste for human blood over-road all other cravings. They were able to blend in by eating regular food when required at social gatherings to maintain their disguise. The werewolves were very hairy human beings with long thick nails, superior speed, superior strength, and an acute sense of smell. For all intent and purposes, they were normal until the full moon. The moon's gravitational pull generates something called the tidal force. The tidal force causes high tides and low tides. The human body is composed of 70% water and when those tidal force changes, the effect on the human body creates moodiness in some humans. For the werewolves, a full moon would cause them to go berserk, and they would kill indiscriminately."

"I'm sure you heard the lore of Van

Helsing. That was our team doing our best to exterminate these uncontrollable variants. If they were benign, we would let them live. Only when they became a threat to mankind's survival did we intervene."

Trinity countered, "Unless it was one of your bioweapons designed to wipe out hundreds of thousands if not millions of people." That statement quieted everyone in the room for a few seconds.

Ryles motioned for Dr. Brenda Calms to take a seat. "As I said before, I did not think we had a choice. Regardless, I cannot change the past, but we can change our approach to this current crisis. So, you can either hate us or work with us on trying to save the human race."

When no responses came, Ryles

continued. "So back to why I went down this path before I finished outlining the plan. Joshua through your martial training, just like so many others martial artists have in the past, you have activated dormant genes and have evolved through training alone. With more training, we can teach you how to fully manipulate your chakras. You and others like you could easily become Home Superior. Now couple this with the activation of certain genes, you will become, as Friedrich Nietzsche described Supermen." A fully evolved Homo Superior race that is so much greater than our species ever could have achieved on its own."

"So, what now?" said Joshua. "What do we do with all this information? How do we stop your colleagues running the Committee from activating the ship?"

"So, what's next? We need your help. We need the people of earth. Earth is about to lose its protection in this intergalactic war. My ex-crewmates are eventually going to win and activate our starship, the Alpheratz. Once the Alpheratz leaves earth's orbit and activates its star-drive, our enemy the Xandurans will be able to trace the drive's unique signature. The crew could also choose to just send a signal if repairs take too long. This will have the same effect as activating the star-drive."

"Part one of the plan. It's imperative that we gain control of at least one of the ship's components. This will give us negotiation power with our old crew mates."

"Right now, as we speak, The Committee is organizing its resources to secure the other missing components. These key ship components came to be known as ancient artifacts by your historians. Overtime, these components became the things of myth and central to religions throughout the world. As you know the Ark of the Covenant was recovered in Iraq. The other components are the Holy Grail; the Spear of Destiny; and Pandora's Box."

"The Holy Grail was fought over for centuries and arguably one of the holy relics in existence. It is said to be the cup that Jesus drank from. It has been rumored to be the blood line of Jesus Christ. The Crusades were the Committee trying to locate the Holy Gail. At the time, the Committee was known as the Illuminati. They campaigned from 1095 to 1291 to seize control of the Holy Land from Muslim rule. It was around 1120 that my team created the Knights of the Temple or Templar Knights, which was founded in Jerusalem to recover the Holy Grail. When the Illuminati succeeded in gaining control of the Middle East, I knew we had to recover the Holy Grail first; hence, the creation of the Templar Knights. Once the Holy Grail was recovered, they left Jerusalem on my instructions and headed to England to hide the Grail. When the Illuminati discovered what had happened, the catholic church developed a plan to eradicate all Templar Knights at one time. The Templars had spread across the globe, so the task at hand was difficult, but the church had unlimited resources. The church gave its soldiers a deadline to locate all the Knights, and on a prearranged date, execute all of them at once. You are very familiar with this day. It was Friday, the 13th of October 1307. A day now that is symbolized as bad luck. Thousands of Knights were killed on the same day, and that day forever more has been associated with bad luck or evil things happening. The Holy Grail which was derived from the ancient French word "Sang Real," which means Royal Blood had nothing to do with Jesus Christ and the Holy Grail is the access key to the ship's navigational system. Its color is ruby red, made of a translucent material. When exposed to sunlight, you can see the superconductive liquid. The fluid is a liquid metal created by fusing the subatomic particles of an alloy that closely resembles the combined atomic structure of zinc, aluminum, andiron then this alloy is combined with ammonia modules to create a superconductive liquid that has the color of ruby red. This liquid metal is needed to stabilize the data storage cube inside of the ship's Navigational Star Chart Module allowing near instantaneous access to the star-maps of the known galaxies. When the Templars were all executed, we lost track of the Grail. My host body was killed and one of my dying instructions was to take the Grail and hide it. When I awoke in my cloning chamber weeks later and made it back to the place of my death, the only information that could gleamed, the Grail was on a ship heading to the Americas, South America to be more specific."

"The Spear of Destiny, believed to give the wielder unlimited power to rule others, was actually our DNA Matrix Sequencer. While it does hold the secrets of life, it's not quite in the way history believed. The DNA Matrix Sequencer enables the crew members to clone themselves in case of emergency when their host body was endangered of dying. Previous expeditions had learned the hard way the dangers inherent to deep space missions that encompassed years. While the hibernation chambers allowed the crew to survive long stretches of time when traveling between galaxies, its functions could not repair severe damage to the host body. The deep sleep allowed the body to quickly heal itself when minor injuries had occurred because all other bodily functions were at minimum functioning. The DNA Matrix Sequencer allowed the host body to be cloned. This piece of technology, we kept with us except during a brief period of our time on earth. During World War II, when Hitler was obsessed with the occult, we lost control of pieces of our Sequencer and cloning technology. On one of his expeditions to Africa he was getting close to finding our headquarters. We were forced to relocate. I split my team and our equipment to avoid being captured. They managed to capture one of our cloning tubes. Hitler's scientists did their best to reverse engineer the technology. While they did not have the DNA Matrix Sequencer, the cloning tube unfortunately was enough. Hitler committed some of the most atrocious crimes against humanity imaginable. Germany's technological leaps and advancements in technology were a direct result of equipment recovered from our crew. They hounded us from one end of this world to the other. At the end of the war, we successfully recovered the cloning tube. When Hitler was killed, they placed him in the tube in the hopes that it would revive him. Little did they know how close they came to reviving Hitler. Had they had a little more time, I believe they would have successfully adapted their technology to activate the tube without the DNA Matrix Sequencer."

"While the DNA Matrix Sequencer is in our control within Mt Everest with us, that component will not stop the Committee from getting into the spaceship. Even though the Sequencer is important, when they realize the Spear of Destiny is inaccessible, they will move on and focus on the other two components."

"Finally, the last artifact is Pandora's Box, which is the matter/anti-matter energy source that powers the star-drive. The star-drive creates a hyperspace window, which allows the Alpheratz to travel faster than light. We initially buried the drive in what is now called the Yucatan Peninsula. You are probably familiar with the race that found it, the Mayans. The fall of the Mayans is one of history's great mysteries. One of the mightiest civilizations in the ancient Americas simply disappeared. There are several theories, but the reality is they found our star-drive and somehow managed to open it. By activating the energy source of the star-drive without being in its magnetic containment shielding, a very small amount of anti-matter was released and instantly annihilated the Mayans through the massive release of gamma radiation.

"The next step in the plan is that we need to prepare this world for an intergalactic battle. Even if the star-drive is not activated, if they are successful in sending out a distress call then you can be assured our enemy will trace the signal back to earth. Rest assured that when they arrive, they will harness this planet's resources thereby wiping out all life on this planet to include ours. Those that are not eliminated in the initial reaping will be assimilated into the Xanduran's ranks. The survivors are infected with an organic virus that rewrites their DNA. It also destroys existing neural pathways. In effect, they lose their sense of self and become part of the Xanduran collective. To prepare this world, we need to evolve mankind from Homo Sapien to Homo Superior. This is going to require the international cooperation of all nations. We need to start preparing the world now so that they know they are not alone in the universe and that a war is coming to their planet. Truthfully, we are going to need Soa'limae's assistance to evolve mankind to the levels we need. On our own, we will turn you into superior soldiers able to do things that until today would have been seen as impossible, but that will not be enough if we want to win this Intergalactic War."

"Finally, we need to resume our original mission to Jupiter to see if we can make contact with the alien species there. It's possible they still don't exist, but with their level of technology we must try. Their technology will give us a clear technological advantage over the Xanduran."

"While the tasks are straight forward, the execution will be near impossible. We're going to have to deal with the ever-changing geopolitical dynamics of one nation seeking to gain an advantage over the other which might possibly trigger WWIII in our efforts to bring the world together. The religious uncertainties will surely drive the world to war almost as fast as geopolitical concerns."

"Trinity and Joshua, if you agree to join our cause, we will immediately start developing detailed plans to execute these changes to our original mission. Our zeal to protect this planet, while harsh by today's standards, was somewhat naive and misguided, especially with all the genetic manipulations that Soa'limae has done to evolve humanity. While the Committee thinks they will be rewarded by reactivating the ship and awakening my old crew, they are deadly wrong. The result of their efforts will be the total abandonment of humanity as the ship leaves orbit. At that point, it is only a matter of time until the Xandurans wipe you out."

* * *

Presidential Emergency Operations Center (PEOC) - Washington, D.C.

All had gathered in the Presidential Emergency Operations Center (PEOC), a bunker-like structure underneath the East Wing of the White House. Everyone stood as President Sartingson entered the PEOC flanked by his Secret Service detail. "Please be seated", said the President after he took his seat at the head of the conference room table.

"Jim, please begin the briefing." Jim Matsumi was the National Security Advisor. "Thank you, Mr. President. Ladies and Gentlemen, in the last 48 hours, the CIA and NSA have been monitoring a growing situation in the Middle East that could potentially start World War III. Both HUMMINT (Human Intelligence) and ELINT

(Electronic Intelligence) have confirmed the development of nuclear weapons in Egypt. It appears that Egyptian hardliners sympathetic with Hamas and ISIS have slowly infiltrated the Egyptian government. Since the 2013 Egyptian coup d'état took place and the Egyptian Army Chief General Abdel Fattah El-Sisi led a coalition to remove the President of Egypt, Mohamed Morsi, from power our influence and traditional relationships in the region have deteriorated. For the past two years, the Egyptian government has closed off entry into the Pyramids of Giza. Originally we thought this was part of a re-construction project, but now we know that it was a cover story."

"What actually clued us in was an intercepted intelligence from Israel. As you know, we routinely monitor Israeli Military and Intelligence organizations. We also have spies within their ranks. One of our operatives reported there was a Gamma spike coming from the Giza Plateau. Israel dispatched a team of Mossad agents to investigate. No one from the team survived the reconnaissance operation, but one agent did manage to get a partial message out to Mossad Headquarters in Tel Aviv before he died. The message basically said that Egypt has been developing a low yield nuclear man-pak weapon within the Great Pyramid of Khufu. Before anything else could be transmitted the connection terminated."

We have been monitoring Israel's troop movement. They have stepped up drone surveillance of Giza. They are in the process of preparing their troops to invade Egypt and secure the Giza Plateau as we speak."

At this point, Calvin Murphy, the Secretary of State chimed in. "Mr. President, if Israel invades Egypt, the entire region could erupt into an all-out war. Iran, Iraqi, Hamas, Jordan, Kuwait, Saudi Arabia, and Syria will retaliate against any Israeli incursion. There is a good chance we can keep Saudi and Kuwait from entering a conflict, but just barely."

"As you know Mr. President, if Israel is attacked, we would have to come to their aid and if we have to attack one of those countries, that will trigger a response from Russia and China. Mr. President, this situation easily has the potential to be the start of World War III."

President Sartingson looked toward the Director of the CIA, Simon Lance. "Simon, just how reliable is this intelligence?"

"Sir, as far as reliability goes, our spy in Mossad has always been above reproach. If he says there is a threat, there is a threat."

The NSA Director, Tyrone Bryant, cleared his throat before he chimed in. "Sir, with the re-tasking of our one of our satellites, we can confirm that Israel is indeed moving assets around. We unfortunately have not been able to determine what's going on in Giza. Even with our ground penetrating satellite, we have only been able to pick up trace radiation from the pyramids."

"Thank you, Gentlemen," said the President. "Now what are our options on a response plan."

Army General Palmer Davis, the Chairman of the Joint Chief of Staff spoke up. "Sir, we are in a no-win situation. Based on the detailed briefing you just received, my staff has been working on preparing contingency plans for the past 24 hours after we were briefed yesterday. Israel will be ready to launch a ground assault in five days."

"General Davis, that makes no sense," said the President. "They should be able to attack in less than 48 hours. Why five days?"

"Sir, Israel has the unfortunate situation of being surrounded on all sides by their enemies. So, in order to launch a successful assault on Egypt, they also have to be prepared to defend their borders and deal with the internal situation in the West Bank with Hamas."

"Mr. President, based on our internal Middle East war gaming scenarios, that we have modified for this situation, the Joint Chiefs of Staff feel a preemptive strike with maximum political pressure is the only solution. We propose to launch an airborne assault on Giza and secure it before Israel attacks. This will accomplish a three-fold objective.

One, it keeps Israel out of the fighting; thereby, we have a chance of keeping this to a contained engagement on the Giza Plateau.

Two, we secure the nuclear man-paks

and control the narrative.

Three, by having a very small footprint, we can defend our position politically as dealing with a very specific threat and once our objective is secured, we will immediately withdraw forces.

"Mr. President, it should take approximately 18 hours to mobilize and start the deployment of the 82nd Airborne Division. We can have troops on the ground in less than 48 hours. We have the 242nd MEU (Marine Expeditionary Force) located in the Gulf of Aqaba. They will be part of the follow-on forces designed to provide armor support after the 82nd secures the Giza Plateau. Prior to the deployment of those assets, we have two SEAL teams from the Lincoln Strike Group stationed in the Gulf that will take out Egypt's Air Defense Artillery's (ADA) capabilities that will pose a threat to the 82nd's C-5M, and C-17 aircrafts. A Delta Unit out of Fort Bragg is already deployed in Syria. They will be picked up and their mission is to conduct a HALO insertion into Egypt to take out Egypt's Radar at the Cairo International Airport. The entire 75th Ranger Regiment will parachute in after Delta and secure Cairo International."

"Mr. President, securing the airport is crucial to all follow-on planes delivering supplies and additional troops and equipment if necessary. Air support will be provided by the USS Abraham Lincoln Aircraft Carrier. The 2/22nd Battalion, 1st Infantry Brigade out of

10th Mountain Division, is currently assigned to the Multi-National Forces & Observer (MFO) mission in Egypt. They are stationed in the Sinai Peninsula and will provide blocking positions for the 242nd MEU coming from the Gulf. It is 422 KM from the Gulf of Aqaba from Taba, Egypt to Cairo. It should take approximately 5 and 1/2 hours for the 1st elements of the MEU to reach Giza. This should be plenty of time for them to arrive and set up defensive positions to counter any Egyptian Armor trying to retake Giza."

Calvin then spoke up. "Our ambassadors to Russia, China, the Middle East, our Nato Allies will immediately engage to ensure we can keep this operation contained once ground operations begin. But Sir, I have to admit this still has the potential to draw Russia into this conflict. And if Russia attacks, the NATO Mutual Defense clause will be activated. We will then be looking at WWIII again."

Sartingson looked directly at Calvin when he next spoke. "Secretary Murphy, I'm going to rely on your ambassadors and you to keep us out of a global conflict."

"General Davis, you have a green light to commence operations. Secure the Giza Plateau and keep Israel from dragging the world into WWIII. You're dismissed and God speed."

The President's Chief of Staff hung around waiting for the room to clear. "Mr. President," Kelly Matthews said. "Should we call a meeting with the congressional oversight leaders, so you can brief them on the operation?"

"Yes Kelly, please schedule that meeting about 8 hours before the air assault operations begin. I want to make sure the SEALs and Delta are engaged first, so there is no risk having to shut down the operation. This is just too critical for partisan politics."

When everyone had left the room, President Sartingson asked his secret service detail to give him a moment. When he was finally alone, the President pulled a nondescript phone from his coat pocket. He opened his phone and rapidly tapped five times on the Google Assistant button. A blank black window immediately opened. President Sartingson put his right index finger on the finger sensor. This action activated the front camera, which scanned his left eye. A text message started scrolling across the black screen. The text prompted the President to enter a 26 alphanumeric password that changed every 30 days. Once all the of these actions were completed, another text message appeared. "This is Operator 36715; how may I help you Mr. President?"

The President then proceeded to type out a prearranged code. "Condor is flying in 18 hours. Condor lands in 36 hours." After five seconds had expired, a reply message appeared on the screen. "This is Operator 36715. Message acknowledged. Out."

President Sartingson immediately closed the text box. In the background operations of the phone, the program erased all evidence of its existence from the system log then uninstalled itself from the Android OS making it undetectable by the NSA system security sweeps performed on all Government equipment. As per standard operating procedures, Committee operatives checked for messages every 24 hours unless they had to communicate in times of extreme circumstances.

President Sartingson put his phone back in his breast jacket pocket then left the PECO heading back to the Oval Office. His Secret Service detail following discreetly behind him.

Somewhere over the Atlantic Ocean - Operation Lasting Hope

The entire 82nd Airborne Division was loaded onto ten C-17 Globemaster III Air Force jets heading toward Cairo, Egypt. The distance was 5,251 nautical miles. The range on the C-17 with a full complement of troops (102 Airborne Troopers) is 5,600 nautical miles. Five KC-130J Tankers were scheduled to meet the C-17s about 1,000 nautical miles from Cairo to commence in-flight refueling operations to ensure the birds had enough fuel if a holding pattern was necessary at any given point. Flight time to Cairo was approximately 13 hours. The soldiers had been trying their best to sleep in the cargo hull of the C-17, but when refueling operations started the troops immediately woke up. The turbulence associated with the weather and refueling operations made it next to impossible to sleep, especially when the soldiers next to you started throwing up. The crew chiefs had already started handing out airbags. They smiled as they always did when this part of the journey began. Even though these paratroopers jumped multiple times a month, whenever the plane started NOE (Nap of the Earth) evasive maneuvers or refueling operations, vomit ensued. Nap of the Earth flying was not for the faint of heart. It is a type of very low-altitude flight course used by military aircraft to avoid enemy detection and attack in a high-threat environment. Troopers usually couldn't wait to jump out of the plane because once the first person threw up, a chain reaction started.

T minus 4 hours and counting until the 82nd Airborne Division launched the largest wartime Airborne Assault insertion since WWII. Six hours earlier two SEAL teams from the Lincoln Strike Group inserted into Egypt. SEAL Team Bravo had inserted to the Suez Canal vicinity and SEAL Team Foxtrot had inserted into the Mount Sinai Mountain range to immobilize Egypt's Air Defense Artillery units at both locations. Egypt selected the Suez Canal because of its strategic importance. The canal is often considered to define the border between Africa and Asia. It is a sea-level waterway running north-south across the Isthmus of Suez in Egypt connecting the Mediterranean and Red seas. After the Suez Crisis in mid-1956. Egypt realized the importance of having Air

Defense assets strategically located to defend their airspace. So, in 1968 the Egyptian Air Defense Forces or EADF, the Anti-aircraft warfare branch of the Egyptian Armed Forces, was formed. It was tasked with the responsibility of protecting the Egyptian airspace against any hostile air attacks. Their main armament is the Soviet/Egyptian S-125 anti-aircraft type missiles. The other location for EADF was the Mountains of Mount Sinai. Overlooking the Gulf of Aqaba, this location offered a strategic vantage point for airborne attacks launched from aircraft carriers.

Both SEAL teams were in place and concealed. The teams had subdivided into smaller units to ensure that every S-125 location could be targeted. The teams would mark their targets with a laser to ensure the Tomahawk missiles launched from the Lincoln Carrier Group would find and destroy their targets. While satellites provide enough information to pre-program the Tomahawks with GPS coordinates, J3 (Pentagon Operations) decided having eyes on the ground was more optimal due to the mobility of S-125 launching platforms. The SEAL teams had set up perimeter security and waited for the designated time to paint their targets. The teams were worried about roaming Egyptian patrols, which was the only thing that could potentially cause mission failure, so they had 100% security for the duration of the mission as per their OPORD (Operational Orders).

General Palmer Davis sat at the

conference room table with the other members of the Pentagon Joint Chiefs of Staff (JCS). They were in the Pentagon War Room, waiting for all assets to get in place. So far everything was going according to plan. Lt. Gen. Peter J. Palings, Director of Operations for the J3 had just given the JCS a briefing about where all the assets were. The 82nd Airborne Division and 75th Ranger Regiment were two hours from insertion. The Navy SEAL Teams were in place. The Delta Force Unit had HALO in from their location in Syria where they were tasked with hunting down chemical munitions. Delta was now in place at Cairo's International Airport and had placed explosives on the radar system. The 2/22nd Battalion, 1st Infantry Brigade out of 10th Mountain Division assigned to the Multi-National Forces & Observer (MFO) mission in Egypt had redeployed to their assigned blocking positions for the 242nd MEU coming from the Gulf. The USS Iwo Jima (LHD-7), a Wasp-class amphibious assault ship of the United States Navy, was almost in position 12 miles from the Sinai Peninsula, where the Marines would deploy in their Amphibious Combat Vehicle (ACV) for the 5- and 1/2-hours journey to reach Giza.

General Davis was very apprehensive about the pending operation. First, they were invading an ally. Second, if anything went wrong, the United States of America would be starting WWIII, but on the other hand if Israel attacked, there is no doubt that WWIII would be initiated by their actions.

T Minus 10 minutes to the commencement of Operation Lasting Hope. Major General Carl E Parker, the Commander of the 82nd Airborne Division, was on the line with General Palmer Davis. "General Parker, the mission is a GO. Godspeed and bring our troopers home safely." "Yes Sir."

Parker stood up and removed his headset and motioned for Command Sergeant Major Brad Parsons to come over. "We have a go, Sergeant Major. Get the troops ready to jump."

"Yes Sir." Said Parsons. Putting his headset on Parsons started issuing commands.

On the lead C-17, the Jump Master started issuing jump commands. These instructions were being repeated on all of the C-17s in the air convoy. The Jump Master yelled "Get Ready". The command was repeated and passed down to all of the troopers. That was the signal for the paratroopers to get ready. "Stand Up." Again, the command was repeated, and all of the troopers stood up and moved to the center of the C-17. The next command was "Hook Up." The troopers then attached their static line hooks to the line running the length of the plane.

"EQUIPMENT CHECK" - The most important command. You are to check your parachute for any discrepancy.

"SOUND OFF, EQUIPMENT CHECK." Despite how simple this command is many tend to mess it up. You are to announce the status of your parachute. The paratroopers will be in a line and this sound off will begin from the rear and work its way up. The last Trooper shouted, "ALL OKAY JUMP MASTER!"

"STAND IN THE DOOR" The first paratrooper stood in the door of the aircraft awaiting the jump command.

The jump indicator status turned from a RED LIGHT to a GREEN. The Jump Master shouted "GO." One by One, the paratroopers jumped out of the plane.

Major General Carl E Parker listened from his console abroad the AWACS airplane. He whispered to himself. "God have mercy on our souls."

Training Headquarters - Waco, Texas

Trinity and Joshua were back at their Texas Headquarters meeting with the team. Since the loss of the Charlie Team, they had to replenish their ranks. With the help of Senator Ryles, they were connected with United States Special Operations Command S1. A shell company was created with the appropriate background in place. Based on Senator Ryles' support, they were now considered one of the top recruiters for special ops service members with their unique skill sets.

Based on the profile that Joshua gave Senator Ryles, Joshua was provided with several potential candidates to choose from. In addition to the military skills, Joshua was also looking for those members who were martial arts experts, but who also supplemented their training with meditation. The last quality Joshua had to discern was the ability of the service members to truly care about others, to have empathy for not just their fellow comrades in arms, but for the plight of those not capable of defending themselves from the monsters of the world. For this characteristic, Joshua had to pour through years of psychiatric evaluations and mission files. Because of Senator Ryles' connections, Joshua was given access to information that normally would have been highly classified, thereby making the final selection much easier. That still did little to alleviate a splitting headache knowing that a wrong decision on his part might be the difference between saving the planet or becoming extinct as a species.

So far out of 100 applicants, he had only found seven that fit the profile he was looking for. Ryles stated he had another batch that was pre-screened and would be delivered within a few days. As Joshua continued his tedious task, the other team members continued to train and hone their skills. When Joshua and Trinity returned, they briefed the team on what was really happening. At first no one could believe what they were saying was real, and they started ribbing Joshua. Senator Ryles knew Joshua was correct when he said his team would not believe him, so he gave Joshua and Trinity a holographic projector that fit in the palm of their hands. Once, the team saw Joshua was serious, the laughter finally died down.

At that point Trinity removed the projector and placed it on the table. Without saying another word, she activated the device, and a surreal picture engulfed the whole room in a life-like visualization of a solar system that was anything but ours. They saw strange new worlds rotating zooming in and out of focus. They saw a meteor impacting an asteroid belt and scattering the asteroids off their course like a cosmic game of billiards. The images were so life-like that several of the men reached out and tried to touch them. Then the whole scene changed and a picture of Alpheratz crew came into focus. These creatures were anything but human. Standing at a little over 7 1/2 feet tall, with a head that was easily 1.5 times larger than an average human head. The eyes were large and round with cat-like vertical slanted pale green iris. There were no visible ears present. They had no nose structure either, but gill-like protrusions on both sides of their neck. There was something that passed as a mouth, but no lips. They had longer arms that extended down to their knees and fingers that were twice the length of a regular sized human's. They were all wearing some type of uniform, so it was hard to tell the sex of the aliens especially since they had no hair. Their skin had a bluish tint. Just as suddenly as the images appeared, they disappeared leaving a stunned room behind.

Joshua then spoke up, "Gentlemen, I hope I have your full attention now. This is not a joke. The fate of the planet literally rests in our hands.

James McKay, the new Charlie Team Leader, an ex-Navy Seal spoke up. "Hey Joshua, why does this task fall upon us? What about getting the US Military involved?"

"Great question James. I truly wish we could, but the Committee as it is now called, has infiltrated every major government on earth. I can tell you without a doubt that President Bill Sartingson is a Committee Member. His elevation to power was a direct result of his predecessor's assassination. Thanks to Trinity, the individual responsible for pulling the trigger is no longer among the land of the living. Unfortunately, the organization is a lot harder to deal with. The news about the existence of alien life is going to come out. Senator Kelsey Ryles is going to deal with the geopolitical ramifications of this news becoming general knowledge. Already there is a major US Military operation that is underway in Egypt to secure the Great Pyramids. That is where their alien spaceship is buried. There is nothing we can do to help stop or hinder that operation. I pray that the Committee will do what's in the best interest of this planet to prevent WWIII from happening. Our job will be to recover at least one of the ship's components to prevent the aliens from leaving the planet. And if what we heard is accurate, if that ship leaves this planet, what follows will wipe every life form including the smallest microbe off the face of this planet. Ryles believes if we can recover one of the components, he will be able to negotiate with his old crew and create a plan of attack that will be mutually beneficial to all.

As the team talked among themselves and asked questions of Joshua, Trinity couldn't help but wonder if this situation was even winnable. What started off as simple revenge for the death of her son Robby had turned into a struggle for the fate of this planet. She carried her doubt, but still pressed on. With Joshua by her side, she felt they had a chance. As slim as it was, it was still something she could hold on to.

# # #

Several weeks had passed and the teams were busy continuing to train and hone their skills. Team Charlie was now operational again with its ranks refilled. Joshua then went about augmenting each team with an additional fire team to increase the lethality and flexibility of each team to handle whatever mission was thrown at them. Joshua also formed a Delta Team consisting of 3 Fire Teams as well. Delta Team was designated as their QRF (Quick Reactionary Force). This team was heavily armored with two M240B machine guns per Fire Team, two M249 squad automatic rifles per team, three snipers, one per each Fire Team armed with a M107 .50 caliber rifle. Fire Team 2 was also armed with a Mark 19 Grenade Launcher. Each Fire Team also carried two FGM-148 Javelin missile launchers, an American man-portable fire-and-forget anti-tank missile. Joshua wanted to ensure that when the QRF was deployed, it could rain down holy hell on whatever force was impeding their mission. The additional funding that Senator Ryles was able to send to the team under the guise of being an elite military contracting unit was put to good use. The team was now outfitted with the latest military gear from assault rifles to the best body armor available. The team was now outfitted in body armor that covered each member from head to foot. that the armor covered the entire torso and head with the ability to withstand a .50 caliber round. The rest of the body armor was rated to stop up to 7.62mm rounds. Most of the team complained about the new helmets because they restricted vision, but Joshua insisted that they train with it to get comfortable with their new gear. The training went as far as to include force on force live-fire exercises in the configurable kill houses. Since the armor was all black, the OPFOR (Opposition Force) all wore white t-shirts over their body armor. For the purpose of these drills, the team members used 5.56mm standard NATO rounds. This also lessened the impact of actually getting shot and it allowed the team to become comfortable with the new gear. The teams agreed only in the event that an actual engagement was imminent would they wear the helmets.

# # #

In the operations center, Bravo Team Leader - Peter Cullum, Charlie Team Leader - James McKay and Delta Team Leader - Mick Sandeski sat down and were finalizing operational plans for the retrieval of the alien artifacts with Joshua and Trinity leading the meeting. Kenny Tahir, Joshua's resident geek was busy tapping away on the computer, bringing up data as it was requested by various team members. Senator Kelsey Ryles, who was the chairman of the subcommittee that funded all black operations used his influence to add an additional member to the unit. Ryles told the CIA Director, Simon Lance, that he needed a liaison to work with a covert off the books elite contracting unit. The liaison officer needed to have the authority to requisition whatever resources this unit needed without question. The person would be on loan and would only report to the unit and himself. Lance had received these types of requests in the past and didn't think anything of it. He selected Susan Pratt, a 15-year veteran Paramilitary Operations Officer (PMOO). She had worked her way up the ranks over the years having been involved in some pretty harrowing missions. Yet she always prevailed against all odds, which led to her continued promotions. Lance knew it wasn't often that someone like Senator Ryles asked for a favor. This was Lance's opportunity to put Ryles in a position where one day he could cash in on this favor.

As Susan sat there listening to the briefing, she couldn't help but to replay the briefing she received from Joshua and Trinity. "Aliens, holy fucking shit. Can this be real?" If not for the holographic technology display, she would not have taken them seriously in the least bit, but now she was part of a team that had the fate of the planet in their hands. The fact that she couldn't trust her own government and that President Bill Sartingson was part of an organization that was responsible for the assassination of the previous president boggled her mind. She looked across the room and recognized the facial demeanor of trained professionals. She had worked with many of these personality types in the CIA. A lot of times, it was these types of people that pulled the CIA's collective asses out of the fire. Her job was to use the resources of the CIA to coordinate assets to move the teams to various locations throughout the world. Team Bravo was tasked with the recovery of the Holy Grail. This device was needed to stabilize the data storage cube inside of the

Navigational Star Chart Module, allowing near instantaneous access to the star-maps of the known galaxies. Team Charlie was tasked with the recovery of Pandora's Box, which is the matter/anti-matter energy source that powers the star-drive. Her job was to initially work with Kenny and track down any leads to the Grail in South America and Pandora's Box in the Yucatan Peninsula. Once located, she would then need to coordinate the logistical resources necessary for them to accomplish the mission.

Joshua laid out the plan for Team Alpha. Their mission was two-fold. Part one, work with Senator Ryles' team of aliens to try and evolve homo sapiens or as Ryles called us hybrid-Sanarians. Their goal was to teach us how to evolve our minds to increase how efficiently we are utilizing its resources. Part two, start putting together an international coalition with the aim of sending a manned mission to Jupiter. Joshua explained how the aliens needed to resume their original mission to Jupiter to see if they, we now, could make contact with the alien species there. It's possible they no longer exist, but with their level of technology we must try. They will give your planet a clear advantage over their intergalactic enemy, when they attack planet Earth."

As she continued to listen, Joshua was now describing the opposition force. They were well trained, mostly ex-special forces like themselves. Unfortunately, they were not given the whole truth about what they were doing. Joshua explains the psychological profile of their team and why he passed over so many other applicants. He needed war fighters that could look beyond the orders and understand the gravity of what they were fighting for. That's why it was crucial to give all the facts, as unbelievable as they are. Their opposition were patriots, who were well paid and told to follow orders because the mission they were on was a continuation of their jobs while serving in the armed forces. But that blind loyalty will unfortunately put them in our cross hairs. You all know the truth of what we are fighting for; they don't, but we unfortunately cannot be sympathetic to their plight because they only see us as the enemy and will kill us without hesitation. We have a planet to save and until Ryles launches his information campaign to enlighten this planet, no one is going to believe us.

Susan was impressed with the team that Joshua had put together. She wanted to be part of this unit to prove herself. She knew their success depended on her as much as their combat skills they had honed over the years. She did not know what was out there in the universe that scared these aliens, but one thing for sure, she did not want to find out.

Operation Lasting Hope - Cairo, Egypt

Operation Lasting Hope was officially underway. The night sky was filled with thousands of parachutes from the 82nd Airborne Division. The army still used the reliable T-10 parachute chutes. The T-10 parachute is a static line-deployed parachute used by the United States armed forces for combat mass-assault airborne operations. The T-10 parachute was introduced in the early 1950s and is still the mainstay for the US military unless you are a member of special operations. Major General Carl E Parker, the Commander of the 82nd Airborne Division, hoped that this one-time Murphy was on their side. Parker remembered being in his philosophy class at West Point. His teacher Major Neil was giving a speech. It was the

first time he heard about Murphy.
"Murphy's Law ladies and gentlemen. What can go wrong, will go wrong. Most mission plans never survive the first rounds of being fired. That's why the mission's intent is so important as well as having well-trained soldiers, so that the mission could still be accomplished even when Murphy decided to rear his ugly head and throw a hand grenade in the best of laid plans."

It was the hopes that by doing this operation at 0200 hours, they would catch the Egyptians off guard and have the Giza secured before they could mount an effective counter strike.

The Naval Seals had done their job and targeted all of the SAMs that would prevent US reinforcements from coming to the aid of the 82nd. At T-Zero Hour, they lased the SAM batteries. As predicted, the Tomahawk missiles fired by the Arleigh-Burke class guided-missile destroyers USS Bainbridge (DDG 96), did their job well. All SAM batteries were destroyed. Sitting in the National Military Command Center watching the satellite feed, Army General Palmer Davis watched the soldiers running from the mobile SAM units. Davis knew by the time the Egyptian ADA soldiers saw the Tomahawks approaching they would only have two choices: run, or die. "Run you fucking bastards," Davis silently screamed. He did not relish seeing any allied soldiers dying this day, but he knew it was distinctly possible. Davis could see most of the soldiers had cleared the blast area when the Tomahawks hit, but a few remained still on the ground. Davis said a silent prayer for them and refocused back on the airborne operation.

The Delta Force Unit had disabled the radar system at Cairo's International Airport as planned and the 75th Ranger Regiment had commenced their jump operations at the same time the 82nd had jumped.

Most armies throughout the world still resisted operating at night. The US Army had trained very hard to be able to conduct night operations with the same effectiveness as they did day operations. All units were jumping at an altitude of 500 ft. At that height, it minimized exposure to potential enemy fire. Paratroopers usually land at a speed of around 13 mph, resulting in a landing force that is comparable to jumping off a 9 to12foot wall. Using the Parachute Landing Fall (PLF) technique, a paratrooper could land with no injuries. The General was doing the mental calculations based on the first commands to jump. "3 seconds before the chute deploys on static line jump, 1.3 minutes to PLF. The General was looking at his watch. Any second now, the first units would be reporting in, that Phase 1 was completed.

SFC (Sergeant First Class) Neal, the Platoon Sgt for 1st Platoon, Alpha Company, 1st Battalion, of 1st Infantry Brigade Combat Team "Devil Brigade," was the 1st paratrooper to land as part of Operation Lasting Hope. Seconds later, several other troopers landed on the sands of the Giza Plateau. After executing his PLF, he released his chute with his quick release clamps at his shoulder. Unlike training operations, he did not bother to collect his chute for recovery and reuse. Headquarters platoon was tasked with that mission. His platoon's mission was to immediately gather his soldiers and secure the Northeast corner of the Sphinx. His platoon was gathering at their rally point (RP) just in front of the Sphinx.

2LT Salazar, the Platoon Leader, had just arrived at the rally point. As per the OPORD or operational order, as soon as the platoon was at 50% strength, they would move out to their sector and start digging in. SFC Neal was designated to stay behind with a rifleman to send the remainder of their platoon to their sector. This location also served as the casualty collection point. As soldiers drifted in, SFC Neal kept a running total to determine who was MIA or KIA. After 30 minutes, the last soldier finally drifted in with a severe limp.

SFC Neal shouted, "Bass, I should have known you would be the last person to arrive. What did you do, take a nap before you got here?"

Bass responded, "Sarge, you are never going to believe this, some idiot drifted into my chute on the way down and both chutes collapsed. Luckily when they collapsed, they separated and mine re-inflated about 100 feet off the ground. The other guy's chute did not, and he hit hard. I hit hard but only had a bad sprain. He had a few broken bones. I followed SOP and marked him with an IR chemlite and started my long limp to our RP."

"Well at least you didn't break anything, you big dummy. When we get to our sector, I'll send the medic over to check you out. Now let's get moving."

Their position was about 300 meters on the Northeast sector of the Sphinx. Intel figured being so close to the Pyramids would slow the Egyptian Forces from engaging with them. When SFC Neal arrived, he found his Lieutenant supervising the platoon getting dug in. The foxholes were mostly dug. It was so much easier to dig in sand vs dirt. The soldiers were now engaged in filling up sandbags to provide additional protection. 2LT Salazar spotted SFC Neal walking towards him.

"Hey Sgt Neal, any casualties?" "Just one sprained ankle. It was Bass. Doc is looking at him now. How's it going over here so far?"

"No complaints. Most of the foxholes are dug. We're filling sandbags. The Squad Leaders are setting out the claymore mines. 1st Squad has linked up with Bravo Company 3rd Platoon and 3rd Squad has linked up with our 2nd Platoon. Can you go around and make sure that we have good overlapping fields of fire Sgt Neal?"

"Yes Sir, LT."

As SFC Neal walked away, he couldn't help but be impressed with LT Salazar. Most Lieutenants come in so green, it takes almost two years to get them whipped into shape. Salazar was pretty squared away from the start. He came to the unit with his airborne wings and Ranger Tab. He listened and learned fast. He did not pretend like he knew everything. They worked well together. When it came to NCO business, LT stepped back and didn't interfere. During one training exercise, when they killed off all the NCOs, Salazar stepped in and executed the duties of the Platoon SGT and his duties without hesitation. Truthfully, he did an outstanding job. Lt Salazar had earned the respect of his soldiers by not being afraid to join his men digging a foxhole, crawling through the mud, or taking his turn on guard duty, but most importantly, he stood up for his men and protected them from the bullshit that some officers peddled just because they had rank. Neal's thoughts turned back to the mission at hand. I hope we survive this mission. Invading an ally was not something one did likely. With that, SFC Neal found the lead elements of Bravo Company, 3rd Platoon.

# # #

The reports were coming in now. Major General Parker was happy that most of the units were now in place. Although Phase II was not finished, if they were attacked now, they could at least defend themselves. The 75 Ranger Regiment had reported that the Cairo International Airport was now secure with five casualties, two KIAs and three WIAs. An airport policeman got lucky and managed to kill two Rangers, one whose chute left him dangling 25 feet off the ground when his chute got snagged on the roof of a building. The other Ranger was killed as he dangled from a powerline. The other three injuries were various degrees of sprains from landing on the drop zone. While every life lost was a tragedy, casualty projections for seizing an airfield put the number killed between 10 to 15% So all in all, the General was pleased with the operation so far. While a 49-minute commute over land in their Stryker Armored Combat Vehicles between the airport and Pyramids was not ideal, it was logistically manageable. With a helicopter ride, they could be there in 15 minutes.

10 minutes after the Rangers had secured the airfield, C-5Ms started landing to offload the famed Pegasus Brigade, the Combat Aviation Brigade (CAB)

for the 82nd Airborne Division. The Air Forces C-5M is a modernized version of the C5 Galaxy used as a strategic transport aircraft. The C-5 Fleet was slated to be retired in 2017, but in 1998, the Air Force began a modernization push to extend the life of the C-5s through 2040. The C-5Ms were perfectly designed to bring in the Pegasus Brigade. Each C-5M could carry six UH-60 Blackhawk helicopters or six Apache attack helicopters. The C-5 also could carry seven Strykers respectively.

Once the helicopters were offloaded, the C-5Ms would immediately take off. SOP (Standard Operating Procedures) only allowed two planes on the ground at a time to minimize catastrophe losses in case the enemy got lucky. The other planes were in a raceway pattern flying overhead.

While it took a day to "fold" the Blackhawks and a day to load the Blackhawks onto the C-5M, offloading them was dramatically easier. The Air Force C-5M Crew Chiefs, the Army Blackhawk Crew Chiefs and the Army Mechanics did not have to be nearly as careful unloading as they did when loading the helicopters. Unfortunately, it was still going to take about 8 to 10 hours to get the Blackhawks ready to fly. The Little Birds on the other hand were a different story. The Little Birds were the first helicopters offloaded. The 160th SOAR crews were very well versed at reassembling the Little Birds & getting them airborne incredibly fast after transport. They were putting that theory to the test today. These versatile little helicopters can be folded for transport and reassembled in about 3 minutes. The goal was to have Delta airborne at T plus 2 hours into the operation.

Once Delta had taken out Cairo International Airport's radar systems, they were to remain in place and link-up with the 75th Ranger Regiment until their Little Birds were ready to fly. Once assembled, Delta would fly to Giza to do a search and find operation in the Pyramids to secure the nuclear weapons. For the purpose of this operation, JSOC, had tasked A Squadron, which was in Jordan to dispatch three teams of 12 men or about half of its squadron, so they could cover all three Pyramids at once. Based on the configuration of troops, the 160th Special Operations Aviation Regiment or Task Force

160 deployed both variants of the Little Bird: the AH-6, which is the attack/ assault version, and the MH-6, which is the assault/transport. Each Delta Team would have one AH-6 for gun support and three MH-6 for troop transport.

In addition to the Little Birds being offloaded, six members of the Nuclear Emergency Support Team (NEST) offloaded too. Two members each would be joining each Delta Team in order to neutralize the nuclear bomb once it was found. The last thing the Pentagon wanted to see broadcasted on evening news was the destruction of the great Pyramids along with the entire 82nd Airborne Division.

The General was amazed at how much misinformation was out there about the famed Delta Forces and Seal Team Six. Task

Force 160 was no different. They are a special operations force that provides helicopter aviation support for general purpose forces and special operations forces. Its missions have included attack, assault, and reconnaissance, and were usually conducted at night. They were the "Go To" for special operations. Task Force 160 is known to have some of the best helicopter pilots in the world.

The Little Birds were assembled, and the AH-6 gunships were already in the air. The three teams of Delta operators were almost finished boarding the MH-6 helicopters. With Delta giving the NEST members last minute instructions on their role during the initial combat assault of the operation. Major Dumfries was the last soldier to board the MH-6. He then took the headset offered to him by the co-pilot and radioed into command that they were enroute to Objective Noble Cause, which were the three pyramids.

The C5's carrying the Stryker Armored Combat Vehicles were the last to start landing at Cairo International. Charlie Company, 2nd Battalion, 1st Brigade, 25th Infantry Division, Stryker brigade combat team (SBCT) was selected to augment the 75th Rangers to secure the airport. 3 Platoons consisting of 4 Strykers each, strategically deployed around the airport as per their operational orders along with the Company Headquarters eliminate. These vehicles were also designated to transport the Rangers as necessary to "Hot Spots" as required.

* * *

# # #

The 2/22nd Battalion, 1st Infantry Brigade out of 10th Mountain Division assigned to the Multi-National Forces & Observer (MFO) mission in Egypt had redeployed to their assigned blocking positions for the 242 MEU (Marine Expeditionary Unit) coming from the Gulf. The Battalion Commander had briefed the Company Commanders that this was a critical mission to get armor into Giza to support the 82nd Airborne Division. While S-2, Intel, did not anticipate any opposition, they should be prepared to engage Egyptian Forces if that became necessary. Each company had been issued their basic MTOE, but to be on the safe side, a double load of ammunition was issued as well.

As Triple Deuce was deploying to their prearranged blocking positions, the 242 MEU radioed that they had just made landfall and were proceeding with all haste to Giza. For the purposes of this operation, the 242 MEU was only deploying their Ground Combat Element. The Ground Combat Element (GCE) is an infantry battalion reinforced with an artillery battery, amphibious assault vehicle platoon, combat engineer platoon, light armored reconnaissance company, tank platoon, reconnaissance platoon, and other units as the mission and circumstances require. The total strength is approximately 1,100 members, including navy sailors. In this partial case those other units included an additional tank battalion consisting of four tank companies, a headquarters and service company, one antitank platoon, and one scout platoon. Each tank company consists of 14 M1A2 tanks bringing the number of M1A2 Abrams tanks deployed to 44.

# # #

Major General Parker was again pleased that so far, the operation was proceeding according to plan. As dedicated by the OPORD, the General picked up the satellite phone and called Secretary of State Calvin Murphy. "Mr. Secretary, this is General Parker, we are now at Phase Line Charlie. Good luck Sir. I hope you are as good as everyone thinks and keep us out of a shooting war."

"Thank you General. If you don't hear from me in the next hour, things didn't go well. Good luck to you and your soldiers as well." With that, the line went died. General Parker hung up his phone and said a quick prayer that Murphy was successful in his conversation with the President of Egypt. The General then directed the pilot to prepare to land, so they could move mobile command to Cairo International Airport.

# # #

As the Little Birds landed, Captain Peele and 1SG Nelson greeted the Delta operators. "We have secured the entrance to all three pyramids. From left to right, 1st Platoon is guarding the entrance to the Pyramid of Menkaure. 2nd Platoon, the Pyramid of Khafre and 3rd Platoon, the Great Pyramid of Khufu. We have the additional chemlights that you requested at each entrance. Each platoon understands, they are under your control and will act as your QRF (Quick Reaction Force) as necessary. If needed, they will enter a designated pyramid and follow the trail of chemlights to your location. After exchanging frequencies, the Delta Operators followed by NEST proceeded to their designated Pyramid. After a few minutes of coordinating with the Platoon Leader and Platoon SGT, the Delta Operatives entered their designated pyramid.

# # #

General Parker's plane landed T Plus 4 hours into the operation. Their TOC (Tactical Operations Center) had already been established in a hanger near the runway. The General and Sergeant Major were escorted to the hanger where the

Chief of Staff Colonel Ben Erikson greeted them and quickly started updating them on the status of all phases of the operation. "Sir", Col Erikson said. "Everything is proceeding according to plan. The only element not in place is the augmented 242 MEU. They are approximately 1.5 hours out. So far, they have lost two tanks and one support vehicle. Triple Deuce is deploying resources to secure those vehicles until they can be repaired. Delta is picking up some residual radiation, but no sign of the bombs or enemy personnel at this point. 3rd Squadron, 73rd Cavalry Regiment has replaced the 75 Ranger Regiment guarding the airport. The Rangers are now re-organizing preparing to deploy as necessary."

"Ben, what about resistance so far?"

"Well Sir, there is a crowd gathering outside of the airport. Mainly individuals who have flights. Of course, the police have arrived and are demanding entrance. The presence of two M1126 Stryker Combat Vehicles, four 50 caliber machine guns mounted on armored HMMWV and a platoon of soldiers is preventing them from trying to breach the perimeter. Our interpreter is trying to assure the police, once the situation was resolved as per the President of Egypt's instructions, the airport would be re-opened. Because of our heavy military presence, the police have not taken any action. Also, the Secretary of State Calvin Murphy along with the US Ambassador just arrived at the President's compound about 5 minutes ago."

"Thank you, Ben. Please let me know

when the 242 MEU is in place. Let's plan for a staff meeting in 2 hours. I need to call General Davis. Please set me up with a secure location."

"That's already been arranged General. Please follow me."

# # #

"Mr. Secretary, it's awfully early for a social visit. What could be so important that you would pay me a visit at 6am? Please sit down and have some tea so we can talk."

Secretary of State Calvin Murphy had war-gamed how this conversation would play out and immediately refused to sit and have tea when President Mohamed el-Klaldi offered. Instead, without the typical pleasantries, Calvin launched into his prepared speech. "Mr. President, as of

0200 hours, the US 82nd Airborne Division launched a very limited military operation to secure the Giza plateau including the Pyramids of Egypt."

The Egyptian President immediately jumped out of his seat where he was preparing his tea and screamed, "What! " Hearing the President scream, the President's elite personal guard, a division of the Republican Guard, swarmed into the room. These guards were specially trained and only took orders from the President. The 2013 Egyptian coup d'état which was led by then Defense Minister, now President el-Klaldi, taught the President the value of having absolutely loyal soldiers around him. His personal guard lived in the finest accommodations. They were paid a small fortune by Egyptian standards and given perks that would make a prince envious. The guards entered the room with weapons drawn and scanned the room quickly for any overt threats. These soldiers trained hard when they were off duty. Each one of them could run a marathon. All were also black belts in Tahtib, traditional stick-fighting martial art of Egypt and Japanese Aikido.

Calvin knew his life was in mortal danger. One false word or move and these soldiers would not hesitate to eliminate him and the Ambassador. "Mr. President, I know this news is upsetting, but please hear me out before you do anything that Egypt can't walk back from."

# # #

At the same time Secretary of State Calvin Murphy was having his conversation with President Mohamed el-Klaldi, the US Ambassador to Israel, Sneed Mandelle was having the same conversation with the Prime Minister of Israel Yitzhak Barah. However, this conversation was delivered much differently.

"Prime Minister, you will stand down your forces immediately!" Prime Minister Barah was not used to being spoken to like this and immediately began to protest. Before he could get a word in, Mandelle continued. "We know about your planned invasion of Egypt. First, are you crazy! How could you think you can contain a conflict with Egypt without every Arabian neighbor joining forces with Egypt? It was only a fluke that you won the 7 Day War, and you know it. We know about the portable nuclear bombs terrorist have been developing. Any minute your defense minister will walk into this room and tell you that the US 82nd Airborne Division has secured the Giza Plateau. With any luck, we will be able to retrieve the nuclear man-pak bombs and be out of the country within a month. Now I will say this again, Prime Minister, stand down your forces or risk bombing American troops. And if that happens, you risk starting a war with your oldest, strongest ally. And I don't have to tell you, that is a war you can't win. So let the United States take the brunt of this disaster and protect our historical ally and friend."

The Prime Minister shook his head and laughed. "Sit down Sneed and tell me how the hell did you find out about our operation. Who's your spy in my cabinet."

"When you tell me the names of your spies, I'll do the same. You up for a shot of some of that premium Johnny Walker Blue Label this early in the morning?"

"The Prime Minister got up and removed a pair of glasses from the cabinet and poured each four fingers of Scotch. Let's hope you have better luck than we would have in stopping World War III, but you know Sneed, we didn't have a choice?"

"I know Prime Minister. I know." With that, both men held up their glass in salute and drained the $800 whiskey.

Gulf of Mexico - Latitude 26.93905139
Longitude -94.68872137

Through a CIA shell company, Brewster Jennings & Associates Susan purchased one the 1,000 abandoned oil rigs sitting in the Gulf of Mexico through their Cayman Island account in the Cainvest Bank and Trust Ltd. This particular oil rig was owned by Exxon Mobil Corporation. Based on operations in both Brazil and Mexico, Susan and Mick agreed this was the most advantageous location for Delta Teams' Quick Reaction Force.

Susan had requisitioned three Bell Boeing V-22 Osprey airplanes. Normally the only aircraft capable of landing on a drilling platform was a helicopter, but Susan needed an aircraft that was capable of flying a little faster than a helicopter. The V-22 is a tiltrotor, which can change from an airplane to a helicopter in just 12 seconds. The V-22 was perfect for landing and taking off from the drilling platform, but more importantly it was capable of cruising, as an aircraft, at 351 mph or 305 knots. The amphibious assault ship USS Tripoli had been tasked with providing aerial refueling for Susan's V-22 via the Marines' V-22 Aerial Refueling System (VARS). Based on the operation plan developed, Delta Team's QRF would use 2 Fire Teams to provide rotating support for Bravo Team in Tapajós, Brazil. Based on the V-22 Osprey specifications, Susan calculated with the distance to Tapajós of approximately 3,054 miles and with the range of the V-22 at 1,011 miles, it would require four ground fueling stops one in Cuba and Puerto Rico, plus the initial one heading down and coming back. It would also require ten aerial refueling, one for the trip and nine so the V-22 could stay on station to quickly provide support for Bravo Team. When briefing Mick, he complained about the delays landing at Cuba and Puerto Rico could potentially cost the team. As such, he requested if Susan could procure the Air Force's variant V-22 or CV-22 Osprey, which had a range of 2,100 miles. Because of his special operations background, he knew the mission of the CV-22 was to conduct long-range infiltration, exfiltration, and resupply missions for special operations forces. So now with the new specifications, Susan calculated seven aerial refueling and one ground refueling in Puerto Rico on the way back. Susan calculated the teams would have about 32 hrs on station before the CV-22 would leave the area of operation. So, each team would have a rotational cycle of about 48 hrs.

Mick liked working with Susan. As far as CIA Liaisons are concerned, she was one of the best. She understood special operations. Joshua had shared Susan's file before his team left to meet Susan at the abandoned oil rig. She had served most of her career in the CIA with the Special Activities Division (SAD). SAD is a division of the CIA responsible for covert and paramilitary operations. Though technically not a military apparatus, SAD has highly specialized, trained, and versatile operatives capable of carrying out some of the most sophisticated top-secret missions in the world. SAD operatives are often compared to elite Tier 1 special forces soldiers such as Delta Force or Navy SEAL. As a paramilitary operations officers, Susan attended the eighteen month long Clandestine Service Trainee (CST) program run by the CIA. Having served in a number of countries as a paramilitary operations officer, case officer and finally as a liaison officer between the CIA and USSOCOM, Mick was more than happy to have her on board. In the follow-up meeting, Susan laid out routes; check points; refueling times; emergency call signs and logistical support. Mick wanted to always have a team on station to support Bravo at a moment's notice. The plan she laid out would accomplish just that.

Thirty minutes later, Mick was on the helipad briefing Delta Team 2 about the mission to provide rotating support for Bravo Team. The risk assessment was low, but just in case the team was packed out with their full MTOE (Modification table of organization and equipment). Mick explained if they need to deploy to provide support, it would be either by fast rope or HALO. He wished Carl, Greg, Norman, Lou and Warren luck as they grabbed their equipment and loaded the CV-22.

Directorate Headquarters - Undisclosed Location Outside of Roanoke, Virginia

Research felt pretty confident about being able to locate the remaining three components of the alien spaceship. Research was able to back into the remainder digits of their location using an algorithm developed by Jamine using what was known about the location of the Ark of the Covenant. As a matter of fact, Jamie mused to himself, the Ark better be known because it was sitting on the conference room table right in front of him. Using a decipher algorithm that Jamie had been working on for the past 6 months, he was able to approximate the last 4 digits of the transponder transmission. Two additional digits to the latitude and two additional digits to the longitude coordinates, he could now pinpoint the Ark to within 1.11 square kilometers. When they first received the Ark, it took them 3 months to bring the accuracy of the search program to 111 square kilometers, then another 2 months to bring the accuracy to 11.1 square kilometers. No matter how hard Jamie tried to pinpoint the location to 3 meters as per Col. Myers' instructions, he just could not. While the program accuracy was down to 1.11 square kilometers, any additional tweaks to the algorithm caused the program's accuracy to decrease by a factor of 10. Jamie finally concluded that the last four digits probably needed some type of alien interface to get within the last 3 meters of accuracy, a device probably still located on the alien ship.

Col. Myers was not happy with this development, but he always had a contingency plan for unforeseen obstacles. Utilizing the financial arm of the Committee, at his direction, Axion Corporation Int'l had been busy buying up property in the Amazon Rainforest when the Ark was first recovered. Col. Myers thought to himself, with over 6,000,000 square km, the Brazilian government could afford to sell 100 square km at the price Axion was offering. With the Brazilian government selling acres upon acres of land to cattle farms, the deforestation of the Amazon Rainforest has been an inevitable forgone conclusion. In the late sixties, early seventies, cattle ranching accounted for about 38 percent of deforestation. As of last year, those percentages are closer to 70 percent. So, these "accidental forest fires" have been consuming more and more of the vaunted Amazon Rainforest. The acreage that Axion burned would go unnoticed in the midst of the other fires burning out of control. Initially Axion had purchased over 100 square kilometers to ensure they could begin searching for the Holy Grail at the Committee's discretion. Unfortunately, Prometheus Unrestricted could not do the same in Mexico's Yucatan Peninsula because in 2011 the Mexico government designation three new protected areas totaling over 76,000 acres on the Yucatán Peninsula. Prometheus had to turn to a tried and tested method of good ole-fashioned bribery. The amount of money they had to give to Mexico's Economy Minister, Juan

Benito Cruz was obscene. It was enough for Juan to buy a small island and for him and his children's children to live a life of luxury without a care in the world. Minister Cruz had arranged for his team to deploy and move without resistance as members of the Mexican Navy special operations force called Fuerzas Especiales, better known as FES. Because the location in the designated 100 square km includes parts of the Gulf of Mexico, the FES was perfect to impersonate. The FES is capable of carrying out non-conventional warfare in the air, sea, and land, by utilizing all means of infiltration available to develop the most variable operational incursions with the use of military diving techniques, parachuting, vertical descent, urban combat, sniping and use of explosives. The units are trained and equipped to operate independently in maritime, lake, riverine or terrestrial scenarios. Col. Myers was pleased with this development, that the Night Stalkers would be able to search via land, sea, and air to find Pandora's Box.

A week earlier Major Wayne Carson, the new Night Stalkers Leader, was called into Myers' office to be briefed on the mission to retrieve the Holy Grail and Pandora's Box.

"Maj. Carson, I hope your teams are ready because it's time to see if the three million dollars in reconstituting the Night Stalkers was worth the investment."

"Sir, I can assure you; we are ready. The teams have been drilling nonstop for three months now. As per our new operating protocols, each team has performed ten combat missions as contractors in Afghanistan. Each mission was either a capture, kill or destroy, and all were performed flawlessly. We are ready for any mission Sir, just tell us when and where."

"Wayne, Research has pinpointed the location of the remaining three devices currently not in our control. The first is in the Amazon Rainforest. The second is in the Yucatan Peninsula, and the final device is in the Mahalangur Himal sub-range of the Himalayas or in other words, the Mt Everest mountain range. Your team is tasked with the successful recovery of each of these devices. All pertinent information has been forwarded to your secure Samsung Galaxy Z Fold 4."

Maj. Carson stood up and saluted sharply, "Yes Sir Col. Myers." As Carson turned to leave, the Col put his hand on Carson's shoulder.

"Wayne, one last order. This one will be a hunt and kill mission for Trinity and Joshua. They have interfered in our operations for far too long. I need them eliminated."

"Yes Sir."

"And Wayne, be careful. Do not under any circumstance underestimate them. They have proven to be deadly adversaries. They are the reason we had to rebuild the Night Stalkers, and you're the new Team Leader. Now good luck and successful hunting."

Anacostia, Southeast Washington, DC

Kenny was staring at the multiple screens arrayed before him. Joshua had tasked Kenny with locating the remaining artifacts. Joshua and Trinity had briefed Kenny on what the Spear of Destiny, the Holy Grail, and Pandora's Box really were. He was told to focus on the Holy Grail and Pandora's Box. Kenny truthfully was stumped for the 1st month trying to figure out the impossible. Then Kenny had an epiphany about a week ago. While he couldn't directly track the artifacts, he might be able to track the groups looking for them.

Kenny thought, "If I can track the group by communication chatter, I might be able to pinpoint the area of operations to at least give our teams a fighting chance." Kenny was actually surprised at how easy the process was going to be. Tedious, time consuming, and impossible, but these are the things that got Kenny excited.

Using the back door Kenny had created in the Dish TV satellite cable network, Kenny started collecting data from the Wideband Global SATCOM system (WGS), a high-capacity United States Space Force satellite communications system. This network of next generation satellites was used in partnership by the United States Department of Defense (DoD), Canadian Department of National Defence (DND) and the Australian Department of Defence. With Dish services being worldwide, it was easy to collect the data feeds from the WGS satellite network.

Kenny was slightly frustrated. Unfortunately collecting the data and decrypting the data were two totally different things. If this was just 6 months earlier, he would have been able to only collect the data. Under the old Defense Satellite Communications System (DSCS), which was the background to the United States military communications system, I could have decrypted the data, Kenny thought.

The old satellites operated on a frequency around 44 GHz. German academics in 2012 theorized this frequency could be hacked into by rapidly speeding up the attack vector. This theory was tested by showing the encryption used in popular Inmarsat satellite phones can be cracked in real time. A publication by two Chinese scientist on "A Real-time Inversion Attack on the GMR-2 Cipher Used in the Satellite Phones" took his research from theoretical to application. The attack method required hitting the DSCS satellite streams hundreds of thousands of times with an inversion attack, which eventually produces the 128-bit encryption key making it easier to hunt for the decryption key, allowing attackers to decrypt communications and listen in to a conversation in real time. Unfortunately, the new satellite system, WGS, uses upgraded Military-grade AES-256 encryption, which was nearly impossible to decrypt. While the conversations were nearly impossible to decrypt, the GPS location data was not.

Kenny theorized that once he started

to process the WGS feeds, he would be able to narrow down the locations of the teams searching for the artifacts. Based on current events, it would be easy to eliminate ongoing military operations for the US, Canadian and Australian military. Once those operations were eliminated, that would only leave special operations and the opposition forces. Only by processing the collected data would he be able to hopefully isolate the opposition forces and thereby the artifacts.

# # #

Kenny's system had been collecting data for the past six weeks. So much data had come in that Kenny had to stop updating Joshua's offline system. At present Kenny had collected over five teraflops of data. His algorithm had been processing data nonstop for the past week. Over 35 major military operations across the globe have been eliminated so far. It was amazing how helpful World Global News Network, Pace News Syndicate, and British News Communications were. Kenny personally felt this whole Freedom of Speech thing was blown way out of control. Some things are meant and should be outside of public purview; however, in this case Kenny mused, anything that makes my job easier, I'm not complaining. There were another 15 clusters of satellite communications that Kenny needed to sort through. Kenny was digging through the dark recesses of the internet trying to understand if there were possible clandestine operations ongoing. While hacking the intelligence and defense communities throughout the world was not beyond Kenny's abilities, he would prefer to find the information a different way. During one of the briefings with Trinity and Joshua, Trinity reminded Kenny to reach out to Senator Ryles to hopefully eliminate any U.S. clandestine operations. With Senator Ryle's assistance, Kenny was able to eliminate another seven locations, leaving eight more clusters to sort through.

After several more weeks, Kenny decided to switch tactics. He had reprogrammed his algorithm to now look for patterns of communication. He theorized teams working together would use standard operating procedures for their communications: duration of the call; preset times of the day to communicate; use of the same frequencies on the X-band.

Using this new tactic, Kenny was able to narrow down the cluster of communications to four distinct areas of operation. Kenny was pretty sure he had pinpointed the opposition forces' location. Kenny was so confident that he called Joshua to arrange a briefing to go over his findings. The other four clusters of communication had no elements of commonality and Kenny easily wrote them off as one-off operations. In most cases, SOPs were an asset to highly trained units. Usually, their training and SOPs were the difference between life and death. In this case, those communication SOPs were being used as a weapon against them. Kenny found the same thing with hackers. They always left a residual footprint or signature based on how their minds worked.

Kenny was always told that he was hard to figure out because his creative brain would always come up with multiple solutions to various problems. Whether it was math or computer programming, it did not matter. Keeping Kenny focused was always a problem for both his parents and his teachers. Kenny graduated High School at the age of 15. Joshua routinely jokes about Kenny running circles around MIT graduates when in reality, he did. Kenny only spent two years at MIT before he dropped out. He constantly butted heads with his college professors because they often clashed over how he came up with answers. Whereas the answers were always correct, his methodology was unorthodox and not the prescribed way to solving problems. Kenny constantly complained to the Dean that the teachers were limiting his creativity by forcing him to comply with antiquity thinking. Kenny finally gave up and quit MIT when his professor of computer programming failed him for not following the prescribed path to completing his assignment. It did not matter that Kenny's program used 68% less code or that it solved the problems 84% faster, the professor wanted Kenny to learn the value of structure. After that Kenny went back home and started writing gaming programs, which allowed him to move out of his house two years later and live comfortably in a modest Brownstone on Nth Street in Washington DC's historical district. The fact that the Brownstone was over seven figures did not matter to Kenny one bit. He loved the historical district of Washington, DC. Looking at Kenny, one would never know that he had a net worth of over 100 million dollars and for shits and giggles, he routinely hacked into the FBI, CIA, and NSA's supercomputers. It wasn't until Kenny met Joshua that his life started to have purpose and meaning. Having been bullied all his life, Kenny finally decided to do something about it. He did his research on martial arts instructors in the area. Everyone had the same BS credentials, lineages that traced back to the supposed founder of the system, national/ international championships, 2nd, 3rd, 4th degree black belts. Karate, Kung Fu, Judo, Muay Thai, Brazilian Jiu-Jitsu, Krav Maga, Aikido, it was all the same bullshit until he came across Joshua. Joshua taught Tai

Chi Chuan, a Chinese Martial Arts and self-defense, but it was the black outs in his background that caught Kenny's eye. He had to hack into the DoD's database to see why Joshua's military records were classified. At the end of Kenny's research, he knew he had to meet Joshua in person to understand how someone with his background would be okay living such an unassuming life teaching people Tai Chi. From that first meeting, Kenny knew he had found his mentor in life. Joshua taught Kenny how to embrace his uniqueness and to not limit himself to what society said was "normal."

Kenny was now a well-paid cyber security expert. He routinely hacked into Fortune 500 companies to expose their weaknesses before other hackers could exploit those weaknesses. Finding patterns in a seemingly chaotic ecosystem was what he excelled in. So, finding this team of elite soldiers was a source of pride for Kenny. This moment took him back to a lesson Joshua was trying to teach him about being fluid like water when fighting using Tai Chi. He used a quote by Sun Tzu in the book "The Art of War."

"Engage people with what they expect; it is what they are able to discern and confirms their projections. It settles them into predictable patterns of response, occupying their minds while you wait for the extraordinary moment -- that which they cannot anticipate."

Training Headquarters - Waco, Texas

Kenny arrived on the first plane out of Dulles International Airport the following day. Joshua and Trinity picked up Kenny from Waco Regional Airport. As was the norm, Kenny could not stop talking when he was excited about figuring out an impossible problem. Trinity tried to get Kenny to focus, but she couldn't make any headway.

Joshua put his hand on her lap and said, "Let him talk. This way when he gives his briefing to the team, he will be more focused and will not inundate the team with useless details. It's his process. The best we can do is to just keep him between the guide rails."

An hour and a half later, they arrived at the training compound to the sound of rounds being fired down range. They exited the Jeep Cherokee and moved directly to the briefing room. Bravo Team Leader, Peter Cullum, who was operational leader when Joshua wasn't there, met them on the stairs to the building. Peter extended his hand to everyone. "Welcome back boss, Trinity, Kenny. As you can see, the teams are training hard and we're ready whenever you give us a mission."

"Thanks Peter. I can't tell you how much I appreciate you picking up the slack in my absence. Hopefully after Kenny's briefing, we can start mission planning. Peter, can you please bring all the Team Leaders in for a briefing at 1300 hrs. By then Senator Ryles should be here."

"Sure thing, boss."

Ryles was talking to Trinity and

Joshua when the rest of the leadership team arrived. "Boss, everyone is here. We can get started whenever you are ready." said Peter.

"Thanks Peter. Everyone, grab a seat. Kenny begin whenever you are ready." said Joshua.

Kenny turned on the micro projector attached to his phone then launched into the briefing. After giving the background for how the data was collected and sorted, Kenny got into the meat of the presentation.

"At the end of the day, there are four teams that I am currently tracking. Three teams are obviously looking for something. Based on their movements, they are conducting a grid search pattern. Here are the locations for three of the four teams.

Opposition Force 1 is located in this two kilometer grid near the Tapajós River in Brazil. The latitude for Tapajós, Brazil is: -4.789969 and the longitude is: -56.62583. Beyond that, I can't get more specific, but it's obvious they are looking for something because the signal GPS locators keep moving in a concentric grid search pattern.

Opposition Force 2 is located in this two kilometer grid near Limones, Mérida, Yucatan, Mexico. The latitude for Limones, Mérida, Yucatan, Mexico is: 21.003204 and the longitude is: -89.646933

Opposition Force 3 is located near Mount Everest, Nepal. Latitude and longitude coordinates are: 27.986065, 86.922623.

Opposition Force 4 is more problematic. I can't discern any particular pattern. They have been hovering around the Metropolitan DC area."

Kenny then overlaid maps of their DC search pattern. "See what I mean. I can't make heads or tails of what they are doing. See here, at times, the Opposition Force 4 team seems like they split."

"They're hunting, Kenny. More specifically, they are hunting for us. Some of those locations are associated with me," said Joshua.

"We have obviously become a thorn in their plans, and they want to eliminate us. So now we have a hunter-killer team on our trail. We immediately need to finish operational plans and split the teams. Know this guys, the same way that Kenny tracked the Opposition Forces, they can do the same to us. We need to move to radio silence and use our email drop boxes to communicate and only use satellite communications prior to engagement or during engagements as necessary."

"Let's start mission planning ASAP. Susan, please coordinate with all teams to ensure they have whatever support is required. Susan, I know we haven't worked together before, but this is probably the most important mission you have ever been a part of. We're all counting on you."

"Yes Joshua." replied Susan.

"Peter Cullum, Opposition Force 1 is yours. James McKay, Opposition Force 2 is yours. Senator Ryles, since you stated you wanted Alpha Team to return to your base of operations, we'll take Opposition

Force 3 in Mt Everest."

Before Joshua could continue Ryles interrupted. "Joshua, that won't be necessary. I don't think you have to assign a team to Opposition Force 3. Remember how you got to our base of operations inside of Mt Everest? There is no way that their team will be able to penetrate our location with earth's present level of technology."

"Good point Senator. I totally forgot about that. The rest of Alpha Team is in for a real treat."

Trinity immediately chimed in. "If you call vomiting and shitting your guts out "A Real Treat" then yeah.... It's going to be a blast."

"Mick, I want you to coordinate with Susan and put a contingency plan in place to split your team as necessary to support both Bravo and Charlie teams. Let's get to it. As always Kenny, outstanding job!"

Somewhere in the Middle of the Atlantic Ocean | Tapajós, Brazil

The Harry S. Truman Carrier Strike Group 8 operating under United States Northern Command (USNORTHCOM) in the Atlantic Ocean was tasked with delivering Bravo Team to Brazil. Carrier Strike Group 8 consisted of the guided-missile cruiser USS San Jacinto, Carrier Air Wing One, and the ships of Destroyer Squadron 28. Destroyer Squadron 28 is a squadron of Arleigh-Burke Class destroyers. It was composed of the following ships: USS Ramage; USS Mitscher; USS Forrest Sherman; USS Lassen and the USS Farragut. Also, part of the Harry S. Truman Carrier Strike Group was the USS Bataan Wasp-class, a Marine amphibious assault ship.

Captain William Mayfield was not

happy about the orders he had just received, but the orders had the correct authentication codes from USNORTHCOM. With everything going on in the world, Mayfield was ill at ease splitting his carrier group, but orders stated the USS Bataan and two Arleigh-Burke Class destroyers: USS Lassen and the USS Farragut were to deliver a covert team of operatives off the coast of Brazil and remain in international waters, but close enough to provide support if necessary. He had been the Captain of the USS Harry S. Truman for just over six months, and he couldn't help but to think this operation was somehow connected with the 82nd Airborne Division's deployment to Egypt. All Captain Mayfield could do was sit and wait for his guest to arrive and pray this operation did not jeopardize his Carrier Strike Group.

Bravo Team landed on the USS Truman at 0200 hrs aboard two Sikorsky SH-60 Seahawk Helicopters. With gear in hand, a squad of Marines immediately escorted Bravo Team to a secure briefing area. From the observation deck, Mayfield watched the team being escorted by his Marines. He had seen their look before. They were professionals through and through. Because they wore nondescript black Army Combat Uniforms (ACU), Mayfield could not tell if they were Delta Force or a CIA paramilitary unit under the Special Activities Center Division. Because of how the orders came through, he was pretty sure this was a CIA operation. Because the CIA had a history of using Special

Operations personnel to include his SEALs from time to time, he could not tell who these soldiers were. He just hoped the mission was worth putting his Carrier Group at risk by splitting his task force.

At 0400 hrs, Bravo Team boarded the same two Sikorsky SH-60 Seahawk Helicopters and ferried over to the USS Bataan. During operational planning, Peter was very specific about the equipment his team would need during this mission. Susan stated whatever he needed; he would have. Peter stated the team would need a Sikorsky CH-53K King Stallion, which was large enough to carry them and their gear and two Rigid Hull Inflatable Boats (RHIBs).

The RHIBs were perfect for navigating the Amazon River. The RHIBs were armed with a M60 7.62mm machine gun, a MK19 40mm, and a M2 .50 cal. machine gun. It was capable of speeds of 40 plus knots with a range of 200 nautical miles. Each boat carried enough extra fuel to triple that range. They also carried double the combat load of ammunition.

After the team landed aboard the USS Bataan, they were escorted to their pre-deployment area, isolated from the rest of the ship. The Captain of the Bataan briefed Peter that they were over 1,800 nautical miles from the insertion point. At flank speed, it would take about 3 days and 10 hours. "Get some rest guys. We have about 3.5 days until we reach our target insertion point. We have a mission brief at 1400 hrs. Until then, rest. Chow will be delivered at 0800 hrs." With that, the team grabbed cots provided and immediately went to sleep. They had learned a long time ago to grab sleep whenever they could. Sleep was a precious gift, as precious as water in the desert. So, when they closed their eyes, most were asleep within minutes. As per standard operating procedures, two men were left awake to stand guard over their equipment. Even in a secure location, they had learned to never leave anything to chance.

The briefing started at 1400 hrs sharply with all Bravo Team Members present minus two members assigned to guard the team's equipment. The S2 immediately launched into the briefing as soon as everyone was seated. "Gentleman, my name is Lieutenant Johnson. While I don't know what your objective is, we will do our best to give you the best Intel possible for the mission. Your area of operation will be the Tapajós river in Brazil. It runs through the Amazon Rainforest and is a major tributary of the Amazon River. When combined with the Juruena River, the Tapajós is approximately 2,080 km long. It is one of the largest clearwater rivers, accounting for about six percent of the water in the Amazon basin."

The team then received a briefing on indigenous life in the area, with more attention paid to the Munduruku tribe. The S2 continued, "In recent years, the Munduruku tribe started conducting guerrilla operations against the corporations that have been building dams to conduct illegal gold mining and logging operations on their land. Especially with the government's failure to protect their forest, the Munduruku felt like they had no choice but to defend their right to live. The Rainforest is their home and provides everything they need to live. The Munduruku tribe have always lived in harmony with the Rainforest. Unfortunately, now gentleman they are defending their lands with blood. At first, their operations only involved sabotage, but when the corporations brought in mercenaries to defend the dams and loggers, the Munduruku started killing in direct response to the mercenaries' tactics. Gentlemen you will be walking into an area that is occupied by three different forces: the Munduruku tribe; the corporate security forces; and finally, the Night Stalkers."

At the conclusion of the briefing, to include an update on the dangerous wildlife and plants in the area, Peter stood up and took over the briefing. "Thanks Lieutenant Johnson. I'll take over from here." With that dismissal, Lt Johnson and his staff exited the briefing room.

"Team, nothing has changed. We have got to recover the Grail first. No matter who we have to go through. The only exception is the Munduruku Tribe. Nonlethal force only if we have to engage them. Max, coordinate with the on-ship armory to get us outfitted with short- and long-range tranquilizer darts in case we have to engage the Munduruku. Stealth is our friend, but we are not natives, which means they have the upper hand. In all likelihood, the Munduruku will have eyes on us from the moment we enter their territory. Hopefully, if we don't directly engage them and they see we are trying to engage the other forces, they will leave us alone. Remember, our job is to recover the Grail. We are not here to engage in random firefights, but make no mistake, if we are engaged, we will use lethal force to eliminate all resistance."

"Questions, gentlemen?" Silence greeted Peter. "Okay. Dismissed. Get your rest. Equipment check at 1500 hrs tomorrow."

# # #

The RHIBs were running silent doing

about 10 knots as Bravo Team navigated the Tapajós river. Kenny had provided Peter with constant updates on the Night Stalker's location. The time was 0300 hrs. Peter wanted the RHIBs off the river and Bravo Team in their hide position for the day. Peter had decided the best way to accomplish their mission was to conduct mainly night operations with small recon operations by day. By 0430 hrs, the team had secured the RHIBs under camouflage netting 50 meters from the river. Bravo Team had finished the construction of their hides: 3 - three person hides and 3 - two person hides.

Three days into the mission, the team had established a pattern of operation. Two recon teams of two soldiers each would go out and search for any signs of the

Grail. If something was discovered that required a deeper investigation, the location was Geo-tagged. Once nightfall occurred, either one or both Fire Teams would go out and investigate. The process was painstakingly slow and so far, the only thing they had to show for their efforts were some of the nastiest insect bites imaginable. Even though the team was using the standard Army issued bug juice which contains 30% DEET, the Amazon Rainforest mosquitoes ate DEET like it was sugar. The mosquitoes in the Rainforest act as the vectors of pathogens that cause malaria and yellow fever. All team members were vaccinated, but that still did not eliminate the team's suffering. Manny, the team medic, finally told the team to stop using the Bug Juice and start rubbing mud on all exposed areas on their bodies. While the sensation of rubbing the mud on their skin was unpleasant, the complaints of insect bites were reduced dramatically.

On day five of the operation, the recon team consisting of Alex and Dean witnessed a confrontation between the Munduruku and one of the security forces and reported the encounter back to Peter. The security forces were unsophisticated, but well-armed. This group of security forces were guarding logging operations. This group consisted of about 20 individuals. The Munduruku employed a simple strategy. They would attack from a position of concealment. Observing the engagement, the Munduruku used a combination of blow-darts and arrows. It was obvious by the way the soldiers reacted that they were struck by blow-darts and arrows that were tipped with a fast-acting poison. The Munduruku would initiate the attack with one volley of darts and arrows then quickly disappear back into the jungle. After losing many tribesmen during previous engagements, the Munduruku learned to immediately leave the area of engagement after their initial attack. What the security forces lacked in sophistication and tactics; they would quickly respond with overwhelming firepower. When they were finished with their response, what was once an area of lush Rainforest, was now a smoking, chewed-up piece of land. After the encounter, there were four security force members on the ground. Ten security members provided perimeter security while the rest of the security members provided aid to the fallen security forces.

After about 10 minutes, the security forces started reacting to the frantic calls for support coming from the logging operations. Based on what Alex and Dean could discern, the Munduruku had used the attack on the security forces as a diversion, so they could attack the loggers and inflict the most damage to stop logging operations. The Munduruku learned killing soldiers did not stop logging operations, but when the loggers were killed, it would take days to weeks before logging operations resumed because it took time for replacement loggers to be shipped in.

On another call with Kenny, Peter had a new sector to explore. They were seven days into the operation and so far, they had successfully avoided any engagements. It was easy to avoid the security forces in the area because of their lack of discipline. The security forces were operating both on the river, guarding the dams, and in the Rainforest guarding the logging operations. During one recon operation, they located the Night Stalkers. Now that the Night Stalker's location had been fixed, Peter kept eyes on them 24 hours a day. Every eight hours, the recon teams were relieved. Peter was impressed with the Night Stalker's operation. They had an engineering team on hand doing the heavy lifting at the direction of a group of archeologists. Once an area was cleared, the archeologist would then come in and do a careful examination of the area. The Night Stalker's security was impressive. There were no deviations in their security procedures. Their security perimeter consisted of three layers. The outermost layer was an electronic perimeter. The Night Stalkers employed a combination of Radio Frequency (RF) sensors, motion sensors, Infrared (IR) sensors, and seismic detection sensors. It was only through sheer luck that Peter's recon team wasn't detected the first day. It was during a security perimeter check to replace a faulty sensor, that Max and Allen had spotted the Night Stalkers. Now having spotted the sensors, they immediately backed away to ensure they did not trigger any of the sensors, especially since they did not know what sensors the

Night Stalkers had deployed initially.

The middle perimeter consisted of trip flares and claymore mines followed by an inner perimeter of roving security consisting of two teams of four members each.

Peter made sure that each recon team assigned to keep eyes on the Night Stalkers were also utilizing the latest sniper ghillie suit specially designed by Kenny. Kenny's suits accomplished two goals: making the wearer virtually invisible and masking the wearer's heat signature. Kenny employed hundreds of tiny cameras that continuously took pictures of the surrounding area and fed the images into the suit's microprocessor, sending the continuous images to LED screens embedded on the ghillie suit. So, in essence, the sniper became invisible by blending in with the surrounding environment. The only drawback to the suit occurred if the sniper had to make rapid movements from one position to the next. Considering the hallmark of a sniper was the ability to move very slowly into their position, quick movements weren't an issue unless the sniper had to E&E (escape and evade) in a hurry. Each recon team operated under radio silence protocol to prevent possible detection. Because the recon teams were operating at the extreme ranges of a sniper in a jungle environment, the use of parabolic microphones were out of the question. At most, they extended the range of the user to listen in on conversation at most up to 200 meters. The recon team, as per their electronic counter surveillance protocols, operated 400 meters away from the edge of the electronic perimeter; thereby, the decision was made to forgo auditory intelligence. To observe the Night Stalker's operation, the recon team used a combination of the Mark 5HD 5-25×56 sniper scope and the M151 spotter's scope. For night observations, the recon teams were using the latest night vision technology developed by Elbit Systems of America. The Squad Binocular Night Vision Goggles were used by the sniper, and the spotter's M151 fitted with a night vision adaptor allowed for the new Enhanced Night Vision Goggles (F6025) to be attached to the spotting scopes eyepiece. So far, three days of observing the Night Stalker's operation revealed they were just as frustrated as his team was.

During one of the recons, Andrew and Billy reported that the Munduruku had been acting very peculiar. On the last recon mission, Andrew and Billy knew they were being followed but because they could not identify their followers, they knew it had to be the Munduruku. The Munduruku had silently followed them for the past 20 minutes. Andrew and Billy stopped, and each took a knee.

"What do you think Billy?"

"Beats me, Andrew? If they wanted to kill us, we would be dead by now. I don't think there is much more that we are going to accomplish today."

"I agree Billy, but if we head back now the Munduruku will know where our camp is located."

"Do you really think they don't already know where we are located?" stated Billy.

"Good point Billy. Maybe we should leave them something to show that we are friendly?"

"Why not Andrew, it can't do any harm."

With that both men took off their rucksacks and removed a few Meals Ready to Eat (MREs). They left only the edible portions of the MRE for the Munduruku, making sure to especially include the candy bars. Andrew deliberately made a show of opening one of the packages and taking a bite of the Maple Pork Sausage Patty. Good old trusty MRE menu #17. Everyone loves Pork, thought Andrew. Andrew then placed the rest of the Maple

Pork Sausage Patty on the wrapper and shouldered his rucksack again.

"Let's go Billy."

With that both men made their way back to the camp.

# # #

Two days later, Andrew and Billy were back out on recon patrol. 30 minutes into the recon, they spotted what could only be described as two packages wrapped in banana leaves directly in front of them.

"What do you think Andrew?"

Andrew took a knee and opened one of the packages to find roasted boar.

"I think we have a definite answer to whether the Munduruku think we are the enemy."

"Well, Mr. Andrew, let's not disappoint them. I don't know about you, but I'm hungry and that roasted boar smells as good as hell."

"Billy, you are always hungry, but I agree. My mouth is watering."

Each man, dug into their respective package. Out of respect for the Munduruku, they made sure the entire meal was eaten. After an uneventful recon, the team returned to the camp where they were debriefed by Peter.

After speaking with Joshua about operational security and Kenny about the customs of the Munduruku, it was agreed that Andrew, Billy, and Peter would try and contact the Munduruku. The next day, the three set out on patrol to contact the Munduruku. About one hour into the patrol, the team, following Kenny's instructions, sat down in the middle of a clearing and removed all their weaponry and sat back-to-back with legs crossed and hands open, palms facing skyward resting on their knees. Kenny stated, this was a sign that they mean the Munduruku no harm.

After waiting for about two hours, three Munduruku tribesmen approached the three seated men with bows slung over their backs. Without saying a word, the lead Munduruku motioned for them to follow. The Munduruku waited patiently while the group put their equipment back on. Once ready, they followed the Munduruku for two hours, stopping briefly to let a boat patrol of security forces pass by. Once the group crossed the Tapajós river, it took another 45 minutes before they arrived at the Munduruku village. Everyone came out of their straw-roofed huts to view the strangers, who walked in the middle of the Munduruku Warriors. The team was led to a larger open structure in the center of the village, where they were instructed to sit and wait. Peter, Andrew, and Billy had numerous encounters throughout their military careers working with various indigenous tribes. They understood the key to a successful engagement was to always remain calm. Even when the situation became tense, lifting a weapon was always the worse thing to do. Peter signaled for the others to remain calm and to lay their weapons on the ground. Peter knew their weapons would not do them much good anyway. If it came to using force, the team would inflict a lot of damage, but the Munduruku had them surrounded. Even though they casually leaned against their spears or loosely held their bows, their posture could easily change in a heartbeat to violence if necessary.

"Welcome gentlemen." Came a frail, heavily accented voice off to their left. In unison, they turned to meet the voice. An elderly man was being escorted to the main structure. A young man acted as a crutch for the elderly man. The team started to rise but were quickly told to remain seated. As the elderly man sat down, he looked up and gave a slight nod of his head to a tribesman standing off to his right. Peter could only assume he was the village chief of staff. The tribesman clapped his hands rapidly three times. As if by magic, ten village females appeared bearing drinks and a light meal. "Please eat and drink gentleman. My name is Maivendo Pai Munduruku, the chief of Munduruku. Eat and drink first then we will talk." Then Maivendo gave a crooked smile revealing a mouth full of bad teeth and said, "I have learned throughout my life it's hard to kill a man that has just fed you. Now eat."

Peter and Andrew ate without complaint. Peter noticed Billy hesitating. It was a simple meal of fish stew with chopped taro leaves as the vegetables. From their Intel briefing, Peter knew the giant taro leaves were eaten as a vegetable rich in vitamins by the indigenous tribes. The briefing also stated, in its raw state, the giant taro is poisonous to humans if eaten in large quantities. Prolonged boiling removes the toxin calcium oxalate. Peter had to assume after all these years of living in the Rainforest, the Munduruku knew this too. "Billy, are you kidding me? The human eating machine is afraid of a little fish soup?"

"Come on Peter, who knows what's in this stuff. I don't want to catch some kind of intestinal bug. My buddy Robert picked up a bug in Panama and had diarrhea for a week out of every month. It took the stupid VA ten years before they finally give him some good drugs that finally killed those little bastards. Can you imagine me with a male period every month? I already shit four times a day. I can't even imagine." With that Billy shuttered.

"Billy, you will be fine. Besides, it tastes pretty good. Now stop embarrassing us and offending these good people and eat."

"Yes, Sir." With that Billy started eating. A few seconds later, Billy looked up from his wooden bowl and say, "Hey guys, this stuff is actually pretty fucking good." Then he immediately went back to eating his soup.

When the village chief put his bowl down, Peter spoke for the first time. "Thank you Chief Maivendo for such an excellent meal. May I introduce me and my men?"

The chief simply nodded.

"My name is Peter Cullum. To the right of me is Andrew Sydney. And to the left of me is Billy Sinclair. We are from the United States here on a mission of great importance. We have seen you make war on the others in the Rainforest. I want to thank you for the peace you have shown us. May I ask where you learned to speak English. I thought the Munduruku people were bilingual, only speaking Munduruku and Portuguese?"

"You are correct Peter. When I was a little kid, the Catholic missionaries would come into our village and tried to spread the message of God. That is where I learned to speak English. Although I haven't spoken the language in many years."

"Our hunters have been observing your men since you first arrived in our lands. You have treated our land with respect. You honor the ways of our ancestors. You live in harmony with nature. Your men don't pollute our lands. You haven't needlessly killed the animals of the forest, but most importantly, you have not tried to make war upon the Munduruku people."

"We know you are looking for something just like the soldiers to the north of our village, but we haven't figured out what. The men to the north destroy our precious forest in their search. We have tried to make war on these men, but their machines alert them, and they respond with deadly force. They are not like the men who guard the dams or destroy our forest. These men have killed over 20 of our hunters, and we have not harmed one of theirs. Once we got close and they did not respond as they did in the past. As we got closer three of our hunters were killed by an explosion that threw many metal balls in all directions. After that, we stopped trying to make war of the men to the north."

"Chief, you must stay away from these men. That explosion was a claymore mine and I am sure they have many more hidden to protect them. Those mines are extremely deadly. I'm sure they also have other booby traps that are just as deadly. Our men only observe them. We are extremely cautious of them and do not try to get close for the same reason your hunters have stopped trying. These men are evil, and they will kill anyone in their way."

The chief nodded his head. "That is wise counsel. We will take your advice."

"So, Peter Cullum of the United

States, why are you in our lands? It's been 15 days now and yet you continue to search for something. What is so important that you would risk the lives of your men to any one of the dangerous creatures that resides in these lands? Have you encountered any of the Bushmaster snakes, the Coral snakes or the Mussurana snakes? What about the Brazilian Wandering Spider or as you might call it, the Banana Spider? It is one of the most aggressive and venomous spiders known to man. Did you know there are eight different species of the Banana Spider? And they all can be found right here in our jungle."

"So, I will ask again, why would you put the lives of your men at risk when it is obvious you care about preserving our jungle?"

Peter knew this question was coming and had already discussed the possibility with Joshua and Trinity. They had agreed to be completely open about what they were searching for, but to leave out the more unbelievable parts of the situation. The consensus was hopefully the Munduruku might be able to narrow down the search area. "Chief Maivendo, we are here to find something called the Holy Grail. Throughout history the Grail has been associated with religious lore. Mainly, it is a vessel that held the blood of Jesus Chris. We recently have come to understand that the Grail is in fact a piece of very sophisticated technology. The men that have killed so many of your hunters have recently discovered how to use this technology and will do anything to recover it and other technology recently discovered. If they are allowed to possess this technology, it will change the balance of global power. Governments will literally do anything to maintain the status quo to include going to war. The only outcome when these governments go to war will be another world war. This planet will not be able to survive an all-out nuclear war."

Chief Maivendo continued to remain quiet and seemed as if he was still processing the information received. Finally, he looked up and stared directly into Peter's eyes. "Peter Cullum of the United States, I have heard of strange things being found by our people in the past. There is a story that has been passed down from old chief to new chief throughout our history. Truthfully at this point, it is nothing more than folklore. The only reason this particular story stands out is that our ancestors found a group of travelers. They found the bones of those travelers. Why these bones stood out from others was because they were encased in metal clothing. Our ancestors searched the area for clues as to who they were, and they found a burial mound nearby. When they searched the mount, they found useless metal trinkets buried. Not understanding why these men would do such a thing, they decided to bury the men with their trinkets. Our ancestors built a shrine to mark the deaths of these strange men, but more importantly to bury the metal clothing that will not return to the earth. They thought leaving the men as they found them would dishonor the spirit of Gaia because the metal prevented the men from returning to the dust from which they came."

"That is the only story that my people know that might hold the answers that you are looking for. I'm sorry that I can't be of more help."

"Thank you Chief Maivendo. You have been more than gratuitous with your time, food, and more importantly, your trust in us. If it is okay with you, we would like very much for your hunters to guide us to this shrine that your people created."

"Meet our hunters at the same clearing you were in today at sunrise. They will take you to the shrine. Please continue to honor and respect our lands. Go in peace and good luck in your quest.

My hunters will guide you back to the clearing when you are ready."

Peter and his men stood. Peter bowed. After he straightened, he said, "Thank you again Chief Maivendo. You have friends with me and my team. Whether we find what we are looking for or not, we will not forget your kindness and generosity."

"Let's go gentlemen." Once geared back up, the men followed the Munduruku hunters back to the clearing where they initially met.

# # #

Kenny had been in overdrive trying to track down any clues that might help corroborate what the chief had told Peter. Joshua didn't want Peter's team to waste time, but at this point, what choice did they have. 16 days into this operation and they had nothing to show for it. If this was the clue they had been needing, then Joshua wanted to make sure Peter was armed with the best information available.

"Okay guys, here is what I have been able to uncover. History believes that the Templar Knights uncovered a holy relic in the late 12th century and unexpectedly packed up and left Jerusalem. Most historians believe it was the Holy Grail that they found. For many years, the knights held unparalleled power in the Roman Catholic Church. On October 13th, 1307, King Phillip IV had his officers arrest hundreds of Knights Templar. King Phillip felt that the Templars had grown too powerful and wealthy, and he felt threatened by them. So, to ensure that no knights would escape, King Phillip dispatched messengers across the continent with a single message. One Friday, October 13th, he arrested all the Templar Knights. No King had ever directly challenged the Roman Catholic Church before. Not only did he challenge the Church, but he also burned the Templar Knights at the stake. Some say that this is the origin where the superstition of Friday the 13th began; a day that would forever be remembered and considered cursed."

"History showed that the Templars had help and not all were rounded up. Historians later discovered King Phillip was actually after the vaunted Templar's treasures. The Knights, knowing that they were no longer in the good graces of King Phillip, started secreting their treasure away. Henry Sinclair the 1st, Earl of Orkney planned to hide this great treasure deep in the new world, far away from everyone. In 1398, Henry Sinclair sailed to North America with 12 ships that were full of riches. He was accompanied by his brothers of the Knights of Templars, and others that were equally loyal to the cause of hiding the treasure so that no man would ever find it. In transit, the fleet of ships encountered a very bad storm. Four of their ships were lost during the storm. At least that's what was recorded in history. There is evidence that one of the ships was blown off course during the storm and eventually landed in South America versus North America. The funny thing is Henry Sinclair, and the men that accompanied him, were the first to discover North America almost 100 years before Christopher Columbus ever set foot on North American soil. Sorry guys, I digress. Back to the subject at hand. If the crew had followed Henry Sinclair's orders, they would have hidden the Knight's treasure that was on their ship. The reason why Henry Sinclair isn't credited with discovering North America is because they never returned, which means they successfully accomplished their mission of hiding the Knight's treasure. Based on evidence I will brief you on later, it is speculated that Sinclair ordered the remaining 8 ships to disperse and find different locations in the New World to hide their respective treasures. Based on how dedicated they were to their mission, there is a high probability that they killed themselves to protect the location of the treasure. That's why there was never any mention of Europeans already living in North America when the British started colonizing America."

"Now we come to the next great search for the Holy Grail. Spain's famous search for treasure in the Americas was Spain's King Ferdinand's attempt to find the Knight's treasure. The conquest started on the Caribbean islands and one after the other, Santo Domingo, Cuba, Puerto Rico, and Jamaica were all drained of their treasures of gold. Spain was ruthless in finding the Knight's treasure. Once they exhausted their search of North America, Spain turned its eyes on Mexico. New discoveries of gold and silver began to flow from the Mexico when the conquistador

Hernando Cortes conquered the Aztec civilization of Mexico."

"King Ferdinand still was not content with the acquisition of the gold of Mexico and Peru because in truth, he could care less about the gold. King Ferdinand was in fact still searching for the Holy Grail. He was convinced that the dense jungles of Central and South America had more treasure that could be found, and with any luck, hold the elusive Holy Grail. Thus, the adventures of Cortes, Pizarro and Quesada famed Spanish conquistadors."

"So, Peter, based on what Chief Maivendo told you, there is a high probability that the men their ancestors buried might very well be the crew of the lost Templar ship. It would make sense if they all were found dead in one location.

If they completed their mission of hiding the Grail, then it only makes sense that they would commit mass suicide to ensure that the location of the Grail died with them."

"As always Kenny, how can we thank you? Great Job!" said Joshua.

"Peter, I think you have what you need. The mission is a go. Good luck and God speed."

# # #

Peter had ordered the entire team minus Jim and Dean, who were observing the Night Stalkers, to assist in recovering the Grail. As instructed, Peter and his team met the hunters at the clearing at 0600 hrs. The lead hunter bowed his head in greeting. Peter did the same. After a two-hour trek through dense jungle, the team arrived at the designated location. The shrine was little more than a mound of dirt with a rusted conquistador helmet marking the grave site. The lead hunter pointed at the mound, bowed his head, and quietly slipped into the jungle to join his fellow hunters, who had already disappeared.

Manny let out a low whistle, "Damn those guys are good. I didn't even hear or see them separate from us. We could definitely learn a thing or two about stealth from them." A few of the guys chuckled at that.

"Okay team, break out your e-tools. We got some digging to do", said Peter. Six hours later Allen called out. "Hey boss, I think I found something." Peter came over to inspect the find. A few hours later, the team had started to uncover the conquistadors' remains. The pace slowed dramatically while they unearthed the bones of the ten conquistadors. To show respect for the deceased conquistadors, the remains were carefully placed in body bags that the team always cared with them as per SOP (Standard Operating Procedure). "No man left behind" was a motto that these men lived and died by. While the hunters were not visible, Peter knew without a doubt that they were being watched and Peter did not want to do anything that would cause disrespect to the Munduruku Tribe.

"Max! Manny! Please start digging a new hole to bury these remains." said Peter. "The rest of you, let's keep working and find the Grail. Hopefully it's not much deeper." It was now about 1600 hrs and the team's efforts had finally paid off. Billy was the first to find the edge of the Grail. After about 30 more minutes, they had excavated the Grail. Unlike the pictures describing it in history. It wasn't a chalice or a cup. It was about two feet long by 1 foot wide. After it was washed off, they could see it was made of some type of translucent material just as Senator Ryles described. Whatever was inside appeared dark in color, but clearly it was a liquid that moved when the device was moved. For a moment, the waning sunlight hit the device allowing Peter to see the color ruby red or "The Blood of Jesus."

Wasting no more time, the device was

quickly stored in Alex's backpack. "Let's get the hell out of here guys. I don't know about you, but I'm getting tired of this damn jungle. Give me a good ole fashion Texas Copperhead any day of the week compared to the things that will kill you in this jungle!" said Peter.

# # #

Across the globe in the Directorate Headquarters - Undisclosed Location Outside of Roanoke, Virginia,

Jamie, the head of Research had been monitoring the various heat signatures in the Amazon Area of Operation where the Night Stalkers were searching. He clearly knew where the Night Stalkers team providing security for their engineers were located. He also knew where the main

Munduruku Tribe lived. Occasionally, the Munduruku Tribe would dispatch hunters. While the hunters were harder to track because their heat signatures would mysteriously disappear, their numbers in the hunting party never presented a threat to the expedition. Jamie continued to stare at the screen. It was the three other groups that merited Jamie's attention. The one guarding the dam was dismissed after the 1st week. It was the other two groups that caused Jamie to frown. Jamie had been comparing the signature recordings from the past week. Both groups appeared to have a main camp with intermittent patrols going out just like the Munduruku Tribe. Jamie kept staring at the screen, something was nagging just outside the edge of his consciousness. Irene was talking to him, but Jamie ignored her and continued to stare at the screen. Unfortunately, the noise all around him became a distracting nagging buzz that stopped him from finding the answer. "Please Irene and everyone else. JUST SHUT THE FUCK UP!" You couldn't hear a pin drop. Jamie had always been quiet. This outburst was so uncharacteristic of him. Even Col. Myers turned his head noting the outburst. Just as Myers was turning his bed back, Jamie jumped up.

"I've got it! Irene, play back the recording from 24 hours earlier of the Munduruku Tribe and put it on screen 2." Irene brought the recording up.

"Now fast-forward to time index 1534.5!" Again, Irene did as requested.

"Now bring up Unknown Group 2, from two hours earlier and put them on screen 1." said Jamie. Col. Myers started slowly making his way over to the Research area. He had seen Jamie do the exact same thing several times when he was on the brink of a breakthrough. This was the only time that Jamie took charge regardless of who was around and of their rank. Col. Myers had been on the receiving end of a few of those outbursts himself. Over the years, having worked with many special forces and CIA operatives, Myers learned to give these guys a certain latitude because they produced results, and that's what mattered. So, when Jamie had these lapses, he took it in stride. Truthfully, Jamie would never apologize for this outburst, Myers thought, thinking back to his file.

Jamie had been diagnosed with Autism at a young age. He was a high-functioning autistic. In Jamie's case his diagnosis gave him an advantage. He was classified as a savant in the areas of mathematics and computer engineering. He graduated from high school at the age of 12. He graduated from Harvard with a double undergraduate degree in Mathematics and Computer Science at the age of 15. He then went on to graduate from MIT with a master's degree and PhD in Applied Mathematics and Theoretical Physics by the age of 24. Just like with so many other high functioning teams, "You give them a mission, then get the fuck out of the way!"

"Col., see how Group 2 splits at time index 1085.9? I completely did not connect the dots earlier because the Munduruku Tribe, Unknown Groups 1 and 2 always had patrols going in and out of their camps. What I missed earlier was the fact that the patrol from Group 2 linked up with a patrol from the Munduruku Tribe. See here?" Jamie advanced the time index forward to 1308.1.

"Two separate patrols from the Munduruku Tribe and Group 2 link up in this clearly. In the past whenever a group linked up with the Munduruku Tribe Hunters, typically you would see one group retreating with quick flashing of heat, indicating a fire fighting. That wasn't the case in this instance. It stood out in my mind, but I was too busy running surface scans for the expedition looking for the Grail to pay too much attention on this incident."

"Okay Jamie, but I still do not see the relevance of what this has to do with the search for the Grail." said Myers.

"Just bear with me Col. for a few more minutes." "Now look here. If we trace the movement on Screen 2 of the Munduruku Tribe Hunters, it's obvious that they are one of the two groups in the clearing. Now watch as both groups move back towards the Munduruku Tribe village. While this is interesting, that's not what interests me the most."

"Irene, move the time index forward another four hours to index 2315.8."

"Col. Myers, look at how the groups go back the to the clearing, split up, then moves back to their bases?"

"Now Irene, fast-forward another

eight hours."

"Col. do you see how the two smaller groups link back up? They then move off in a North by Northwest heading? After about three hours, the group splits off again. What does this behavior remind you of Col.?"

The Col. looks Jamie confused at first then it hit him. "Damn it, they found the Grail. The Munduruku Tribe Hunters led this group to the Grail."

"Sir, I believe the people in Group 2 are most likely members of Joshua and Trinity's team. Now everything makes sense. I have been seeing two to four intermittent heat signatures around our base camp. I wrote it off as animals initially, but now I'm pretty sure that their team has some sort of technology that masks their heat signatures. Regardless, we need to alert the Night Stalkers' commander and inform her of the new developments."

"Thank you, Jamie!"

"Christopher, contact Barbara and tell her I need to speak with her in 15 minutes."

"Yes, Sir." replied Christopher.

"Jamie, I need you to prepare a briefing with coordinates for Barbara and her team. We need to give her everything we have. I want the Grail in our control in the next six hours." The Col. didn't wait on a response, but immediately headed to the SCIF (sensitive compartmented information facility) conference room.

15 minutes later Jamie was finishing his intelligence briefing with Barbara

Nelly and her second in command, Masters Parker. "Barbara, I'm going to assume that they have the Grail at this point. Based on our previous encounters, I don't think we have the numbers to reliably guarantee the outcome. I will not underestimate them again. I want you to secure the Munduruku Tribe Village. Only casualties as necessary. We need to use the villagers' lives to trade for the Grail."

"Yes Sir." came the reply.

"Jamie, I want you to send out a general broadcast message stating our terms. Turn over the Grail or the entire village will be destroyed. Every man, woman, and child. Period. No Exceptions!"

"Barbara, break camp and get our engineers back home, and at all costs, secure the Grail. You have three hours and 40 minutes. Get it done now." Everyone immediately started moving.

# # #

Peter had just hung up the satellite phone. The conversation went well. The carrier group had been alerted and told to double the CAP (Carrier Air Patrol). The Marines were on standby just in case. To be on the safe side, Joshua had deployed part of the team's QRF Delta Team, Fire Team 2. While Peter thought this was overkill, he learned a long time ago when the stakes were this high, having more resources wasn't necessarily a bad thing.

"Everyone let's pack up. Time to go home."

"Andrew, reach out to Jim and Dean,

and instruct them to return back to base."

"Yes Sir."

Just as Andrew was about to transmit, a call came in from Dean.

"Rain Man Actual, this is Over Watch 1 over."

"This is Rain Man Actual. Go ahead."

"Boss man, we have some serious activity going on over here. It looks like the Night Stalkers are breaking camp. Did something happen?"

"Fuck!" said Peter. "We found the Grail, so that must mean somehow we are compromised. Get back here on the double. We need to vacate this area of operation (AO) ASAP."

"You got it boss. Over Watch 1 Out."

"Guys, we've got a problem. It looks like the Night Stalkers are on to us. We need to be prepared to leave as soon as Jim and Dean arrive. Alex, make sure their gear is packed. I shouldn't have to say this, but let's be prepared for a fight to get out of here. Now move!"

The RHIBs were exactly where they left them. They were successfully navigating the river making their way back to the ocean. Peter was glad that the Delta QRF was enroute about two hours away just in case they needed the extra firepower.

20 minutes from the ocean, the team received a call on the team radios. It was broadcasting on the NATO international frequency. It was being broadcast in the clear. "Attention forces that have recovered the Grail. You have 15 minutes to acknowledge acceptance of our terms and

another one hour to meet us and turn over the Grail. If 100% compliance to our terms are not met, we will kill every man, woman, and child in the Munduruku Tribe Village. If you hand over the Grail, they will be released with no additional casualties. The coordinates will be broadcast as soon as you acknowledge receipt of this message."

With that Peter recognized the village Chief's voice on the radio a few seconds later. "Please Peter, listen to these people. If it was just my warriors then I would tell you to keep going, but they already killed one woman and one baby to prove they were serious. So, we were forced to put our weapons down. In addition, they have already killed ten of our Hunters trying to protect our village.

You have already proven that you are an honorable man. I would not ask this, but our people will become extinct if these people do as they stated."

# # #

The RHIBs had pulled over and Fire Team 2 minus team leader Alex had fanned out about 100 meters to pull perimeter security around the RHIBs. Peter had just finished speaking with Joshua. There was no question about what to do next. Peter would have been surprised if Joshua and Trinity had decided anything else other than to turn over the Grail. Delta's QRF was simply too far away to do any good before the deadline expired, and while air support was available from the USS Truman, it would do little good other than to kill the villagers as well.

"Alright listen up gentlemen. It's a no brainer. While we might be trying to save the world, there is absolutely no way we will sacrifice an entire village to secure the Grail. Karl, get the on the NATO international frequency and broadcast our acceptance of their terms."

"Roger Boss."

30 minutes later, the team was five minutes from the rendezvous point. Karl transmitted the same. To ensure the Munduruku Tribe were safe, two MH-60R Sea Hawk helicopters were hovering over the station. The Night Stalkers balked at this, but Peter insisted this requirement was the only way they would take possession of the Grail. Peter had deployed two sniper teams in over-watch.

He walked alone up to the rendezvous point. The rest of the team was split to the north and south of the rendezvous point, ready to come to the aid of Peter should anything go wrong.

There were only two people at the rendezvous point, a woman and a man. As Peter got closer, he stopped dead in his tracks. "What the fuck! Barbara, what are you doing here? Are you running this operation?"

"Yes, Peter. Now hand over the Grail."

"Why are you working for these people? Do you know who they are and what they have done? We have known each other for years. We went through hell and back in Iraq. Your CIA members were embedded in my Delta Squad. How could you possibly threaten a whole village?"

"Peter, you have no idea what's at stake here. The people you are working for do not see the bigger picture, and I have no time to bring you over to our way of thinking. So, either hand over the Grail or we will kill those villagers. We have two Cruise Missiles already inbound to the village and this location in case you decide to kill us. If I do not send the abort code in the next ten minutes, we will all die Peter. This is no game and my employers do not accept failure. We cleared out the rest of my team as we promised. As soon as we have the Grail, the men I left behind at the village will leave as instructed. You have my word."

Peter placed the Grail on the ground and walked away without a second glance.

While he did not know why Barbara was working for the enemy, he knew Barbara always kept her word.

# # #

Three hours later, the team was back on board the USS Truman being debriefed by the Commander and S2 along with Delta Team's QRF. The mission was classified a failure, but the cost of success was simply too much to bear for any of the team members. Susan had just communicated that she was arranging transportation for the team. Now the Commander was giving his normal spill to classified operators returning from a mission. "Until you depart my ship," the Commander told them, "You are quarantined from the rest of the ship!" The Commander raised his voice and looked directly at the men all clad in black body armor. "This area has been deemed off limits to the crew except as required to ensure your comfort. Meals and cots would be arranged for you all ASAP."

Under his breath Manny laughed, "I don't know about Commander, but Allen is in serious need of a shower. He stinks!" Several of the men laughed.

"Did you say something soldier?" said the Commander.

Peter quickly stepped in. "No Commander. Thank you for the accommodations and your sailor's assistance during this past mission." With that, the Commander left.

After the Commander had left, Peter first shot Manny a look then turned to the

Delta QRF Team Leader. "Okay Carl, what gives? What was up with the Commander eying you all down? And why are you and your team still in full body armor?"

Removing his mesh black helmet, Carl signaled for the rest of the team to do the same. "Honestly Peter, I have never liked the smug way that those Marines think they are superior and bossed our teams around when I was back in Special Ops. You should have seen the way they reacted when we just stood there indifferently as they ordered us to follow them. Then one stupid Corporal decided to flex his muscles and level his gun at us. We still did not move. Being in a diamond formation, the Corporal assumed the point person was the leader. He was correct. After barking orders at us for five minutes to grab our gear and fall in, the Corporal finally worked up the nerves to grab me by an arm and drag us to the waiting area. Just as this was happening a Gunnery Sergeant was walking up and was telling the Corporal to stand down, but by then it was too late. I had the Lance Corporal on the ground and my pistol pointed at his face. The Marine Squad immediately pointed their weapons at us. Through our internal comms, we were dying laughing as we all drew our weapons as one and sighted each Marine in the escort."

"The Gunnery Sergeant immediately took charge and started yelling orders for the Marines to stand down."

"Come on Carl. Tell me you didn't do that?"

"You're damn straight I did. You know

how much fun that was to finally give those damn Marines something to worry about? Within minutes, the USS Truman had sirens blaring and the squad of Marines was reinforced with the rest of their platoon. Then some butter bar LT out of breath came sprinting to the front demanding to know what the hell was going on. I still did not acknowledge their presence other than to shift my fully visored helmet from the stupid Lance Corporal to the LT then back to the Corporal."

"Finally, I spoke. I used the amplified speaker function of my helmet to ensure everyone heard. Gunny, please advise your Marines to back away before someone gets hurt and it won't be us. The LT was very upset that he was being ignored. In a squeaky voice, he said, "I don't know who the fuck you think you are, but your ass is mine." As he started walking up to grab me, Gunny pulled him back and said "LT, please let me handle this." With the mic amplification on, Carl clearly heard Gunny telling LT just how quickly things could go bad for his platoon. "Sir, of all the special operators I have seen in the past 20 years, these guys are radiating energy that says, "Do not fuck with us." They will probably kill everyone in your platoon without one casualty on their side. Sir, look at their body armor. That's state of the art. Nothing short of a .50 Caliber machine gun will penetrate it. Lance Corporal Peters has a big mouth and probably deserves to receive a piece of humble pie. Take the platoon and counsel him. I'll deal with these guys." Hesitantly, the LT retreated with his platoon in tow.

"After a few minutes of joking around with Gunny, I ordered the men to follow Gunny to the debriefing room. No one was hurt but having spent a few days in the brig before because some stupid Marines had a hairball up his ass, I decided today was time for payback. I had lost a few buddies on a mission and truthfully, I was fucked up and didn't like the attitude of that Lance Corporal, so I punched him in the face. I spent two days in the brig until my CO finally got the Commander to release me. So yeah, this was worth it."

"I will admit Carl, when Joshua was making us wear that equipment in training,

I was hesitant but seeing your team all decked out. I have a newfound respect for the effect it will have on the enemy."

# # #

"Col. Myers, we have secured the Grail and are enroute back. ETA is 15 hours. The engineering team will be boarding a ship in the next four hours. The ship is scheduled to depart at 0600hrs tomorrow. It should take about 10 days for it to make port in Charleston, SC.," said Barbara.

"Good job Barbara. Get back here as soon as possible so we can secure the Grail!" With that the line went dead.

Unfortunately, this encounter left a few doubts in Barbara's mind. She had been through hell and back with Peter and his team when he was back in Delta. He was a straight shooter. She never in a million years would have thought Peter would be working for the enemy. His moral character was beyond reproach. She had seen him take on a Full Bird Colonel and won because he wanted them to clear an objective so he could call in an air strike. Peter disobeyed the direct order and was brought up on charges, which were later dismissed. When CID finished the investigation, the evidence proved Peter was right to disobey the order. It was in fact an unlawful order. There were too many children and innocents in the village, and Peter's team did accomplish the objective and eliminate the target eventually with any collateral damage. Barbara let the thoughts and doubt go, but promised herself when she had time, she would get to the bottom of why Peter was working for the enemy.

* * *

Pandora's Box - Yucatan, Mexico

Night Stalker Team Force 2 had set up its base of operations in two locations in Mexico. One was at the Mayaland Hotel & Bungalows in Chichén Itzá. It was home to the Pyramid of Kukulkán. The other was at the Auto Hotel Frances in Palenque, Mexico, located near Palenque an important Maya City know for The Temple of the Inscriptions. The Night Stalker Team Force 2 had deployed a force of about 100 operatives and scientist for this mission. Each team would deploy with a force of 25 operatives and 25 scientists to each site.

Prometheus Unrestricted had reserved both hotels for the next 3 months. When initially contacted, the hotel manager at Mayaland Hotel & Bungalows resisted the thought of one company monopolizing the entire hotel for so long. Nancy Saunders was the VP of Logistical Support Operations (LSO) for Prometheus Unrestricted. LSO was responsible for running logistical support for the Night Stalkers whenever their operations intersected with commercial enterprises. Colleagues would describe her as a force unto herself. She was recruited right out of Harvard Business School after receiving her MBA. She was so excited to receive an offer letter for $75,000 working as a Commercial Asset Property Analyst. 10 years later, she was the VP of Logistical Support Operations making $300,000. It was her 6th year at the company that her boss at Prometheus Unrestricted finally read her into the real mission of the company. After signing an ironclad Non-Disclosure

Agreement two inches thick, her boss Preston offered her a job as the Director of LSO. She knew things weren't quite what they seemed at LSO. There were too many meetings that she was excluded from that she should have been part of. It was her curiosity and drive that finally made her a candidate for recruitment.

Miguel Alvarez, the hotel manager, insisted booking the hotel simply wasn't possible. Nancy smiled to herself after she hung up with Miguel. Obviously, Miguel, like so many others before him, underestimated her will to accomplish whatever mission was put before her.

"We'll see about that, Miguel." thought Nancy. After speaking with the owners, and three million dollars later, Miguel was a changed man. He bent over backwards to accommodate any request from Nancy thereafter.

The Mayaland Hotel & Bungalows was perfect for the team. It was spacious with 52 rooms and several conference rooms. It would accommodate the full complement of Night Stalkers plus the scientists deployed for this mission. Nancy had insisted on discretion from Miguel, and if everything went well, he would personally receive a bonus of $100,000.

It had taken the team a full week to move in and set up operations. Nancy had assured Miguel the local government was fully briefed, and permits were issued. The weapons were for the protection of the scientists who were doing research on the Mayan Pyramids. With the local drug cartel kidnapping tourists and holding them for ransom, they were not going to take any chances with the lives of scientists. This was a multi-million-dollar research project that might help potentially explain what happened to the Mayans once and for all. While nervous about all the guns, Miguel had accepted the explanation and assured his staff these men posed no danger.

The Auto Hotel Frances in Palenque, Mexico was much easier to book. Business had been down recently, and the hotel manager had no reservation about Prometheus Unrestricted reserving his hotel for the next three months. The $25,000 bribe went a long way towards accepting their offer to reserve the hotel. The Auto Hotel Frances only had 20 rooms, but that was more than enough for their contingency of operatives and scientists. Unfortunately, the operatives would be sleeping three to a room and the scientists doubling up in each room.

# # #

James McKay was briefing his team again on Pandora's Box. Susan had procured a temporary base of operations at Rancho El Colorado located just outside of Tizmin.

"I'm going to turn over the briefing to Susan to discuss the Intelligence surrounding the Night Stalkers. Susan!"

"Thanks James. As you all know, on every operation so far, we have always been one step behind the Night Stalkers. So far, they have recovered two of the four artifacts. Unfortunately, in direct action, the Night Stalkers have beaten us twice because they are willing to cross lines that we are not. While the DNA Matrix Sequencer is firmly in control of Ryles and his crew, it is not a necessary component to make the ship operational. The last component on the chess board is Pandora's Box. We have to gain control of this component if there is any hope of negotiating with the crew on the ship as Ryles hopes to."

"The Night Stalkers are already in the country and setting up operations. They are operating out of the Mayaland Hotel & Bungalows in Chichén Itzá and the Auto Hotel Frances in Palenque, Mexico. They are going to focus their operations on the Pyramid of Kukulkán and the Temple of the Inscriptions. Both locations have been the home of many archaeological studies in the past. In 1947, there was a fringe physicist, who used archeology to prove what we call new science is actually old science just being rediscovered. His name was Dr. Milo Nachtnebel. Dr. Nachtnebel had some very interesting theories about the Pyramid of Kukulkán. According to legend, twice a year when the day and night are in balance or equinox, this pyramid is visited by the God Kukulkán. On the equinox, Kukulkán returns to earth to commune with his worshipers, provide blessing for a full harvest and good health before entering the sacred water, bathing in it, and continuing through it on his way to the underworld. Dr. Nachtnebel thought this was nonsense, but he could not dismiss the fact that land around the Pyramid of Kukulkán yielded some of the best crop harvests in the country. Also, the average lifespan of the people in the surrounding area lived on average ten years longer than the national mean average. During one of his visits, he noticed exotic particle readings during the equinox. To his knowledge collisions at high-energy particle colliders were the only traditionally source of exotic particle. Most people had never heard of particle accelerators until the 600-MeV Synchrocyclotron came into operation in 1957. This was CERN's first accelerator even though accelerators have been around since the 1930's. In 1930, inspired by the ideas of Norwegian engineer Rolf Widerøe,

27-year-old physicist Ernest Lawrence created the first circular particle accelerator at the University of California, Berkeley, with graduate student M. Stanley Livingston. In theory it was possible for these particles to have been produced artificially. Except one important fact, the first Van de Graaff particle accelerator in Latin America was installed at the Universidad Nacional Autónoma de México in 1952. Considering the year was 1949, Dr. Nachtnebel knew without a shadow of a doubt, whatever was occurring, it was something that occurs naturally in nature, which wasimpro bable, it was alien in nature. For the next two years, he searched the pyramid in hopes of discovering the source of the energy source. Finally, he gave up and hypothesized that whatever the original source of the energy had left a residue charge in the stones of the pyramid. Over the course of six months, the energy levels intensified to a point where the stones could no longer contain the exotic particles. In 1968, three years after Dr. Nachtnebel died, his thesis about the disappearance of the Mayan people was discovered. He postulated that whatever was strong enough to leave this kind of residual energy years later likely was the answer as to why the Mayans mysteriously disappeared. He believed that at some point the energy source must have been released at full power, and that release literally vaporized the entire Mayan civilization. As we know, Ryles confirmed that is exactly what happened to the Mayans. Guys if you want more proof, Dr. Nachtnebel died at the ripe age of 118 years old."

"The Temple of the Inscriptions", on the other hand, is a potential search site because of some interesting hieroglyphics found there. The entire structure was specifically built as the funerary monument for K'inich Janaab' Pakal. A few interesting facts, the sarcophagus lid weighs as much as five tons. Can anyone guess what was engraved on it?"

Oscar raised his hand.

"Put your hand down Oscar. It was a rhetorical question." said James.

Everyone laughed.

"Gentlemen, have you ever seen the History Channel's Ancient Aliens series?

The focus of the show was how this world has been visited by aliens throughout our history. The show discusses unexplained occurrences including leaps in technology. Well, on the sarcophagus lid was an image depicting what people believe is an Ancient Astronaut. It is possible that what they saw were images from Pandora's Box. Maybe even instructions on how to safely activate the matter/anti-matter engine with the proper spacesuit on."

"Our intel tells us that we can assume the Night Stalkers have a military presence of about 30 - 40 operators and 20 - 30 scientists on station. Due to the Night Stalker's presence, we are not going to be able to actively search these sights. They just have too many people in the field. The only thing we can do is survey the Night Stalkers, and if they find Pandora's Box then our mission is to go in and capture the component at all costs."

Oscar raised his hand again. Everyone immediately started laughing.

"Really Oscar?"

"Weren't you embarrassed enough last time?"

"You always were a glutton for punishment."

"Seriously guys, I have a legit question. Trust me!" said Oscar.

"Yes, Oscar?" said Susan.

"If this mission is simply a recon, snatch and grab, then why did we deploy with all of this scuba gear?"

Susan looks at James, who returned the look.

"James, do you want to answer his question?"

"No, continue with the background briefing Susan. I'll take care of the tactical briefing after you finish, but Oscar that is a very good question."

"See, I told you it wasn't a stupid question!" Oscar said as he flipped off the room.

"As a matter of fact, Oscar, it's a very relevant question. Most of you probably don't know this; NSA makes a habit of routinely monitoring satellite scans of the earth taken throughout the world. On July 15, 2022, CERN launched its first satellite for studying space-based radiation. During one of the calibration tests, using earth as the calibration source, the satellite picked up strange reading coming off the East Coast of Mexico near the city of Río Lagartos. That's approximately one hour from our base camp."

"So why aren't the Night Stalkers exploring this area as well?" said Oscar.

"Oscar, you're on a roll now. Maybe you should take over the briefing." joked Tyrone.

" Oscar, you are asking all the right questions. The CIA and FBI jointly maintain a Fringe Department. Think X-Files and Project Blue Book! Whenever a fringe activity occurs, it is initially investigated and categorized then flagged for any future occurrences. Well Dr. Nachtnebel's research was classified as fringe, and when the calibration test reported similar readings as Dr.

Nachtnebel's, the scans were immediately routed to the Joint Task Force Fringe Department (JTF-FD). I can guarantee you Oscar, we will be the only group searching Río Lagartos. JTF-FD immediately re-tasked a classified NSA satellite to do a deeper water scan of the area. The NSA acquired the patent plans from a company called DeepBlue, which developed an underwater satellite designed to scan the sea floor areas in high definition, as well as lake bottoms and riverbeds. It makes use of advanced imaging and underwater navigation, and its software is based on machine-learning algorithms or artificial intelligence. Because it's the government and they own the keys to the patent office, in times of national security matters, the government will simply take patents based on eminent domain. During the scans, we discovered an underwater pyramid roughly the same size as the Pyramid of Kukulkán.

Height

24 m (79 ft), without temple

30 m (98 ft), with temple

6 m (20 ft), Temple itself

Base

55.3 m (181 ft) on all sides

Slope

37°29'44" (edges)

47°19'50" (sides)

"And guess what Oscar? There is a steady radiation signature that matches the data that Senator Ryles gave us. At this point, I will turn the briefing over to James to discuss the tactical aspects of the mission."

"Thanks Susan." said James.

"Gentlemen, what we are looking for is Pandora's Box. It is the matter/anti-matter energy source that powers the star-drive of their alien spaceship. As stated, the star-drive creates a hyperspace window which allows their spaceship to transition into a slipstream or wormhole allowing them to travel faster than light. Senator Ryles stated it was initially buried in the Yucatan Peninsula. The Mayans discovered it at some point. Somehow, they managed to open it. By activating the energy source of the star-drive without its magnetic containment shielding, the resulting cosmic radiation released instantly annihilated the entire Mayan civilian. When we find Pandora's Box, do not attempt to open it.

Immediately call the team of scientists that Susan has procured for us."

"For this mission, we will be operating about 500 feet below sea level. We are going to get to test some of the newest toys that have ever been invented. You will be using augmented reality diving masks, which will significantly improve underwater operations. The mask will be equipped with HUD (Heads Up Display). Divers will be able to get data about time spent underwater, depth, pressure, and temperature. The coolest part of this technology is that the sensors on the mask act like a dolphin's echolocation system. The sensors emit an ultrasonic pitch. Employing artificial intelligence, the sound waves returning from the object provides information about the object's distance, shape, and size. The sensors also use a combination of thermal imagery and night vision technology embedded in the AN/PVS-14s. Based on these three sensory inputs, the AI will create digitally enhanced images for your HUDs that can be magnified for more clarity. Because the image you are seeing is not the actual object, the clarity and sharpness will be beyond anything you could imagine. Seeing at a depth of 1,000 ft will be easier than seeing with AN/PVS-14s while conducting normal night-time operations. And as is normal with night vision operations, everything will be cast in your favorite hue green."

"As for your dive suits, you will be outfitted in the latest that NASA and the US Navy has to offer. You will be using the experimental Paragon Suit. Due to the potential exposure to cosmic radiation, we need to use a suit that not only protects you from the depth and cold of the sea, but radiation as well. The Paragon Suit provides "space-suit-like" isolation, delivering safe breathable air to the diver. The surface air-supplied system collects exhaled air and returns it to the surface to eliminate ingress pathways of hazardous agents through a prototype Regulated Surface Exhaust Diving System. The suit is currently being evaluated by Navy divers at the Navy Experimental Diving Unit facility in Pensacola, Florida.

"The contaminated water diving technology that Paragon developed for the Navy came about as a result of its partnership with NASA. This joint partnership strove to find a better way to protect Navy divers enabling them to complete missions in extreme pressure, temperature, radiological, biological, and chemical environments. This was accomplished by using NASA's operational know-how that allows astronauts to work in the extreme environment of space while using existing deep suit dive technology."

" We're going to be real-life astronauts!" said Tyrone.

"Pretty much." responded James.

The entire Charlie Team in addition to Delta Fire Team 3 will deploy to Río Lagartos. Charlie Team will immediately start getting familiarized with this new dive equipment. Susan has arranged for a team of Paragon technicians to teach us the operational use of the equipment and operate the Regulated Surface Exhaust Diving System up top. Sarah, your Fire Team will provide security on site. Mick, I want your remaining two Fire Teams to maintain eyes on the Night Stalkers at the Pyramid of Kukulkán and the Temple of the Inscriptions. If by chance they happen to find Pandora's Box, you are to immediately contact us and engage the Night Stalkers if they try to leave the compound. We will deploy and support you. Remember, they cannot be allowed to escape with Pandora's Box.

# # #

It had been two weeks since the operation in Mexico began. Col. Myers, despite the assurance of Jamie, the Head of Research, was still not sure if they would ever find the matter/anti-matter drive. While he could marshal unlimited resources to deploy to the search, there were only so many people that could physically fit inside of these structures. They also had to be careful to follow the guidelines set forth by The Instituto Nacional de Antropología e Historia. Myers knew ultimately, he could violate those guidelines, but without anything to show for it, he was not in the mood to justify his decisions to the Committee. Continuing to look at the daily briefing reports from the scientist at the dig site wasn't going to help them find the artifact any faster, so he turned his attention back to a more manageable problem, how to find and destroy Trinity and Joshua.

Myers seriously had underestimated Trinity and her ability to convince others to join the cause to avenge the loss of her son. As Myer's old Command Sergeant Major used to say, "Everyone is a genius with hindsight 20/20 vision. We can only do the best we can in the moment and let God sort it out in the end."

Myers pressed a button on his intercom. "Brenda, get Maj. Wayne Carson on the line. Let him know I need an update on the search for Trinity and Joshua at 0600 hrs tomorrow morning."

"Yes Sir!" said Brenda.

Myers immediately hung up the phone then picked up the daily Intel feed from the Department of Homeland Security. Unbeknownst to Homeland Security, which provides a daily consolidated intelligence briefing to the White House from all the three letter agencies. His group was considered a classified black ops group working within the CIA which was approved to receive the daily briefings as well. Myers might not like the fact that the Committee members were unknown to him, but he did admire how they operated. His organization had high-level contacts in just about every government in the world including just about every intelligence agency as well. As he sat back and started reading the daily briefing. Col Myers then lit a Cuban cigar, his trademark practice since he joined the Marines. He savored the taste, fragrance and feel of the cigar in his mouth as he continued to read.

# # #

* * *

James coordinated the efforts up top with the Paragon techs, Sarah's QRF Fire Team, Intel briefings from Kennedy, and Mick's surveillance operations. Fitzgerald was the lead diver for operations at Río Lagartos and focused on controlling dive operations below. So far, the suits had worked like a charm. The augmented reality face mask worked beyond expectations. James was almost jealous that he wasn't leading dive operations. The pictures from the face cams were so clear and detailed it was hard to believe they were operating in near pitch-black conditions 1,000 feet below the surface. The team was now exploring the underway pyramid making good progress.

That wasn't the case one and a half weeks ago. Initially when the team was introduced to Susan Pratt, James had doubts about working with a CIA spook again. But he had to admit, each time she was given a request, she pulled through with flying colors. He grudgingly let go of his past and accepted her as a member of their team. So had the others. The current ship they were on was again a testament to her abilities. She had commandeered a vessel from Gulf of Mexico Express Company or CMA-CGM. They were using a ship that was undergoing its maiden voyage shakedown. The COSCO NASHVILLE was a new class of vehicle that CMA-CGM was fielding. Oceanic research was one of the fastest growing revenue streams. CMA-CGM felt by having the most advanced ship on the water it would guarantee a steady stream of revenue for the foreseeable future. The ship was equipped with both the Model 985B Sidescan and an ROV. The sonar was the next generation in high resolution Sidescan sonar. It was specifically made for the COSCO NASHVILLE. The ship also carried two commercial ROVs. Oscar and CJ were both ex-Navy SEALs. When they saw the ROVs, they were speechless. James remembers going up to them.

"What gives, guys?"

"Boss. This shit is cutting edge. These aren't your typical Inspection and Observation Class ROVs. They are equipped with advanced sensors, samplers, powerful manipulator arms capable of construction, welding, and more versus the typical ROVs. These ROVs could easily cost you millions of dollars. When we were going through our specialized operation training, we got to play with a prototype of this baby. This mother looks like it's been on steroids since birth." joked Oscar.

When operations commenced, it took the team about two days using the Sidescan sonar to pinpoint the exact location of the pyramid buried by a few centuries of silt and sediment. It took another day and a half for the ROVs to find the opening of the pyramid. That was the easy part. The most crucial part of the operation was to determine how to remove all that sediment without anyone noticing it was being displaced. They discussed two options for this part of the operation. Either use powerful blowers to remove the sediment or vacuums to suck it up. The team finally decided on the vacuum option and to relocate the sediment two miles further out into the gulf using two 30-inch-wide interconnecting pipes for the transportation. How Susan had procured this much pipe, again, was beyond James. The reason they decided to transport the sediment two miles away was to mitigate their operation being discovered if massive amounts of sediment started washing up on shore.

Four days into the dredge operation, the team had successfully cleared the interior of the pyramid. Now the scientists and archaeologists gathered around the bank of the monitors to look for clues as to where Pandora's Box was located. While some of the archaeologists, mainly Dr. Salem Navee, wanted to be down there touching stones that haven't been seen in over 2,000 years, they also realized just how dangerous it was down there as well. On one occasion, Rob from Fire Team 2 had to be rushed to the local hospital with a severe case of the bends. During a dive, his oxygen line got cut when a shark got tangled up in his lines. Part of Delta team's responsibility includes guarding against sea born threats as well. Sarah and Jalen were already in their scuba suits and immediately responded. The shark was tangled in Rob's lines around 100 ft below the surface. Using their spear-guns, they tranquilized the shark, but the damage was already done. The shark had already cut the oxygen line and they could not cut the shark out or risk the blood drawing more sharks to their area of operation.

Fitzgerald had communicated to James that Rob was in trouble and would need to be immediately evacuated to the local hospital. Their normal ascent protocols for the operation would take approximately 35-40 minutes. Rob had to immediately seal his suit as per emergency operating procedures. With a sealed suit, he had approximately 15 minutes of reserve air in his suit. Fitzgerald had to detach his ascent cable and attach it to Rob's because the tangled shark made it impossible to bring him up on his line based on the feedback from Sarah. Just like ever trained special forces operator, Rob did not panic and trusted the team would take care of him when he surfaced.

Rob lost precious time getting into the hyperbaric chamber at Hospital General

San Carlos 54 km away. The local hospital Centro de Salud de Rio Lagartos only minutes away was dealing with an unstable power supply from their back-up generator. The hospital staff explained 30 minutes earlier, there was a car accident that brought down the power line running into hospital. Jalen had called James with the news that the doctors assured Rob would make a complete recovery but would be in the hyperbaric chamber for the next three days.

Every time the team discovered something interesting, Dr. Salem Navee so badly wanted to be down there instead of watching the discovery from the monitors, but Rob being rushed to the hospital doubled up in pain, stopped those thoughts immediately. The idea of killer sharks did a lot to dissuade those thoughts as well.

# # #

Across the globe in the Directorate Headquarters - Undisclosed Location Outside of Roanoke, Virginia, Jamie, the head of Research was called over by one of his Senior Analysts.

"Hey Jamie, I'm not sure, but I think you might need to look at this. You know how you told me to flag any unusual occurrences in our AO (area of operation)?"

"Yeah. Go on."

"Well, there was an incident at a local hospital. A patient was admitted to Hospital General San Carlos for a severe case of the bends."

"What's so interesting about that

Amy?"

"Jamie, in and of itself, nothing. But one of the queues we started running in an effort to find any of Joshua and Trinity's teams, were to flag any ex-special forces operators that were detained by local authorities or hospitalized in or around all Night Stalker operations."

"Amy, when was this flagged?"

"30 minutes ago, Jamie."

"Get a message over to Captain Miguel Martinez ASAP to start an immediate sweep..." Before Jamie could finish his sentence, Amy interrupted.

"Jamie, it's not that simple. I think we have a bigger problem. When someone is admitted to the hospital or detained, one of our analysts immediately filters the person based on age. This very quickly filters out individuals that are too young to have served or too old to still be a threat. One of our Junior Analysts then runs an extensive background check to make sure their identification passes mustard. A patient by the name of Nate Banes was admitted eight days ago. Unfortunately, it took until 30 minutes ago for Drew to come back with a positive match for Rob Snyder, a former member of the Navy Seals, who specialized in deep sea dives. Whoever created his fake ID was good, and I mean good. The problem Jamie is that we don't know how long they have been operating in our AO. I'm asking for permission to immediately re-task an NSA satellite into a geosynchronous orbit, so we can have 24/7 cover over the area. Plus, I think you should also deploy a counter surveillance team to see if we can locate them and see what they are up to."

"Approved. Make it happen immediately Amy!"

# # #

It was around 1400 hrs on the 10th day of operations that the team was entering a secret chamber of the pyramid. Dr. Salem Navee had been going over the video logs of the previous days when he noticed something that was previously missed. What was initially passed off as simple hieroglyphics was actually a keypad. Dr. Salem Navee had seen something similar in the Amazon Basin when exploring a newly discovered ancient pyramid. There were only nine possible combinations based on the three hieroglyphics. It was decided to use the ROV to enter the nine possible combinations in case there were booby traps. On entering the 8th combination, a trap was triggered, and a one-ton stone hidden in the top of the pyramid crushed the ROV flat as a pancake. It took the rest of the allocated dive time for the day to remove the stone with the help of the larger ROV.

The following day, Fitzgerald took the lead and entered the last combination. Fitzgerald tensed expecting another stone to come crashing down. Instead, a section of the wall slid open to reveal a hidden chamber. Immediately radiation alarms started going off. Fitzgerald was pretty sure they had found Pandora's Box. James ordered the immediate evaluation of the pyramid to give the scientists time to evaluate if the suits would protect everyone. While everyone was excited, they were also disappointed by the news, their suits would only give them about ten minutes of protection before they received lethal levels of radiation. James asked Susan to perform another miracle. They need another smaller ROV flown in ASAP. The larger ROV could not fit in the 6 meters wide by 3 meters high doorway. James was frustrated. They were so close to completing the mission, yet so far away. A smaller ROV drone revealed the Matter/Anti-Matter drive in the chamber. It was made of a black material that seemed to absorb the light from the chamber as the drone illuminated it. Its dimensions were 5 meters wide, 2 meters high by 10 meters long. It was initially unknown how large the drive was, so the scientists were of one mind to complete final construct of the containment unit on the ship. They used lead and tungsten titanium alloy 1" thick sheets to assemble a containment unit. Based on their calculations it would take 2" of lead and 4" of the anti-radiation tungsten titanium alloy plating to properly contain the radiation. Susan again not only procured the sheets of material based on the scientists' specifications but had procured a local warehouse with the necessary fabrication equipment to construct the containment unit.

James looked at the box. It wasn't pretty, but the scientist assured James that it would work. The box itself probably weighed about two tons by itself. Ryles stated the Matter/Anti-Matter drive only weighed about 250 lbs. The Paragon technicians supervised the installation of the anchor points, six in all.

With everything in place, the operation to retrieve Pandora’s Box could not happen fast enough for James. Two nights in a row the team had to collect and remove dead fish floating on the surface of the water. No one planned for the radiation killing the fish in the immediate vicinity, and the cargo hold of the ship was almost out of capacity. With the addition of the smaller ROV, the scientist successfully managed to loop a cable around Pandora's Box, and the larger ROV dragged the box out of the pyramid.

The scientist used a 200-foot cable to ensure the large ROV would last long enough to put Pandora's box in the containment unit. Based on their calculations after about 15 minutes of exposure, the radiation would penetrate the shielding on the ROV electronics and eventually fry the circuit boards. The small ROV already was becoming non-responsive to commands.

The Paragon technicians had successfully lowered the containment unit to the ocean floor while the ROVs were positioning Pandora's Box. With everything in place, the large ROV used its heavy lift crane to place the Box and place it in the containment unit. Unfortunately, with that act, the ROV died before it could close the lid of the containment unit. Without hesitation, Fitzgerald and Mack quickly closed the distance to the containment unit. Knowing that if they did not close the lid in time, the suits would not protect them, and their lives would be forfeited. Fitzgerald reached down and summoned all his collective willpower from surviving years of countless battles throughout his career. The will to endure and graduate from some of the hardest training the US Military had to offer, so that he could summon the strength to close the containment lid with the help of Mack knowing that it might cost him his life.

When radiation levels dropped to zero, James immediately ordered his men and the containment unit to be brought back to the surface.

Pandora's Box - Yucatan, Mexico

"Col. Myers, we have something. As you know, we have been monitoring one of Joshua's teams. We verified that Joshua and Trinity are not amount this team. Based on satellite imagery, it looks like they have recovered Pandora's Box. Our counter surveillance team could not get close enough to their ship, but at the warehouse, they witnessed the construction of a radiation containment unit. As of 0900 hrs, our satellite confirmed that a box fitting the dimensions of the containment unit was indeed removed from the ocean floor and loaded on the ship. It appears they have a C-130 waiting at Cancun International Airport."

"Jamie, how long do we have before they arrive at the airport?"

"Sir, they still need to dock the ship and unload the containment unit. I estimate that will take another three hours. Based on drive time to Cancun International Airport, it will be around 1600 hrs before the containment unit is loaded on the C-130."

"1LT Brennen!"

"Yes Sir!" said Col Myers' aide.

"Get Captain Martinez on the line ASAP. They need to prepare to engage and retake Pandora's Box."

"Yes Sir!"

Ten minutes later, Captain Miguel Martinez was on the line.

"Yes Sir, how can I help you?"

"Captain Martinez, I need you to immediately halt all search operations. We have new intelligence that says Joshua's team has recovered Pandora's Box. They will be leaving their current location in Río Lagartos, Yucatan, Mexico in about one hour heading to Cancun International Airport. At all costs, I need you to intercept that convoy and recover Pandora's Box. Jamie will link to your iPad and give you real-time coverage of the convoy. Unfortunately, you will not have any air support for this operation, but you have overwhelming numbers on your side."

"Yes Col Myers. We will immediately cease search operations and put together a hasty ambush and recover Pandora's Box."

"Captain?"

"Yes Sir?"

"Failure is not an option Captain. Do you understand me?" Before Captain

Martinez could answer, the call was terminated. Miguel understood exactly what was required.

# # #

Sarah came running up to the second HUMVEE that carried James. "James!" yelled Sarah. "Both Mick and Carl just reported in. The Night Stalkers from both camps are hastily breaking camp, preparing to leave."

"Fuck!" replied James. "You can bet that somehow they know we have Pandora's Box and are preparing to ambush us enroute to the airport."

"Fuck!" said James again. "What can go wrong will go wrong. I fucking hate Murphy. What's your thoughts Sarah?"

Sarah unfolded her Samsung Z Fold 4 and pulled up Google Maps. "I really need to get one of those Sarah. Compared to my iPhone 13, the screen size just doesn't compare."

Sarah looked up and gave James a brief smile. After a few moments, she drew a circle around El Pocito. "If I was going to conduct an ambush, this is the spot where I would hit the convoy. After El Pocito, two major routes exist that will allow us to get to the airport as quickly as possible. This way they will not have to split their forces to maximize the possibility of successfully securing Pandora's Box. Based on the terrain, I would probably set up an L-Shape Ambush with one team set up on the North side of Highway 1800 and other team set up facing

West to engage the convoy head on. I would suggest that we ambush the ambushers, have Mick and Carl follow their perspective Night Stalkers. I'm pretty sure they have satellite coverage of the AO at this point. Fortunately, I doubt they have spotted our teams conducting reconnaissance or else they would have engaged them by now. You may not know this, but prior to this deployment Kenny upgraded our MTOE with one additional item. Each team member has been equipped with the modified ghillie suit he designed for our snipers. Kenny's suits accomplished two main goals: making the wearer virtually invisible and masking the wearer's heat signature. Kenny employed hundreds of tiny cameras that continuously take pictures of the surrounding area and feed the images into the suit's microprocessor, sending those images back out to LED screens on the suit. In essence, our men are virtually invisible to the naked eye and their thermals show up as the equivalent of field mice."

Sarah continued, " Susan and I continued to speak after the briefing. Most people are not aware, butthe CIA had its own privately funded technology organization called In-Q-Tech, formerly named Peleus. It's an American not-for-profit venture capital firm based in Arlington, Virginia. It invests in high-tech companies to keep the Central Intelligence Agency, and other intelligence agencies, equipped with the latest in technology in support of United States intelligence capability.

Immediately after our initial briefing with Susan, she contacted In-Q-Tel and put in a request to have Kenny's suit's technology retrofitted on the M1126 Stryker Combat Vehicle. Now instead of casting an image of what’s behind the vehicle, the processors will instead generate an image of our choice. To the casual observer, the Stryker will appear to be a rusty pickup truck as long as no one gets too close. Our teams will stay far enough back, but close enough to deploy and hit the Night Stalkers from the rear. Once the ambush commences, the convoy should immediately set up a defensive position around the containment unit and engage the Night Stalkers deployed on the North side of the Highway. My team will engage and attack the Night

Stalkers on the East side cutting off our route to the airport. Once we eliminate their blocking force, you need to drive like hell to the airport as we engage and eliminate the other team. With our enhanced armor and heavy weapons, we should be able dispatch the Night Stalkers, even though they have superior numbers on their side."

"Sarah, I like it. I even have a few surprises, courtesy of Susan as well. We have about five drones that are packed with C4 loaded with impact sensors. Basically, they are high tech suicide bombers. When we get close to the ambush site, we will deploy them at high altitude. The Night Stalkers will be engaged with our forces and never see the drones until it is too late."

"James, how much longer before the convoy is ready to deploy?"

"Another 60 minutes and we should be on the road."

"Perfect, that should give my team just enough time to mount some tungsten titanium alloy plating to the front of our HUMVEEs."

"Sarah, we don't have time for that."

"Believe me James, we need to make time. While our armor should protect us, for this plan to work, we need to engage the blocking force as quickly as possible and that's not going to happen if we are on foot. We have to provide some level of protection to our HUMVEEs or they won't make it 100 yards before they are rendered useless. It doesn't have to be pretty. We just need to weld a few plates on each

HUMVEE, and we will be good to go. 45 minutes is all I'm asking for."

"Make it happen Sarah and good luck. Use whatever resources necessary to get it done ASAP."

# # #

Mick had signaled to Sarah that his team was in place about one click behind the Night Stalker blocking force. Their Night Stalker group was moving into final position for the ambush. Carl signaled that their Night Stalkers were about 15 minutes from the Northern position. Sarah related this information back to James.

"Damn, you're good Sarah. I wish you were running intel when I was back on the Teams. They are setting up exactly as you predicted."

"Truthfully James, these guys are mostly ex-special operators just like us, so predicting them is actually pretty straight forward."

"Don't sell yourself short Sarah. I wouldn't have guessed right if it were me. So good job Sarah!"

Sarah briefly flashed back to a conversation that she had with James after she put together their hasty Operations Order when she asked James if he was going to challenge any of her assumptions. "Sarah, Mick told me to rely on your judgment when it comes to tactics because you're one of the best. He also said, if it wasn't for the stupid "No females in combat arms" rule, you would have been one of the finest SEALs that he ever served with. As it stands, even though you were a product of the CIA, he has the utmost respect for you when you saved his team's bacon back in Iraq on a joint CIA/SEAL operation. I trust Mick implicitly and if he tells me to trust you, then without pause, I will trust you as well." Things were so much different serving with Joshua and Trinity. Everyone here was a different breed of human. Their morality was impeccable. She felt fortunate when Mick reached out to her a few months ago. She was so disillusioned with politics and sexism in the CIA. With hyper-politicalization of appointees designated to run the US Intelligence Agencies, the leadership slowly became infiltrated by "Yes Men" vs professional that actually understood the business of keeping America safe.

* * *

# # #

All members of Delta Team had suited up in their full body armor. This would be their first test in battle conditions. Tension was high, although everyone appeared to be relaxed. This was no different than any other battles in the past. Susan was anxious to engage the Night Stalkers and let her training kick in. Thoughts were the mind killer before any battle; over thinking if you were ready; if your training was enough; if you thought of every contingency that the enemy might employ. Worst of all was Murphy's Law. Carl had called in about ten minutes ago to say that the Night Stalkers were in place, and they were waiting for their Go signal to commence their attack.

With Sarah's last communication, Mick launched all five drones. Mick radioed to all team members. "Here we go team. Heads on a swivel. Remember ambushes only work when the element of surprise is there. We know when and where the ambush is going to happen, so this is a movement to contact operation. Stick with your training and we will be okay. Good Luck and see you on the other side!

# # #

Captain Martinez had just spotted the lead vehicle in the convoy. Captain Martinez had deployed with the team on the Northern side of Highway 1800. If everything went well, this would be over in a matter of minutes. Jamie had assured him that his spies in the area had confirmed Pandora's Box was secure and protected. It should be able to withstand direct hits from their 50 cal. Sniper rounds. Unfortunately, all their explosive ordnance was off the table for this operation, but with their superiority in numbers, the battle should still be brief.

"Fire!" shouted Captain Martinez. Immediately after the rounds started going down range, Captain Martinez knew something was terribly wrong when two explosions went off within their ranks. Calls started coming in for the medics. The blocking force was also taking causalities. As Captain Martinez was trying to ascertain where the bombs were coming from, one of his men went down directly in front of him. Captain Martinez started immediately issuing new orders when his Stalker fell forward instead of falling backwards.

# # #

As soon as the drones attacked Carl gave his sniper the order to fire. Norman had his first target sited in. He was looking for the Night Stalker commanders, but because of their hasty set up, he would have to find the commanders once the fighting started. As soon as he fired, he realized the commander was to the right of the man he had just shot because he immediately issues orders for part of his men to turn and engage the unknown forces behind him.

# # #

* * *

In a matter of minutes, Captain Martinez realized half his men were down and only a few minutes had passed. The convoy had circled their vehicles around what could only be the vehicle carrying Pandora's Box. His unit was pinned down by fire from the convoy and some heavily armed force to their rear. Captain Martinez had called Col. Myers, but without air support they were SOL (Shit out of Luck). His men were getting hit with a combination of M240B machine guns, and .50 cal sniper rounds. His armored HUMVEEs were lying in smothering ruins by what could only be FGM-148 Javelin missile. The blocking force was in much worse shape. They were being attacked and the attackers were closing in to destroy them. Two vehicles had broken away from the convoy. When they dismounted, they were armored from head to toe. Even though they were taking directs hits, it only momentarily slowed them down. They would drop and immediately get back up. His guys were going down one by one, and there wasn't anything he could do about it. Even with the tragic deaths all around him, one thought drowned out all other concerns. "Failure is not an option Captain. Do you understand me?" With that last thought, Captain Martinez ordered his soldiers to attack knowing the inevitable outcome of the battle.

# # #

As soon as the blocking force was eliminated, James followed the plan, drove to the airport, and was safely on the plane heading to England. It was predetermined that the safest place would be Senator Ryles' secure location inside of Mount Everest. The only viable transition portal was Stonehenge. Ryles stated he would have a full contingency of men there to meet the plane and provide an escort. Sarah had linked up with Mick and it was with sadness that they closed in on the remaining Night Stalkers. The fight was no contest, but the Night Stalkers refused to give up. They had no choice but to eliminate them to ensure the success of the mission. With a heavy heart, they engaged and destroyed the remaining Night Stalkers. The global stakes were just too high.

Mount Everest Latitude and longitude coordinates: 27.986065, 86.922623

Joshua, Trinity, Ryles and his team were assembled at Stonehenge. The team seemed to be hovering between anxious anticipation and excitement. Paulie looked over at the body language of Joshua and Trinity, noting the tension.

"Guys, are you alright? It can't be that bad, can it?"

Joshua looked at Paulie with obvious disgust. "When you finished cleaning the shit off yourself in a few minutes, then you can tell me how bad you think it is!" Joshua turned around and started pacing again.

Ryles turned to the group. "We're ready. I just received the go signal. Please stay within the circle. Prepare yourselves."

The air around the 12 individuals begins to vibrate then hum. The air finally begins to shimmer and sparkle. One moment they were at Stonehenge, the next they were standing in a sealed room. Having gone through this before, Trinity and Joshua did not eat prior to the trip to Stonehenge. It still did not matter; both were on their knees throwing up bile and simultaneously losing control of their bowels again. Again after a few minutes, everyone seemed to have recovered. Everyone followed Joshua to what appeared to be changing stations and started to remove their soiled clothing before heading toward a communal shower. After the second experience, Trinity didn't care about being modest. The need to clean herself and put on a fresh set of clothes was simply overwhelming.

Dr. Brenda Calms met the team as they exited the changing room. Please follow me to the conference room. "Hi, I'm Dr. Brenda Calms. I know you have been briefed by Kelsey about the procedure I will be attempting, but if you follow me, I will give you a more in-dept briefing on the procedure." The team followed Dr. Calms and took a seat. After about an hour, the team members were escorted to their rooms to rest before the procedures started tomorrow.

Trinity quietly knocked on Joshua's door. When Joshua didn't answer, Trinity slowly opened the door and whispered if it was okay to come in. Trinity saw Joshua sitting in a half lotus seated position meditating to some frequency meditation music he had been using recently. Trinity came up and touched him on his shoulder as she sat next to him. "Sorry to disturb your meditation Joshua, but I thought you might like some company and talk before the procedure tomorrow."

"Thank you, Trinity. I am fine. I was just sitting here shutting my conscious mind down, trying to access the universal knowledge source to see if what we are doing is in fact the right thing. This is all so confusing, but I do know if we do nothing, humanity is doomed."

"Joshua, do you mind if I sit and meditate with you?"

"Of course not, sit and see if we can meet on the astral plane and connect to our higher purpose."

With a laugh Trinity said, "Whatever

Joshua, let's go walk the astral plane together." With that, she assumed a full lotus position across from Joshua, closed her eyes, and started meditating.

# # #

Joshua was unconscious sitting in a medical chair with a multi-probe harness attached to his head. Dr. Calms had explained in order to ensure the accuracy of the neural pathway mapping, Joshua would need to be placed in an induced coma. It was asked, "Why not just sedate him?" She went on to explain, Joshua needs to be in a deep coma that goes beyond flatlining. During this state of a deep coma, cortical activity revives. When your brain reaches this state, electrical waves called Nu-complexes waveforms are generated by the brain that are absent during known coma states, sleep or wakefulness. It is only in this state that we can do deep mapping of Joshua's neural pathways.

Trinity stared at Joshua because she was grateful for his guidance and teachings as she dealt with the loss of Robbie. Now that they were dealing with this global/interstellar threat trying to save humanity, at least Robbie's death now had meaning and it wasn't for nothing. That's how she was able to bear thinking about him being gone, and there wasn't a day that went by that she didn't think about her son. Without a doubt, she knew she would have ended it all if not for Joshua's intervention. Robbie's death was beyond bearable on its own, but her ex-husband's accusations and blame only added to her guilt. Jamison, her ex, was mentally abusive to begin with and knew how to make her feel incompetent, inadequate as a spouse and mother. He was a bully growing up, the local football star, whose life peaked in High School. Like so many other bullies, joined the local police force so he could still feel important and relevant in life. Now he could legally bully people for minor legal infractions. He thrived in environments where he had control.

Trinity remembered when she left Jamison. She did it over a note while he was at work. She and Robbie left with only the possessions she could fit in two suitcases. She finally listened to her parents and moved back in with her after the numerous times she had confided in her mother and eventually her father about the mental abuse. Jamison was smart; he did not need to hit her. Breaking her down into the shell of the person she used to be was enough for him.

When Jamison got home and found the note, he immediately tried to call her. As per her parent's insistence, she turned off her phone, and his calls kept going to voice mail. He used his resources on the force to put out an Amber Alert on her car. It did not take long to track her vehicle back to her parent's house. He immediately called her parents' house and the father picked up. Yelling in the phone, Jamison told Bob to put Trinity on the phone now. It was decided from the beginning to have Bob answer the phone. Of the three of them, he was the most level-headed in the heat of an argument. Having served three tours in the Vietnam War, a lot of things simply did not faze him. Bob calmly, but firmly told Jamison. "Son, I am not sure who you are talking to, but no person has the right to talk to another person the way you are currently talking. And let's be clear about something, you are lucky that you never laid a hand on my daughter. So many times, Martha stopped me from coming over there and taking my daughter from the house of an asshole who thinks it's okay to mentally abuse my daughter. She is the same person that I entrusted in your care eight years ago."

"Old man, I don't know who the fuck

you are talking to, but I will put you six feet under if you ever set a foot in my house."

Trinity was sitting next to Bob and could hear everything Jamison was saying because of how loud he was yelling.

Again, in his calm voice, Bob addressed Jamison, "Son, I have seen more death and fucked up shit in my lifetime to know a frightened little man when I see one. You think that badge protects you and gives you the right to do whatever the hell you want. Well, I'm here to tell you, I'm not afraid. True, you have youth on your side, but you think it's a foregone conclusion that you will kick my ass."

Her dad's voice got very quiet and while he did not shout, the threat and menace in his voice was palatable and real. Trinity tried to retreat further in her chair away from the threat then she stopped. She became proud and smiled. She had always thought of her dad as the most gentle, lovable man in the world. She was his princess. From her earliest memory, he always was a gentleman, holding the door for mom, carrying the heavy stuff, massaging mom's feet after a long shift as an ER Nurse. She always felt safe when he was around. When they asked the kids in school to talk about their hero, she would always talk about him and relate the good stories she would overhear when his military buddies came into town. He was one of the reasons she married someone like Jamison. Her father always carried himself with an air of authority. It didn't matter who was in the room. He ran a small road construction company, and everyone loved him. On the wall in his office, he had a sign from his days as an Infantry Officer in Vietnam. "Mission First, People Always!" They would do anything for him because he took care of them.

Now for the first time, she saw a side of her dad that both scared her and made her proud.

"But let me tell you something son. I have had over 15 near death experiences in my life and guess what? I am still here. I have had mobsters threaten me and guess what? I am still here. So little man, be careful who you are threatening. You just might be the dog that finally caught the car and not have a clue what to do with it."

For a moment, Jamison did not say a word. Finally, he worked up the courage to speak. "She can't take my son away from me. Rest assured I am going to make her regret ever walking out on me."

"Son, for the last time, you had better stop writing checks that your body can't cash. That's the last threat you will make to my daughter. And just so you know, this conversation has been recorded!" With that, Bob hung up the phone. Before Bob could fully turn around, Trinity leaped into his arms crying uncontrollably. The last five years of her life had been hell living with Jamison. He cut her off from all her friends. He forced her to stop working after Robbie was born. She felt trapped and alone. Only the strong ties with her parents saved her from having a complete mental breakdown. Through the sobs, Trinity finally managed, "I love you daddy!"

"I love you too my precious little girl. I'm just so sorry that it has taken you this long to finally leave that asshole, but I also understood I couldn't force you to leave him either. Your mother managed to penetrate my stubborn thick head and convinced me if I forced you to leave, you would resent me for it and want to go back to Jamison. Only when you reached your limit, would you finally see that you deserved better. Your mother is a smart woman. That's probably why I married her. Not too many people can change my mind when it gets made up, but Martha has a way about her." Bob said with a slight laugh.

"Don't worry Trinity. We'll get through this. We just have to stick with the plan." Trinity recalled the meeting she had with her parents six months prior. Bob's longtime friend and lawyer recommended a specialty divorce lawyer, who was also at the meeting. The lawyer told her to place hidden cameras throughout the house. Because of Jamison's contacts and influence, the only way to win the pending child custody battle would be with hard evidence. True to his word, the police & child protective services showed up at her parent's house. Bob had previously spoken to the local police chief, another longtime friend and golf buddy, about the pending conflict. So, when the Amber Alert came through, Chief Tommy Santis called Bob and gave him the heads up. Robbie's bag was already packed, and Trinity had explained to Robbie what was about to happen. Initially Robbie clung to his mother and cried uncontrollably because he did not want to stay with daddy. By the time Child Protective Services (CPS) and the police showed up, Robbie was just sniffling. The police served the warrant to Trinity, for unlawfully removing a minor across state lines without a parent's consent. While the police were talking to Trinity and Bob, CPS was preparing Robbie for transport.

# # #

The divorce proceedings and trial were nasty. Trinity cried every night. The endless psychological evaluations for her and Robbie, the supervised visits with Robbie, and the hostile arbitrations were pushing Trinity beyond her emotional limits. Every night the crying had become a part of her routine of how she coped with everything. More than anything, the supervised visits were beyond painful because every time Robbie hugged and cried at the end and begged her to go back home with her. All she could do was promise Robbie it would happen, but she needed a little more time. Her lawyer told her to be patient. Her time in court would come.

She remembered clearly it was a chilly March morning. She and her parents went to the courthouse. Her lawyer was brilliant in the way that he introduced the video evidence to the judge. Jamison's lawyer, Tom Synderson, immediately objected saying these recordings are not admissible because she did not have the client's permission to record him.

Tom immediately started quoting statutes for the District of Columbia as it relates to One-Party Consent. "Your Honor, I'm sure my esteemed colleague must have forgotten that DC is one of thirty-eight states that are covered under One-Party Consent, which means that an individual can record conversations they are a part of without the other person's consent."

"But your Honor," Mr. Synderson said "Mrs. Trinity, seek to disparage my client's..."

"Your Honor, please understand." continued Trinity's lawyer, "If my client was trying to taint Mr. Winter's reputation, she could have easily released these tapes to the local news outlets and through social media. All my client wants to do is to show the court all relevant evidence before a decision is made on what is in Robbie's best interest."

Jamison's lawyer immediately countered. "Your Honor, in order for photo and video evidence to be admissible in court it must meet two basic requirements: relevance and authenticity."

The Judge had had enough. Addressing both lawyers, "Gentlemen, please approach the bench. Let's address the easy question first. How can you prove the video recording is authentic?"

"Your Honor, the video was taken off the client's home security system that was installed in the home of residence. It was installed by Mr. Winters for their protection since he is a police officer. I have a certification from Home Security and Monitoring Services (HSMS) that they were the ones that pulled this particular video from the client's system, and that the system has not been tampered with, and the video is unaltered in any way."

"Please hand over the Letter of Certification." said the Judge. After reviewing for a moment, the judge passed the document over to Jamison's lawyer.

"Your Honor," said Jamison's lawyer. "Whatever is on the video is not a reasonable representation of my client and may result in undue prejudice against him. This is only one moment in time, your honor. Anyone can have a bad day, and I feel that Mrs. Winters will only present the worse moments of my client. Without context, anything viewed will only create more prejudice against him. Besides, your Honor, the video isn't relevant to these hearings. We are discussing the custody of Robbie, not the relationship between my client and Mrs. Winters."

Jamison sat listening to the exchange. He felt Trinity might pull something like this. He had assured his lawyer that he has never been abusive to Robbie. He admitted to having major arguments with Trinity, but who doesn't have arguments with their spouse from time to time?

"Your Honor," said Trinity's lawyer. "This video is in fact."

Before he could continue, the Judge

held up her hand. Gentlemen, this is not a criminal proceeding. We are trying to determine what is in the best interest of Robbie. I will allow the video to be presented, as long as it's relevant."

"I assure you it is your Honor."

"Your Honor, can we have a 30-minute recess to review the video first? The judge allowed the recess, and the parties exited the court room. 15 minutes into the recess, Trinity's lawyer received a call. After listening he said, "Give me a few minutes and I'll call you back."

"Trinity, they want to negotiate a settlement!" Bob shouted yes, and Trinity started crying with tears of relief that this 4-month nightmare was finally coming to an end.

Both parties were standing before the

judge. "Both parties are agreeing to these terms?"

"Yes, your honor." Both lawyers said in unison.

"So be it. On this day, March 13, 2015, I am awarding full physical and legal custody of Robbie Dewayne Winters to Trinity Winters. Mr. Jamison Winters, you will have supervised visits at minimum every other week or as agreed upon by Mrs. Winters. You also agree to pay $1,000 a month for child support until Robbie graduates from High School. You will also contribute $250 a month to Robbie's 529 college savings account."

"Yes, your Honor."

"Mrs. Winters, you are agreeing to no alimony or any entitlements to Mr. Winters retirement pension."

"Yes, your Honor."

"And you both are agreeing to sell the house, or the other party buys the other out. The house proceeds will be split 60% to Mrs. Winters and 40% to Mr. Winters minus any applicable fees and taxes."

Trinity continued to reminisce about her past, thinking about her journey up to now. She knew her failure to become a field agent for HLSORD (Homeland Security Operational Response Division) was a direct result of the mental trauma she had experienced during her relationship with Jamison. While outwardly she looked fine, her self-confidence still wasn't there. She had trained hard and was in the best physical shape of her life, but that did not help her fully with the mental trauma, when she applied to be a field agent. His words of being inferior, inadequate, a loser, a bad mother always lingered in her mind. When Robbie died, Jamison twisted her inside and out with guilt and blame. He almost convinced her of killing herself because without Robbie, she had nothing left to live for. He had almost succeeded. Thank God for the man sitting in that chair. He sacrificed everything for the love of country when he served in the military. Now because of her, he was sacrificing himself for all of humanity.

She knew without a doubt, she was a different person already because of him. Now she would be receiving all his martial skills thanks to this amazing technology.

40 minutes into the procedure, Dr Calms indicated that the procedure was

completed, and Joshua would be coming around any time now. Trinity was sitting beside Joshua as he opened his eyes. Dr Calms looked away from the monitors and handed Joshua a glass of water. Joshua immediately took it and downed the entire glass before he said, "Thank you."

"Sorry, Joshua. That's one of the side effects of the procedure, an overwhelming thirst afterwards." She handed Joshua another glass of water. "Based on the scans, the procedure was a complete success. First thing tomorrow, we will start overlaying your neural pathways on to your team. Trinity volunteered to be the 1st patient." said Dr Calms.

Joshua looked at Trinity. "Really? Why not let one of the others go first?"

Trinity returned Joshua's stare

unflinchingly. "After all I've been through, and all we have been through to get to this point, I wanted to be the first. I started everyone down this journey, and I'm ready to complete what we started. And if these newfound skills will make this journey less arduous then I'll volunteer to be first every day of the week. We will not lose this fight Joshua. We have already lost too much, Robbie and the loss of Charlie Team. No more!"

Joshua closed his eyes and nodded. He fought back the tears, the sorrow, the guilt of losing his comrades in arms. They had each survived numerous deployments in Iraq and Afghanistan just to lose their lives on US soil, fighting for a cause that most Americans were clueless about. His nod was one of understanding for the pain he could see in Trinity's eyes, for wanting to do anything to tip the scales to gain an advantage or edge that could be the difference between life or death, good versus evil, and ultimately us versus them. Joshua had done the same thing when Delta asked for five volunteers to train Tai Chi Chuan with Sifu Jia Peng. Most of the soldiers laughed at the prospect of learning Tai Chi, but not Joshua. A few of them joked Tai Chi was for old people and women in the park. Most Delta operators were very skilled in various styles of Martial Arts. Most chose styles like Krav Maga, an Israeli martial art or Brazilian Jiu-Jitsu, which emphasizes grappling with a focus on ground fighting. The five volunteers all had a Martial Arts background in various Chinese Kung Fu disciplines. Joshua's was in Wing Chun.

Delta was structured with various cycles of readiness: three months on deployable status on various missions throughout the globe, three months in training phase/QRF (Quick Reaction Force) in order to provide back-up for team missions, and finally three months on R&R (Rest and Relaxation).

During the R&R phase, soldiers are given two months of a mixture of leave and/or continuing educational courses followed by one month of training to get ramped back up for the deployment phase. During one R&R phase Joshua chose to go back to China and get additional training with his current Wing Chun Master Lo Chen. During this trip, Joshua got an opportunity to visit an exclusive Kung Fu tournament. Various styles of Kung Fu were represented. There was only one Tai Chi participant in the tournament. Most of the participants and spectators laughed and gave the Tai Chi participant no chance of making it through the 1st round of tournament. To everyone's surprise, he easily defeated a Hung Gar contestant with seemingly little to no effort. After his win, Sifu Xue's name was being whispered on everyone's lips.

Joshua was fascinated. During each round that Sifu Yuhya Xue participated in, Joshua watched this unassuming Tai Chi practitioner defeat opponent after opponent. Regardless of martial style, size of the competitor, or speed of the contestant, the results were the same. They were all defeated. He moved with a grace that was almost supernatural. It looked like he knew what technique his opponent was going to use and countered it or simply was somewhere else as the contestant delivered what was seemingly a knockout blow. It looked like Sifu Yuhya Xue was playing. Not once did he get hit by his opponent. During the final round of the competition, Sifu Yuhya Xue was slated to fight Sifu Li. Sifu Li used to be Joshua's teacher when he trained Wing Chun under the tutelage of Master Lo Chen. Sifu Li was Master Lo Chen's number 1 student. Joshua remembered being defeated daily learning Wing Chun from Sifu Li with bruises to show just how powerful and fast Sifu Li was. Joshua looked forward to being paired with Sifu Li because even in defeat, he learned so much.

Sifu Li and Sifu Xue bowed to each other in the center ring. This truly was going to be a match of Kung Fu Masters. Two minutes into the 1st of three rounds, there were no points scored. Each strike was blocked. Each counterstrike was blocked in turn. The contestants were seemingly evenly matched. The timekeeper hit the desk three times with his hammer to indicate 15 seconds remaining in the round, at which point, Sifu Li unleashed a barrage of lightning-fast hammer strikes. It was all Sifu Xue could do just to block each strike. Sifu Li sensed an opportunity and landed an outside dragon kick to Sifu Xue's inner right thigh, which sent Sifu Xue to the ground right as the bell rang. The round went to Sifu Li. Joshua found himself cheering wildly like everyone in the arena.

Round Two went similarly to Round One. Again, in the last minute, Sifu Li landed a blow as the bell rang. Joshua could clearly see that Sifu Xue was frustrated. Halfway through the 3rd and final round, Sifu Xue countered a series of strikes from Sifu Li at which point something happened that changed and shook Joshua's understanding of Kung Fu. Sifu Xue hit Sifu Li with what seemed like a push that literally threw Sifu Li 20 feet across the ring and into the 1st row of spectators. Sifu Li was knocked out cold. The problem was Joshua knew without a doubt that Sifu Xue's hands never connected with Sifu Li. It was like a magnet had repelled Sifu Li across the ring. What happened next was just as surprising. Sifu Xue rushed to Sifu Li's side and put his hands on Sifu Li's heart and a spot right around his navel. He later found out these spots were Sifu Li's 4th and 3rd chakras respectively. Again, Joshua saw something that he did not understand. Sifu Xue's hands looked like they were glowing. A few minutes later, Sifu Li opened his eyes and sat up. Sifu Xue started apologizing profusely to Sifu Li. Sifu Xue then helped Sifu Li to his feet.

Both contestants then made their way back to the center ring, so a winner could be announced. Before the judge could raise Sifu Xue's hand as the winner, Sifu Xue disqualified himself and withdrew from the competition. By default, Sifu Li won the tournament. The crowd was initially stunned then applauded because both contestants had given a spectacular demonstration of martial skills. Joshua had to understand what he had just witnessed, so he searched the crowd for Sifu Xue. He finally spotted him walking on the road leading back to the town square. Joshua had to run to catch Sifu Xue. Joshua questioned him with his rudimentary mandarin as to why he disqualified himself. Sifu Xue stopped and looked directly at Joshua. "I might have won the match, but at what cost. Tai Chi is about balance. I was out of balance and became angry that Sifu Li was defeating me. His Gung Fu was superior to mine this day. Sifu Li taught me on this day, that I needed to train harder."

Joshua interrupted, "Sifu, I don't

understand. You threw him 20 feet across the ring. Your skills are clearly superior."

"Young Master, I used Qi to defeat a worthy opponent. This is a violation of my path. My life was not in jeopardy. I was not coming to the aid of one in need. Qi is universal energy that is all around us to be used for either good or evil. This competition was about demonstrating martial skill. Qi gives me an unfair advantage. That I used it on Sifu Li is a stain on my karma. By using Qi to heal Sifu Li, I removed some of that stain. By withdrawing from the tournament, I removed more of that stain. To remove the rest, I need to continue my training and meditate to remove my ego to regain my balance. In defeat, you learn. My ego prevented me from accepting that on this day, Sifu Li's martial skills were superior to mine. Now I must depart to immediately confess to my teacher Sifu Jia Peng and accept his guidance on how to continue my journey."

Joshua left the encounter with Sifu Xue puzzled, but also in need of a deeper understanding of Tai Chi and this mysterious energy called Qi. So, when Command asked for volunteers to learn Tai Chi under Sifu Jia Peng, being first to volunteer was a given.

When Joshua looked into Trinity's eyes, he simply nodded his head clearly understanding why Trinity had volunteered to go first.

# # #

Dr. Calms was turning from one

mounted flat panel screen to another monitoring the team's vitals. She was looking for signs that Joshua's mapped neutral pathways were degrading or the activation of some of the so-called junk DNA was failing. The DNA Matrix Sequencer had performed just as she had hoped. Unfortunately, Soa'limae was the expert in this area, so she continued to monitor closely for signs of rejection even though they were three weeks post treatment and recovery. She only hoped that based on the numerous captured humans with DNA anomalies over the centuries, that she had properly isolated the DNA strains that Soa'limae had altered in those specimens.

Dr Calms remembered the conversation she had with Joshua's team three weeks earlier about the procedure they were going to undergo. "Bridging Soa'limae intellectual gap around DNA manipulation and my understanding of human DNA, I'm going to use the DNA Matrix Sequencer to create a retrovirus to rewrite specific strains of your junk DNA."

"Excuse me Ma'am. Not wanting to sound stupid, but what is a retrovirus?" asked Paulie.

"Actually, that is a good question. A retrovirus is a virus that uses RNA as its genomic material. RNA or ribonucleic acid is a nucleic acid present in all living cells. Its principal role is to act as a messenger carrying instructions from your DNA in order to control the synthesis of proteins. Whenever you hear about diseases including AIDS and some forms of cancer, that is a person's DNA producing the wrong types of proteins. Left untreated, those proteins will alter a person's cells and ultimately kill them."

Paulie continued, "Not trying to sound like the Debbie downer here, but how do you know which junk DNA to activate? I personally don't want to be walking around with tumors all over my body and the strength of Sampson."

"Please Paulie," said Sean, "It's not like you get any action now. As a matter of fact, it might be an improvement on your looks!" With that, everyone laughed and released the tension that was building.

"That's actually a fair question. I was one of the main scientists that worked on the Human Genome Project. The project was an international scientific research project with the goal of determining the base pairs that make up human DNA. To include identifying, mapping and sequencing all of the genes of the human genome from both a physical and a functional standpoint. While I relied on a lot of the data generated from this project, with our technology, I took it one step farther. This is where we truly understood what Soa'limae had done to the human genome. Do you wonder why humans and chimpanzees are almost genetically identical? In 2005, the NIH published a research paper by an international research consortium. It was the first comprehensive comparison of the genetic blueprints of humans and chimpanzees, which shows our closest living relatives share perfect identity with 96 percent of our DNA sequence. So, before you can ask the question Paulie," Dr Calms said with a wink. "I'm going to address the 5,000 pound elephant in the room. My colleague Soa'limae combined our alien DNA with that of a chimpanzee."

Immediately, everyone started talking over each other. Senator Kelsey Ryles stood up. "Please everyone calm down! If you would let Dr Calms finish, she will answer all of your questions."

Joshua also stood up. "Guys, my teacher once said. Wishing something isn't true does not make it so. In order to confront the battle ahead, we must be armed with facts. No matter how painful or unbelievable. Do you remember when Trinity and I first briefed you all on the reality that there are aliens among us? It wasn't until Trinity activated the holographic technology that your minds accepted this reality. This is no different. How we became who we are today is irrelevant. We can't change that. All we can do is focus on the future and what we can change."

Trinity then chimed in. "I remember when Kelsey first met with Joshua and I and told us everything. Joshua and I were confronted with the unworldly truth of our existence and the degree by which our history has been shaped by his crew's warring factions. I was pissed. I remember Joshua saying something about fighting for the human species. I remember yelling at him that we can't even use that word human because we are nothing more than intergalactic mutts used as playthings for these aliens. Of course,

Joshua with his usual calm demeanor brought me back to my senses. He said emotions cannot be allowed to override logic. I have had time to reflect upon this journey that we now find ourselves on. I hated Senator Kelsey Ryles and his crew for the deaths of untold millions over the course of our existence because they wanted to stop us from evolving and providing aid repairing their spaceship. Because in the act of leaving this planet, a far greater threat would be unleashed upon Earth. One that will wipe us out of existence. While on a logistical level, I get it. Kill a few now to protect the future of the many, but let me repeat this again, I will never forgive you and your kind for what you have done."

Dr Calms tried to reassert control of

the meeting. "Please understand, what we did, we did out of arrogance, because in essence, we created you."

Again, everyone started speaking over each other. Kelsey started to rise, but Dr Calms motioned for him to remain seated with a slight shake of head.

"If you would please allow me to continue, I assure you, I will answer all of your questions. Please." Brenda just stood there silently until everyone quieted down. Once all eyes were on her, she began again. "Before we arrived on this planet, your ancestors were nothing more than chimpanzees that walked the face of this planet content eating bananas and grooming each other. Senator Ryles, our Commander, knew we had the ability to immediately evolve the chimpanzees to become a work force capable of helping us mine the rare materials we needed to harvest and process in order to repair our ship. These various materials were scattered across the globe. We would need millions of laborers to accomplish this. Kelsey and the others you have met instead chose to stay true to our oath as officers of the Sanarian Empire and not alter in any way the natural evolution of indigenous lifeforms on other worlds. This led to the mutiny aboard our ship. By taking the artifacts that your other teams are now searching for, we felt Xan'lima, the ship's First Officer and Soa'limae, the ship's Scientist Officer would not be capable of doing any harm to this planet. We were wrong. No one knew just how brilliant and cruel Soa'limae was. To make a long story short, Dr. Soa'limae killed thousands of chimpanzees until he succeeded in creating a hybrid Sanarian using chimpanzee DNA. This new species would be called Homo Sapiens."

"We kept an eye on our mutinous shipmates throughout the years. It was on one of our missions when we first found out about Dr. Soa'limae's cruel experiments. At that point, there was nothing we could do. They had control of the ship and thereby, superior weaponry. Without the aid of the DNA Matrix Sequencer, trying to find the right DNA combination to evolve the chimpanzee was going to be a time-consuming process, if it was possible at all. So again, we did not think they would be successful. While we felt bad for the chimpanzees, we also knew they were only animals and not worth losing our lives in order to protect them."

Sam O'Donnell immediately yelled, "So, we were not worth trying to save?"

"You misunderstand what I am trying to say Sam. Look at it this way. While some of your species might want your cattle to be treated humanely, there are others who could care less. And then there are those who could care less how that juicy mouth-watering hamburger made it to their plate. The only thing they care about is that they are hungry. This thinking is no different than ours. Your race at the time of our crash did not exist and the chimpanzees were inferior on the evolutionary scale. Think about your cattle, pigs, chicken, fowl, fish and many other animals in your food chain. Do you think about the comparative morality of weighing the cost of their lives versus the billions that need to be fed. There are some scientists that have even genetically modified those animals to make the food cycle more efficient: chicken, cattle, pigs, and salmon hatcheries. What about other genetically modified food? Did you know that almost 60 percent of American sugar originates from genetically modified sugar beets thanks to an herbicide sprayed to protect plants? This means that when you eat processed foods like snack foods, soups, canned sauces, cereals and breads, you are eating genetically modified food. What about corn? GMO corn makes up about 80 percent of the American corn market. I could continue with all the genetic modifications your scientists have made to your food chain, but I think you get the point."

"I do have a question for you Sam. "What do you think all these GMO products have done to your bodies? Why are do think obesity rate in the United States has tripled in the last 50 years? Let's not even mention the rise in heart disease and Type 2 diabetes. It is estimated that worldwide there are 937 million adults that are overweight, and 396 million that are obese. Were these statistics a product of greed or in the name of some greater good? Who stands up and fights for the rights of the animals or for you to eat non-genetically modified foods? Let me answer my own questions, just a handful of Eco-terrorists and activists, while the rest of humanity enjoys their hamburgers and High-Fructose carbonated drinks." At that point, the anger left Sam's eyes and he looked down.

Trinity's expression became one of deep contemplation. "Are we really any different than these aliens? Is all evolved life in the universe this cruel?"

"I digress. Please forgive me. Back to Dr. Soa'limae. Not only did he have to figure out the correct genes to turn on, but he would need the patience to let the hybrid-Sanarians stabilize before the next round of experimentation could begin. While cruel, our primary mission objective was to ensure the planet was protected from our ancient enemy, and it was."

"Every ten thousand years or so, Dr.

Soa'limae would wake to check on the development of the hybrids. If the DNA combinations developed sufficiently during those periods, then the next round of generic manipulations would begin. Archaeologists have been successful at tracking Soa'limae's work. The distinct phases of the hybrid's evolution are now known as Ardipithecus, Australopithecus, Homo Erectus, and finally Homo Sapien. Once the hybrids evolved to the stage of Homo Sapiens, Xan'lima started using telepathy to manipulate the direction of human development. The minds of humans were still very fragile at this point. Some of your world's greatest prophets went crazy trying to write down the mental instructions of Xan'lima before the human brain evolved enough to handle telepathy.

The ones that did not go completely mad initially, eventually went crazy as well. Some were chained to post living out their lives in monasteries. In some ways, the whole reason monks existed was to create a safe haven for these instructions to be captured and the information controlled. Once the human brain evolved enough, some noted prophets were produced: Nostradamus, Miriam the Prophetess, and Edgar Cayce to name a few. It is through these writings that the group you are currently fighting formed and evolved through the centuries. Originally known as the Illuminati then the Light. Every global conspiracy can be traced back to our shipmates' manipulation of small groups of humans. Today, they are known as the Committee and they are on the verge of succeeding in doing something we have worked a millennium to prevent, the re-activation of our ship."

"Now Paulie, back to your question. It is true that the DNA matrix sequencer was not designed to utilize a retrovirus to manipulate DNA strands. In truth it was designed to repair our bodies and create clones in case of a catastrophic emergency, where the original host body was destroyed. With the use of neural mapping, the host's consciousness would be imprinted upon the new clone body. With my knowledge of the human genome, I will be using a retrovirus to rewrite parts of your junk DNA to evolve you to what you were already evolving into: Homo Superior. Through the unique combination of our alien DNA and this planet's environmental anomalies you have already been evolving into a new species, Homo Superior. Just look how much stronger, faster, and smarter you are getting every generation. What you call extreme sports today would have been called superhuman just 50 years ago. This evolution would have happened in a matter of centuries, but I'm going to speed up the process with this retrovirus created by the DNA Matrix Sequencer. Basically, I'm going to infect you all with a retrovirus using the flu virus as the delivery platform. Upon infection with this retrovirus, your cells will convert the retroviral RNA into DNA, which in turn will overwrite the junk DNA of your host cells. The cells will then produce more retroviruses which will infect other cells throughout your body. Based on the characteristics we targeted from

Soa'limae's work, after you recover from your brief flu- like symptoms, each of you should have increased speed, enhanced strength, and superior vision to include night vision. Your bodies will heal in a fraction of the time. A broken bone should heal in hours instead of months. Wounds should heal in minutes. You will even be able to effect healing in others. You will have a sense of smell and hearing on par with that of wolves. You should also have extrasensory perception or ESP abilities from telepathy: the ability to know another person's thoughts. Precognition: the ability to see into the future. Telekinesis: the ability of one's mind to have a direct effect on an object without the use of any physical energy; and finally Pyrokinesis, the ability to start or control fire with your mind. These are just a few of the known enhancements, but truthfully there might be more abilities that we are simply not aware of. Remember, just because you will have these abilities, you can still die. With enough trauma to the body, it will not be able to heal."

Unable to contain herself any longer, Trinity finally blurted out the question that has plaguing her subconscious since she became aware of these aliens' involvement in mankind's development, "Dr Calms, I understand the why of what you did, but I have got to ask the question. At what cost? How many inferior Homo Sapiens have died in your quest to cull the cattle population over the centuries in your so-called war?"

The question came out before she could stop herself. The self-righteous superiority of these aliens was more than she could take. It came out with such venom and hatred, it shocked everyone including her. Having said it, Trinity tried to take it back. "Please forgive me Kelsey and Dr Calms. Hearing all this for the first time or even the second time, it's a lot. I don't."

Dr Calms interrupted Trinity. "Please don't apologize, Trinity. You have no idea the nightmares I have had over the centuries about what it is we have done to your race. You don't know how glad I am that we are now sitting in this room together. It is fitting that the species we once thought of as no more than cattle that needed to be culled are now our salvation against our ancient enemy. While your evolution started off as a tool to help us get back home, it has become so much more. Our war has spanned thousands upon thousands of years, species throughout the galaxy have come and gone. It is the universe's strange twist of fate that brought us to this back water planet at the time of our crash. The fact that our crew fought is why we are now here with the potential answer to save the galaxy. For surely, our ancient enemy will eventually eliminate all sentient life in the galaxy to include Earth after they defeat us."

"To answer your question, I have tracked the destruction that I have brought upon this world and if it wasn't for the fact that I believed at the time, it was the only way to save your planet, I would have ended my life a long time ago for my part in the deaths that I have caused." Dr Brenda Calms hit a button on her controller for the holographic viewer. Like before, the team was immersed in an artificial reality taking them back to each plague.

ANTONINE PLAGUE (165 AD): Death Toll: 5 million

PLAGUE OF JUSTINIAN (541-542): Bubonic Plague: Death Toll: 25 million

THE BLACK DEATH (1346-1353): Bubonic Plague: Death Toll: 75 - 200 million

THIRD CHOLERA PANDEMIC (1852-1860): Cholera: Death Toll: 1 million

FLU PANDEMIC (1889-1890): Influenza or "Asiatic Flu" or "Russian Flu": Death Toll: 1 million

SIXTH CHOLERA PANDEMIC (1910-1911): Cholera: Death Toll: 800,000+

FLU PANDEMIC (1918): Influenza: Death Toll: 20 -50 million

ASIAN FLU (1956-1958): Influenza: Death Toll: 2 million

FLU PANDEMIC (1968): Influenza: Death Toll: 1 million

HIV/AIDS PANDEMIC (AT ITS PEAK, 2005-2012): HIV/AIDS: Death Toll: 36 million

An hour later when the holographic images stopped everyone sat in stunned silence. Many were weeping openly. "At least once a week since I started engineering death, I have relived what my creation has done to the species of this planet. Some days it is almost too much to bear." There were tears in her eyes as she addressed the team. "It's easy to just look at these events as numbers on a screen. I felt each individual deserved to be remembered as a life lived and how they died. While it would be impossible to capture each singular death, I did my best to capture the time period and what my engineered death took away from those that survived."

Addressing Dr Calms by her Sanarian name Ce'limae, Kelsey stood up to go comfort her. Brenda held out a hand to push him away. "I had no idea Brenda, the toll this took on you. I don't have the words to express my sorrow and regret." The team then observed something they didn't quite understand, but it moved them profoundly. Kelsey made some type of jester with his hands then knelt at Dr Calms feet. He held something in both of his hands outstretched to Dr Calms. While Joshua didn't know exactly what he was seeing, he was pretty sure that Kelsey had just placed his life in her hands. While not the same, he had seen similarly events in the Asian cultures as a way to regain their honor at the cost of their life.

Not knowing exactly what was being said, in the singsong Sanarian language, Ce'limae addressed Be'lima. He refused to look up at her until she placed a finger under his chin. Tears were streaming down both their cheeks as she sank to the floor in front of him. She closed her hands around his and what could only be interpreted as another part of this formal ritual. She touched her forehead to their hands, then they both embraced each other for a few minutes before rising.

The anger that Trinity had felt toward this alien was no longer there. She remembered how she had felt when Robbie had died. The nightmares she had experience when SFC Daniels had died at her hands. Even though he deserved to die, that still did not relieve her of the guilt of taking a life. When she asked Joshua how he got over the lives he had taken in war, his answer was simple. "You don't unless you are a monster. You just pray that you did the right thing for the greater good and try to lessen the karmic stain by living the rest of your life in service to those that are in need." She could clearly see that this must be a universal truth by the burden that Dr

Calms still carried. Trinity now understood, her initial judgment of Dr Calm's character was far from the truth. Her hard cold exterior was her way of coping with the untold horrors that she had witnessed over the centuries. Silently in the recesses of her mind, something gave, and she realized that she had forgiven Brenda and Kelsey.

# # #

Refocusing back on the banks of monitors, it had only been three weeks post the team receiving the retrovirus that they were now testing their newfound abilities in the training room. The results were beyond expectations. She and Kelsey watched the team perform feats that were beyond believable. The holographic simulator created realistic scenarios. Against Kelsey's better judgment, the safety protocols were turned off to give the team a 4D experience that could actually hurt them, but not kill them. Joshua had reasoned that to truly understand the limits of their new abilities, they needed to believe that their lives were in mortal danger or else they would hold back. It was Brenda that convinced Kelsey that Joshua was in fact correct. With the combat that these soldiers had seen, if they knew this was simply a simulation, they would hold back knowing they wouldn't be hurt. She needed their adrenaline and cortisol levels to spike to see what effect this would have on their enhancements.

Kelsey watched them move from one battle simulation to another. They no longer used radios to communicate. They were honing their telepathic abilities. In some simulations, they went into the mission armed with nothing more than a combat knife. It didn't matter. The Tai Chi Chuan styles they had acquired from Joshua's neural mapping proved to be just as effective as the gene modifications. They wore body armor and a few times, team members had gone down with gunshot wounds to limbs during training but managed to heal in minutes. A few days into running these simulated drills, training was paused at one point while Mike healed. He had suffered an injury that nearly tore his forearm completely off. It took him about 2 days to fully heal. At that point, the team took the simulations a lot more seriously, but the traumatic injury served its purpose. They were starting to realize just how enhanced they were now. They pushed the limits of their new abilities. Jumping from a 6-floor building was the equivalent of jumping off a table now.

In order to gain the Expert Infantryman Badge, a soldier candidate must complete a ruck march of 19 kilometers or 12 miles within three hours, carrying a rifle and 40 lb. rucksacks. Joshua's team now were doing 30-mile ruck marches in under 60 minutes carrying 200 lb. rucksacks.

With their enhanced vision, the team members were now effectively able to outperform the specifications of the Barrett M82 .50 caliber sniper rifles they were using. Before the enhancements, the world record for the longest confirmed kill in military history was by a Canadian sniper with an astonishing distance of 2.2 miles (some 3,540 meters). The longest confirmed sniper shot by a U.S. soldier came in 2004, when Sgt. Bryan Kremer killed an Iraqi insurgent from 2,300 meters or 1.42 miles. Joshua's team could now reliably hit targets out to the maximum range of the .50 caliber round of 4 to 5 miles or about 8,000 meters.

The simulation drills were comprehensive and exhausting, but every day seemed to unlock some new enhanced ability. The last drill was the most challenging of all. The team was on a CIA cargo ship in the Gulf of Aqaba preparing for an insertion by sea into Jordan to neutralize a chemical munitions plant. While doing equipment checks, the ship was struck by AGM-88 HARM missiles from two Royal Jordanian Air Force F-16 Fighting Falcons. The team received an alert from the bridge that hostels were engaging, and countermeasures had failed. Because this was a disguised CIA cargo ship, they were in a secret compartment deep in the bow of the ship. Even with their enhanced speed, the ship was struck multiple times before the team could get to the outer hull compartment that housed their scuba gear. The AGM-88 HARM missiles struck true because the ship immediately started to take on water via multiple entry points. Knowing that the situation was dire, Joshua called everyone in a quick huddle. For a second, Joshua just shook his head at how realistic the simulation was and the fact that this 220,000-ton cargo ship was sinking to the bottom of the Gulf of Aqaba.

"Alright listen everyone. I think it is kind of obvious that this baby is going down and going down fast. Trying to get to our scuba gear is useless at this point. The compartment and our gear were on the side of the ship that got struck and likely was destroyed. We are definitely below the surface by the rate in which the water is flowing into the ship. Our best option is to blow a hole in the side of the ship with C4 and using our enhanced abilities swim to the surface. We unfortunately are going to have to use our enhanced strength to fight the incoming water pressure. We can't wait until the ship fills or we will likely be on the bottom of the Gulf, which is 6,070 ft or 1.14 miles down. Even with our enhanced abilities, I don't think we will be able to make that swim. The deepest scuba dive record is a little over a 1,000 ft. By my calculations, by the time we blow a hole in the ship, we will be about 1,000 to 1,500 ft down. The swim should be doable. If Herbert Nitsch can dive 702 ft and hold his breath for 9 minutes, this shouldn't present us with any problem with our enhanced abilities. While this is a simulation, we can still drown and truthful at this depth, we might even die. Watch out for your dive buddy. Remember to continuously exhale all the way up or the compressed air in your lungs will expand too rapidly as you approach the surface, and your lungs will explode."

After the successful completion of that simulation drill, Dr Calms worked with the team on honing their psychic abilities during the morning hours, and Joshua took the team through Tai Chi Chuan drills in the afternoon.

Six weeks after the team had arrived, they were back on the teleportation pads, ready to get back out into the world and use their new enhanced abilities. They all said goodbye and thanked Dr Calms for all of her assistance. One minute, they were staring at Dr Calms, the next they were back at Stonehenge in the same disgusting state when they initially arrived at the Senator Ryles base Head Quarters in Mt Everest. They were wearing special suits this time designed to keep from contaminating their transportation vehicles, but otherwise, they stewed in their own feces for the next hour until they arrived at Senator Ryles safe house in England.

* * *

Mount Everest Latitude and longitude coordinates: 27.986065, 86.922623

Night Stalker Team Force 3 had been in Nepal for the past four weeks looking for the Spear of Destiny. Jamie, the head of Research insisted they were in the correct location. Captain Samuel Farley and his team were beyond frustrated with this mission. While they had the equipment to deal with the inhospitable temperatures, being cold constantly made for low troop morale. For the week and half that they circled the base of Mount Everest, the average temperature was in the 20s during the day and single digits at night. Once they moved to Base Camp the temperatures dropped to minus 15 degrees. During the week the team searched while at Base Camp, two team members suffered from pulmonary edema and had to be evacuated back to Virgina for treatment. The team suffered five more casualties as they searched the Summit where the average temperature was minus 42 degrees. The team split up into four groups to cover more area. Team Delta had not reported in for over four hours. Using the teams' location beacons, Captain Samuel Farley identified that his team was located at Khumbu Icefall, the most dangerous part of Everest. Unfortunately, a storm had moved in, and it would be another three hours before they could reach them. By the time they linked up with Team Delta, of the eight members on the team, only three survived. All had extreme altitude sickness and cerebral edema. Fluid had been leaking into their brains for the past two hours. They were barely conscious and close to death like their other five teammates. After conferring with Colonel Myers, Maj. Wayne Carson had ordered an immediate evaluation of Captain Samuel Farley's team. Wherever the Spear of Destiny was, it obviously was inaccessible. Four weeks into the operation, the best troops on the face of this planet had suffered five fatalities and eight members were hospitalized and being treated for cerebral and pulmonary edema. Maj. Carson had convinced Col. Myers that if they couldn't find the Spear, no one could. On the flight back to Virgina, Captain Farley struggled with the loss of his team members. This mission had been a complete and utter failure. Major Carson stated his team's casualties would immediately be replaced and they would go into a training cycle. Captain Farley wanted to unload his weapon in frustration, but instead focused his anger inwardly waiting for the time and place where he would get a chance of avenge whoever or whatever were responsible for the death of his teammates.

Training Headquarters - Waco, Texas

Alpha Team was back in the states training, continuing their journey learning to move as a cohesive unit unlocking the full potential of their newfound abilities. While the team members carried conventional comms to communicate back to the TOC, they only used their psychic link to communicate to each other during operations. As they pushed the boundaries of their new abilities, team members more than once had to use their enhanced healing abilities. Alpha Team no longer used their body armor during these exercises. Before the enhancements, Joshua already could focus his Qi and harden his skin against physical blows. Now his skin could with 7.62 rounds up to a 7.62mm resulting in slight bruising. Joshua taught the team this technique as well. While the team had new neural pathways with this knowledge, some of it still needed to be unlocked because it was still new. Joshua explained while they were not indestructible, they were damn near it, but a .50 caliber round to the head was still a good way to die. Limbs could heal, but if the brain was too severely damaged, then the body would not recover.

"Boss, enough of this training. I want a live field test to see what these abilities can really do.", joked Mac.

"Mac, can't you be serious about anything?", said Joshua.

"Not if I can help it!"

In addition to battle stimulations, the Alpha Team practiced Tai Chi Chuan twice daily. During the fifth day of training Tai Chi, the team discovered something profoundly spiritual for a lack of a better word. While practicing the Tai Chi Yang Family 108 Step Traditional Form as a group, the air around the group literally crackled with energy. Kenny commented that he received a nasty static shock when he entered the training room. Team members stated they felt this shared connection beyond the psychic links. Joshua explained, on a lesser level when Tai Chi practitioners train together and move in sync, they are practicing group QiGong. The breath, the synchronized movements, coupled with an individual's Qi will elevate the collective group's Qi or energy. Admittedly Joshua confessed, their enhancements were taking this practice to a whole new level. With practice, Joshua theorized they could probably join their collective Qi and use it as an energy weapon if necessary. In addition to the Tai Chi practice, Joshua led the team through intense meditative practice because several members on the team complained of headaches due to the constant noise of other individual's thoughts. Being a natural empath, Joshua had learned over the years to erect mental barriers to prevent himself from being bombarded with the emotions and thoughts of others. After about a month of practice, the team could successfully communicate with each other without invading the private thoughts of their teammates. Alpha Team was itching to get back into the fight to save the world. So, in between training, the team got caught up on the news of the world. The discovery of the alien spaceship had turned the world upside down. Pandora's Box had successfully been recovered and was enroute back to Florida. Alpha team was packing up preparing to meet Charlie & Delta Team at Eglin Air Force Base. James McKay & Mick Sandeski briefed Joshua & Trinity on the battle for the Matter/Anti-Matter drive in Mexico as they flew back to Florida. Senator Ryles made it clear that without the successful retrieval of one or both artifacts, a truce would be impossible with his ex-crew. Joshua wasn’t going to take any chances. The Night Stalkers had taken possession of the Holy Grail and the fierce battle for Pandora's Box wasn't over until it was safely returned to their compound in Waco. It would be all hands-on board. Bravo Team Leader under Peter and Delta Fire Team 2 under Carl were already enroute back to Texas from Brazil with the mission of fortifying the Waco compound against a full attack. Susan Pratt was coordinating to have a platoon of Abrams Tanks and Bradley Fighting Vehicles shipped to the compound at Joshua's request. When Susan asked, who would man and drive the tanks, Joshua assured her that his men were more than capable. Although, he did request a maintenance crew to accompany the tanks.

"Joshua, Trinity. The 5-Ton trucks are waiting out front. We have a 4-hour drive to Red River Army Depot in New Boston, TX. There we will meet up with four MH-47 Chinook helicopters. Joshua, before you say it, I unfortunately could not secure a military airplane for the trip; hence, why the MH-47s. Talk about strange. It was like someone put in requisitions for every C-130 and C-17 planes all at once."

"Susan, the typical range of a fully fueled Chinook flying at its max speed of 136 mph is 345 miles, which means we need at least one refueling stop.", said Joshua.

Before he could continue Susan interrupted him. "For this mission, you will have a refueling stop in Jackson-Medgar Wiley Evers International Airport in Jackson, Mississippi. From there it's a direct shot to Eglin AFB.

# # #

* * *

Col Myers was surprised at the tempo of operations at Head Quarters. The Night Stalker Human Intelligence (HUMINT) network had finally pinpointed Joshua and Trinity on a ranch in Waco, TX. Maj. Wayne Carson, the new Night Stalker Leader, was assembling a team more than capable of destroying them this time. Mexico and Everest had been a disaster. The Night Stalkers wanted payback. Captain Farley and his newly reconstituted Night Stalker Team Force 3 of thirty-two members augmented Maj. Carson's team for a total of sixty-four Night Stalkers. With overhead satellite coverage of the compound now, Col Myers informed Carson that Joshua and Trinity's team had just left the compound. Based on their current direction and rate of speed it looks like in four hours they will reach Red River Army Depot in New Boston, TX ago. Jamine informed me that a requisitioned for four Chinook helicopters at Red River Army Depot. We are pretty sure they are heading to Florida to escort Pandora’s Box to their compound in Waco.”

"Based on the current satellite trajectory of the plane coming out of Mexico, in all likelihood its heading to Eglin AFB in Florida. From there, they will probably transfer the Matter/Anti-Matter drive to the Chinooks and head back to their compound. Your mission is to intercept those birds during refueling and destroy Joshua and Trinity's team with extreme prejudice. Once accomplished proceed to Florida and secure Pandora's Box at any cost."

"Carson, we intentionally eliminated their teams' ability to use any Air Force assets. They had to requisition four MH-47 Chinooks. Based on range and fuel specifications, they will need at least one refueling stop. We believe that stop will be at Jackson-Medgar Wiley Evers International Airport in Jackson, Mississippi. Let's set up our ambush right after they refuel enroute to Florida. Based on the range of a Chinook and their flight time to Jackson-Medgar, they should be arriving around 2200 hrs. Your team will arrive on site two hours before them. Plenty of time for you to set your ambush."

Carson studied the map then called Sergeant Major Nasir Sykes. "Hey Top, what do you think about turning this area into a kill box." Carson finger was pointing in the middle of a spot East of Route 13, West of Route 35, and North of Route 80. The computer identified the exact longitude and Latitude coordinates as: 32.400977, 89.569831.

"Sir, I like it. It's an isolated location making it hard for local law enforcement to respond. We have clear lines of sight. I recommend that we use four Stingers missiles per Chinook. The missiles should have no issue locking onto their heat signatures because there are no other competing heat signature for miles. I would recommend splitting the team into three groups. I'll take 22 men to the West end of the kill box with Captain Farley leading 22 men on the East end. Finally, Sir, I recommend that you setup with 21 men North of Route 80. My team will take out the trail Chinook. Captain Farley will initiate the ambush by destroying the lead Chinook. Sir, your team will take out the middle 2 birds."

"I like it Top. Make sure you get me a few of those British-made Starstreak missiles. While the Stinger is my primary choice, I want something that I know will defeat any countermeasures on those birds if the pilots get lucky. The Starstreak cannot be jammed by infrared countermeasures or radar/radio countermeasures. I don't want to take any chances with Murphy rearing his ugly head. Also Top, let's preposition men from each group near the kill box so we can quickly conduct mop up operations and get the hell out of there so we can get to Florida and retrieve Pandora's Box."

# # #

The Chinooks finally lifted off from Jackson-Medgar Wiley Evers International Airport. Joshua projected his thoughts directly to Trinity. "So far so good. We have approximately three more hours of flight time before we arrive at Eglin AFB. How are you doing?"

"This has turned into so much more than when we started back at your studio. I can't believe everything that has happened since then." Laughing, Trinity said, "I'm basically a walking talking mutant now. Robby loved the X-Men. If he could only see me now."

Joshua felt the wave of sadness

emanating from Trinity before she could close off those emotions. He reached out a hand and placed it on her leg. "There is no need to hide your emotions from me. Everyone needs help. We started this journey together and we will end it together."

Trinity squeezed his hand to acknowledge her gratitude for his friendship.

# # #

Col Meyers was watching the four helicopters take off in real-time. "Is Maj. Carson's team receiving the satellite feeds yet?"

"Sir, as of five minutes ago, we finally got them patched in. They had an authentication protocol error that took a few minutes to resolve. Sorry Sir."

Myers ignored the apology and immediately refocused on the screen. Keying his mike. "Good luck Maj. Carson and happy hunting. Target will be in range in ten minutes."

"Roger that Sir!"

# # #

As soon as Trinity squeezed Joshua's hand, she immediately sensed something was wrong. Joshua turned to her as he sensed it as well. "Everyone prepared yourselves. I sense imminent danger!", shouted Joshua in their minds.

Everyone heard on the headsets at the same time. The crew chief, with his head out the door, was shouting on comms. "Two missiles inbound on the starboard side."

"Fuck Murphy and the horse that he rode into town on! Why can't one mission go as planned", thought Joshua just as the pilot released a series of flares and banked hard to the port side. The MH-47 was not built for aerial combat. For all intent and purposes, in hostile engagements its ability to evade the enemy could be compared to the maneuverability of a beached whale. While not a combat helicopter, the MH-47 did have upgraded armament versus the CH-47 its sister. It is armed with two M134 7.62mm electrically operated, air-cooled mini guns and two M240 7.62mm belt-fed machine guns mounted on either side of the fuselage at the forward and rear sections. Since 2006, the

MH-47s have been equipped with the AIRCMM solution. The Army tested these new Infrared Countermeasure flares to enhance aircraft survivability against the most sophisticated IR guided missiles. These flares when combined with the older M206 Aircraft Countermeasure Flare, have proven to drastically increase the survivability of aircraft and aircrew employing it during missions over hostile areas.

Joshua took a deep breath and sent his thoughts out to the team. "Expect nothing, be prepared for everything. We got this team. Relax and trust our training and new abilities."

# # #

It didn't surprise Carson that all

four Chinooks survived the initially volley of missiles. The secondary missile teams were already set up prepared to fire. This time however, each Chinook would be targeted by another two Stingers and two Starstreak missiles.

"Fire!", commanded Carson.

"Now let’s see you survive this.", thought Carson.

# # #

There was mass confusion over the net. Everyone was over-talking everyone else thought Joshua. "Guys, this isn't over. We're not going to get off this easy."

Just then, the crew chief yelled again, "Multiple inbounds on the starboard side!"

Flares were ejected again, and two missiles veered their course and exploded as the Chinook banked hard to port again. Unfortunately, one missile followed their Chinook into the banked turn.

"Nickleback!", the call sign for the pilot, yelled the crew chief. "One missile is still tracking us."

Nickleback immediately turned the bird to starboard and dove for the treetops hoping to confuse the missile. Unfortunately, it didn't work. The rear rotor was hit, and everyone was thrown forward. In the headset Nickleback yelled, "Brace, Brace, Brace!"

"Mac, you just got your wish. Team prepare for combat. Rally point be 100 meters north of our landing point."

* * *

# # #

The Night Stalkers quickly closed in on the four down Chinooks. They moved in formation of four teams of 12. One team for each helicopter. 16 of the Night Stalkers, who fired the missiles, were now with Top as the Quick Reaction Force. Reports were starting to filter in that there were no signs of Joshua and Trinity's team. The only bodies they found at each crash site were the pilots and crew chiefs.

"Okay guys, this has now turned into a search and destroy operation. Let's move out." As per SOP, the four teams of 12 now split into two sub teams with one moving to contact and the other in over-watch position.

"Col. Myers, this is Carson. No sign of our targets. We are now transitioning to search and destroy operations. Please give my pad a wide view of the kill box and switch over to thermals."

"You got it Carson. Happy hunting."

Inwardly, Carson was a little concerned about only finding the pilots and crew chiefs dead, but he immediately dismissed the concern because it didn't matter. He fell in line as he flipped his NVGs over his eyes.

# # #

Joshua felt lucky that his team was in the middle two helicopters. It made linking up much easier. Most escaped the crash with minor injuries. A few burns, cuts and bruises that were already mostly healed. Sam from Joshua's Fire Team suffered a broken arm. After it was set and a bandage applied, the healing process had already begun. In another hour, it would be completely healed. From Fire Team 2, Paulie suffered 3rd degree burns to over 50% of his body. While not life threatening, he was in no shape to fight. He needed about half a day to recover. Dan's injury was a little more serious. A rod had penetrated his chest. Normally the protocol would be to leave it in and immobile him as much as possible, but they no longer were bound by normal protocols.

Mike, the team medic, mentally projected instructions to Tom, the team leader for Fire Team 2. "Tom, I recommend removing the rod, so his body can start healing. If you leave it in and wait for help, there is a high possibility, he will bleed out because the rod will prevent the wound from sealing."

Even though Dan was unconscious, he work when Tom pulled the rod from his body. Bennie had to cover his mouth to muffle the scream from Dan until he passed out again.

Joshua projected his thoughts, "Team, I want half of you to reduce your thermal signature by ten degrees. Use the biofeedback techniques we practiced. I want them to find us and think we lost half of our force. When they get close, I want you all to then reduce your thermal signature to that of a squirrel then we will go hunting. Once the Night Stalkers close in on you guys playing dead, we ambush them from the front and back. Once they turn to engage us, we will put them in a pincher maneuver. Let's take them out quickly and silently. Knives only.

# # #

Carlson didn't think there would be any problems taking out the remaining Tangos. Based on thermal imagery, it looked like half of their team was down and the other half appeared to be attending to them.

Now that all the down copters had been searched, Carlson consolidated his four teams into two elements with Top still waiting in reserve with the QRF. Carson and Farley were leading one element each. Farley from the West and Carlson from the South. This was a simple search and destroy mission now. Just as the lead elements from each team were set to engage, the point man from each team halted. The updated satellite imagery showed half of the tangos had simply vanished from their screens. The other half were still lying in the prone position where they were being attended to.

"Sir, we have a problem. Half the targets simply vanished from our screen. What do you want us to do?"

"Sweep through and clear the objective. Make sure they are all eliminated with no exception. Stay alert for the other members. We have seen them use high-tech concealment suits before."

* * *

# # #

After reducing their heat signatures, the team immediately took to the trees then leaped from tree to tree until they were behind the advance elements. On Joshua's mental command, the team went into action. In the first two seconds of the engagement, six of the Night Stalkers were down without a single sound being made. five seconds later, another six Stalkers were down.

# # #

"Sir, we have a serious issue.", said 1LT Brennen, Col Myers' aide. "In the last ten seconds, we lost the vital signs of 15

Night Stalkers and it's not an equipment error. We are still receiving a transponder signal from each of the units, but they are no longer transmitting vitals. Sir, we have 15 men down. Wait, now make that 22 men down."

"Fucking Murphy!"

"Carson, I don't know what is happening, but your men are dropping like flies. 22 of your 48 men are down and a shot hasn't been fired."

Carson immediately went into action. Shouting through the team comms, "Tactical lights on now! They're mingled within ranks."

As soon as the tactical lights were on, all hell broke loose. The remaining Night Stalkers opened fire on Joshua and Trinity's team. Carson was stunned. He had never seen anyone move that fast. One second they were in his sights, the next second, they had disappeared. He received a message that another three of his men were down. Just as he was sighting in on another target, one of men were literally thrown 30 feet across the clearing slamming into the Oak tree so hard, he could hear his spine snapping from where his stood. It was obvious he was dead before he hit the tree because he didn't make a sound. Carson followed the trajectory of the thrown soldier. At the other end of the terminus point, Carson spotted Trinity. She was engaged with another of his men with her back turned to him. As he had been trained some many years before, time slowed down as he exhaled and slowly squeezed the trigger. A three-round burst hit Trinity dead center of her back knocking her down face first into the dirt.

# # #

Trinity felt the impact of three rounds tearing into her back. Based on training, she could tell she was hit by 5.56 mm rounds. As she was going down to the ground, her opponent took his opportunity to finish her. He started lining his Hecker and Koch MP5 for a head shot. As he squeezed the trigger, time slowed down. Trinity looked around and everyone was moving in slow motion. Joshua discussed that everyone now had this capability, but only under certain conditions where your fight or flight response kicks-in would you potentially experience it.

"This effect is called Tachy Psyche effect or Tachypsychia.", quoted Joshua. It's a neurological condition that distorts the perception of time, usually brought on by physical exertion, physical stress, a traumatic event, or a violent confrontation. It is believed to be caused by a combination of high levels of dopamine and norepinephrine in the body. While none of my teachers would say it, I believe that Tai Chi Chuan was designed specifically to promote Tachypsychia? The average human has about one random thought every three seconds or about 50 thoughts per minute. The practice of Tai Chi allows the brain to have about 6.5 thoughts per minute. Tai Chi has been called moving meditation or active meditation. In a combat situation, Tai Chi Chuan trains the mind to stay focused on one thing and one thing only. Survival. The brain is more powerful than any intelligent machine in existence. With around 100 billion cells, it is more complex than just about any computer created. The problem is distraction and random thoughts, but when you put the body into a fight or flight situation, all useless thoughts are discharged all that processing power goes toward surviving.", said Joshua.

Trinity was amazed as she experienced the Tachy Psyche effect for herself. If she wanted, she could have counted the sweat beads dripping off the soldier's chin. She saw the soldier's eyes sighting in on her head as his intended target. The

Hecker and Koch MP5 swung toward her head in response to his eye movement. She could see the flexor muscle of his index finger pulling the trigger to fire 9 mm rounds into her head. Without seemly any thought, she thrust out her left hand and used telekinesis to send him flying backwards where his head exploded against the tree directly behind him. Trinity immediately turned to the next threat to her left.

# # #

Carson couldn't believe what he was seeing. She was down. He saw it with his own eyes, but now she was up after literally throwing one of his men back into a tree, who was going to finish her off with a head shot. And to make matters worse, she hadn't even touched him. Across the clearing, what he was seeing wasn't making any sense. Nothing in his 20 years of service could have prepared him for the carnage unfolding before his eyes.

"Col Myers, the carnage is unbelievable. My men are being slaughtered. We shoot them, yet they keep getting back up. They haven't fired one round, yet everyone is dead. Sir, they are dead!", he screamed into the commlink.

Carson's mic was still hot. "Fuck you, Joshua!" All Col Myers' could do was watch through the helmet cam as Carson unloaded his magazine into image that disappeared then reappeared on another part of the screen. Somehow, Carson managed to reload and fire another entire clip before all sound ceased. The last imaged on the screen was Carson's cam showing his body still standing upright and blood shooting from his body where his severed head use to be.

"1LT Brennen, get Top and the remaining 16 Night Stalkers the hell out of there."

"Yes Col."

"Jamie, get me a fucking answer on what the hell just happened to 48 of the meanest baddest motherfuckers on this face of this planet. How the hell did they all go down in less than 60 seconds!?"

For all of Jamie's quirks, he knew not to try and answer the Col's question because, it wasn't a question that had a logical answer. He watched the same live feed as everyone else. One helmet cam after another showed images of things that were not possible.

# # #

48 hours after initial contact, Col Myers' was receiving an After Action Review, that shook him to the core. There was no doubt that somehow Joshua and Trinity's team were now Meta-human. Jamie had explained the team's helmet cams were using some of the most advanced cameras on the face of the planet and this event was recorded in excess of 250 fps. Carson's last recording gave the best example of just how fast their target was moving. Initial engagement put the target about 100 meters away. While the bullets were faster than the target, the target was moving faster than Maj. Wayne Carson could

track. His eyes were tracking at between 30 to 60 frames per second. Col Myers knew he had a major problem. 15 minutes into the briefing, it was clear these soldiers were now faster, stronger and had the ability to heal incredibly fast. Several had been shot point blank with little or no effect. Col Myers was dreading the report to the Committee.

# # #

The team was successfully back at their ranch in Waco. For the first time since the search had begun, the entire team was back together again. Senator Ryles was briefing them on the events that had occurred in Egypt. The Matter/Anti Matter drive was now secure in their compound. And after the showing in Jackson, Mississippi, Joshua was pretty sure the Night Stalkers would think twice about attacking them again.

Giza Plateau - Cairo, Egypt

Major Dumfries, the Delta Squadron Leader was monitoring comms from the three teams currently searching the pyramids. Each team had set up repeaters at regular intervals to ensure adequate communications as the teams ventured deeper into the pyramids. So far there was nothing of interest to report. The teams were also leaving a trail of chemlights at each turn they made within the maze of tunnels. Picking up his satellite phone, Major Dumfries called Col Myers and reported the same to him. "Nothing to report yet Sir!"

"As soon as you get anything, I want to know immediately Fred. Is that clear?", said Col Myers.

"Yes Sir!" With that, the line went

dead. Fred was thinking back to this incredible journey that had led him to this point in his life. He was a veteran of multiple campaigns in the "War on Terrorism" over the past 15 years that he had been in. He was on the promotable list to be a Lieutenant Colonel. His next assignment in two months would be the S3, Operations Officer, with the United States Special Operations Command or SOCOM out of Tampa, FL. This would be his last opportunity to be in the field with troops. No true war fighter ever wanted to be sidelined as a desk jockey, but that was going to be his faith in a few months. He remembered when he was first recruited at West Point by a Captain, who taught history. Fred still remembered the class with fondness, "War Technology and Society

Minor". This class was about teaching Cadets how social systems, human agency, politics, laws, and technology have impacted warfare. It was his questions that caught the attention of Captain deVandercamp. Captain deVandercamp offered up his home over the weekends for Cadet Dumfries. During those many hours of historical and philosophical viewpoints of war, Captain deVandercamp recruited him into the Night Stalkers. The moto of the Night Stalkers was "Those, who hold the watchers accountable!" Cadet Dumfries was amazed to learn of the lineage of the Night Stalkers. Whereas the history of the Rangers can date back to Roger's Rangers during the Revolutionary War, the Night Stalkers' became the very secretive enforcement arm of the Freemasons. Captain deVandercamp told Cadet Dumfries that there were members embedded throughout the military forces of the world. During his summer vacations, Cadet Dumfries met with other cadets from various academies as well as other West Point Cadets. It was strictly forbidden to interact with each other. Each cadet was given an email address that would only be used as a means for drop communications. They were taught a secret cipher that was based on their birthday and current date of the year to embed messages in case the email address was ever discovered.

During his time as a Platoon Leader with the 82nd Airborne Division, time served in the Ranger Battalions and now with Delta, he had performed hundreds of missions for the Night Stalkers. Most of the time, his missions were a slight addition to an existing mission already scheduled. He had total faith in the absolute morality of the Night Stalkers' missions because how else would they always know what missions he was on, when 1/2 of his missions technically never existed. Although this mission was the craziest of them all. He still had a lot of skepticism about there being an actual spaceship underneath Cheops, or the Great Pyramid, but he wasn't going to start doubting his orders now. Over the past two years, he was ordered to place other Night Stalkers in key leadership roles. Captain Kyle Franks, the leader of Team 1 and SFC Petter Nettles, the Team's NCOIC were two that he had placed. The NEST scientist, Nancy Harkness PhD, with Team 1 was a famed archaeologist. Unfortunately, she was famous because of her outlandish theories about the pyramids being built by aliens. Based on this current mission, maybe she wasn't as crazy as folks thought. Even though he was taking reports from the other teams, and he reported them up to Major General Carl E Parker, he was only focused Team 1 in the Great Pyramid.

# # #

Nancy stopped along with the rest of the team. They were all examining the hieroglyphics on the wall. They had come to a dead end, but there was a radiation reading emanating from beyond the wall. Nancy Harkness just shook her head at the improbability of standing inside the great pyramid staring at this wall. She had waited her entire adult life to be back in the pyramids with an opportunity to uncover the secrets of the pyramids. As a teenager, her family took a vacation to Egypt to visit arguably the most famous pharaoh that was uncovered; Tutankhamun or King Tut, but it was the tour of the great pyramid that had sealed her faith to become an archaeologist. She had climbed the stairways made of wooden planks and handrails with her father. Her mother had refused to go because she was claustrophobic. When they finished the tour, her father did nothing but complain about the higher they climbed, the thinner the air felt and that the entire pyramid smelled of mold. What fascinated Nancy was the fact that every chamber they entered was empty. Her brain postulated that if King Tut's treasures were found in a hidden chamber then what else was hidden in the great pyramid. Based on its size alone, she knew the pyramids had to hold so much more. It was at that moment her destiny was set. Armed with a PhD in Archaeology with a focus on Egyptology from Cambridge University, Nancy was sure she was up to this task. As a matter of fact, it was her thesis and several published papers that caused her to come to the attention of the Night Stalkers. Her thesis focused on all theories surrounding the purpose of the pyramids.

She studied the various theories of pyramid construction. From the belief that huge stones were carved from quarries with copper chisels, and these blocks were then dragged and lifted into position to the fringe that stated aliens or residents of Atlantis, or another highly advanced civilization that lived more than 13,000 years ago built it. Nancy also researched the purpose of building such giant structures. One such theory was the ability of the pyramid to focus electromagnetic energy. That its entire design was based on the principle that the pyramids conducted electricity. At one point, the great pyramid was covered in white tufa limestone, which does not contain magnesium and has high insulating properties. This insulation prevented the electricity inside the pyramid from being released without control. Of course, the alien theorist suggested that the coating of the pyramid was to signal any passing alien spacecraft. The fact that Nancy was on this exploration mission confirmed what she had always believed. She believed the removal of the limestone during the era of Tutankhamen, when the pyramids were already 1,200 years old, was a conscience act to make sure no alien came to investigate the signal being generated by the structure. Even Nikola Tesla believed the Great Pyramid was more than just a structure to house the remains of the pharaohs. In keeping with his theories of giant transmitters, he claimed that his Tesla Towers were inspired by studying the Pyramids. While others felt the structures were designed to resonate sound at a certain frequency to allow for harmonic healing.

Nancy’s journey down memory lane

quickly came to a halt as Captain Franks raised his voice again to get her attention. "Nancy, I will ask again. Do you have any clue as to how we should proceed? We are on a tight timeline and if you don't have an answer, I will have my sapper friend here put a hold in this wall."

"And Captain, if you do that, we will have a million tons of rocks come crashing down on us. These pyramids were designed so that if one of the corner stones is misaligned by just half an inch, the whole structure will collapse and Captain, this wall is adjacent to the corner stone over there. So, please just give me a few minutes. See these series of indentations. I need to press them in the correct order and this wall should retract and allow us entry. So please give me a few minutes. I have been studying all my life to accomplish this very task. Your expertise is to conquer enemies lurking around the corner. My expertise is to defeat mysteries that are thousands of years old."

Silence ensued as Nancy continued to study the hieroglyphics on the wall. This wall was focused on Anubis, also called Anpu, the ancient Egyptian god of the dead. Nancy was cycling through all her knowledge as it related to Anubis. Anubis was represented by a man with the head of a jackal. His prominent role was a god who ushered souls into the afterlife by measuring the hearts of the dead on the Scale of Justice. Nancy knew that the heart was the key. Anubis weighed the heart. During the embalming process, all organs in the abdomen and chest were removed through a cut on the left side of the abdomen. They only left the heart in place. The heart, rather than the brain, was regarded as the organ of reasoning. As such it would be required in the afterlife, when it would testify to the goodness of the deceased; hence, why Anubis weighed the heart. They knew the dimensions of the heart because they were highly skilled surgeons of the dead.

Nancy was moving without thinking. She was in her element, her zone. Nothing existed but the mystery in front of her. Nancy had a photographic memory, and in her mind, she visualized the human heart. The heart length, width, and thickness are 12 cm, 8.5 cm, and 6 cm, respectively, but she knew the Egyptians did not use the metric system. She immediately converted the numbers to the Egyptians base 10 system of hieroglyphs for numerals. Her fingers started touching the corresponding indentations as if she had done this a million times before. Everyone around her was mesmerized as they watched Nancy work. It was clear, she was in a near trance and when she pushed the last indentation on the wall and lowered her hands, everyone held their breath with anticipation, but nothing happened.

"Well Nancy?", said Captain Franks. "Nothing is happening. So much for your expertise Nancy. I knew we should have just blown a hole in the wall. Cody! Get up here and prepare a shape charge. One that will not move the cornerstone."

"Yes Sir!", said Cody.

"Franks, just give it a minute. This wall probably hasn't been opened in over 3,000 years.", said Nancy.

Just as Franks was about to respond, a rumbling deep within the heart of the pyramid started vibrating the floor. A puff of stale air escaped as a crack widened at the bottom of the wall. The gap became larger as the wall retracted into the ceiling.

Nancy cleared her throat, but before she could say anything Captain Franks spoke. "My humblest apologies Nancy and please don't rub it in. We have a long night still ahead of us."

"No worries Franks and to be honest," Nancy said with a slight laugh, "I had no clue if it was going to work either."

As per SOP, one man took point and proceeded down the dark tunnel. Moses was this man. An E-6, with an impressive career and numerous encounters the survived that the team gave way, when he volunteered to take point. Moses was their good luck charm, having saved the team's bacon through ambushes and room clearings. The team had discarded their NVGs pretty early on. NVGs required some light to work. In these tunnels, there was no ambient light, so they used their tactical flashlights instead.

"Cody, brace the wall to make sure we don't get locked in here.", said Franks.

Cody immediately used one of the hydraulic jacks to brace the wall that had recessed into the ceiling. This jack was rated for 10 tons. There was no way it should fail.

Using the rely system setup, Franks radioed in the latest update to Major Dumfries and told him, they were proceeding on.

While Moses was point man, Nancy was just a few steps behind him. This wasn't an option. While Moses was looking for current threats, Nancy was trying to make sure the team wasn't killed by a booby trap created thousands of years ago that only she could decipher. Together they had led the team through five such traps. They had steadily been angling on a 15-degree downward slope. The air was very stale and getting difficult to breathe. Franks had ordered the team to dawn their Draeger LarV rebreather about 30 minutes ago using them intermittently. They were using 15 minutes on, 30 minutes off cycle. This would extend the four-hour life of the rebreather to about nine hours. Each team member had a spare, but they had no clue on how long this mission would take.

Four hours later, nine more booby traps successfully navigated, the team was stopped. All stared dumbfounded at what appeared to be a hatch in the center of a metallic room. As one, they all turned to Nancy. "Well?", said Moses. "What do we do now?"

Never been accused of being shy, Ramirez spoke up. "I say we open the hatch. I am kind of excited to see why there is a modern looking pressurized hatch in the middle of a 4,000-year-old pyramid."

Nancy looked at Franks. "I think we

should tell them everything at this point."

Franks gave her a sharp look, but Moses, Jacobs, Cody, Ramirez and Pulaski all caught the look and folded their arms and simply starred at the two.

"Look Captain. I understand the need for compartmentalization, but we are two miles below the surface and standing in the middle of a metal box. So how about you tell us the story that we all kind of figured out already. We have all watched Ancient Aliens. We have seen some of the hieroglyphics on the wall. So, tell us Captain.", said Ramirez.

Letting out a huff and one final stare at Nancy, Franks started to speak. "Team this is a mission that is classified above Top Secret. The hunt for the man pack nuclear bomb was a ploy. Our actual mission is to find an alien spaceship that potentially has been buried under the pyramid thousands of years before they were ever constructed."

Nancy quickly chimed in. "If I'm correct, what's beneath that hatch is an advanced spacecraft that's been here on planet earth for over 300,000 years. This is a mission of First Contact. My team member Gregory and I have special equipment specifically designed to allow us to make First Contact."

Gregory had been quiet this the entire mission up until now. "Gentlemen, my name is Gregory Nevinski. I have a PhD in both Astrobiology and Quantum Mechanics. My team has been scouring the planet looking for ancient artifacts that are actual components to this spaceship. We don't know how these components were separated from the ship, but we have been tracking signals that have allowed us to track these components and triangulate the originating signal back to this location. The components are legendary throughout our history imbued with magical powers. The Ark of the Covenant. The Holy Grail. The Spear of Destiny. And Pandora's Box. With me on my rover, I have the Ark of the Covenant, which will allow us to make contact safely with the aliens. It is our belief that the aliens have been trying to communicate with us over a millennia and only now have we evolved significantly enough to understand what these signals mean."

"Enough!", said Franks. "Our job is

to do or die. Not to ask the reason why. We have a mission to complete and just like every other mission, we will accomplish it."

It was Ramirez, we broke the silence. "Readily will I display the intestinal fortitude required to fight on to the Ranger objective and complete the mission though I be the lone survivor. Rangers lead the way!" "So, let's ruck up and open that hatch. I'm kind of excited to meet ET!"

"Everyone, MOPP 4 before we proceed. We have no clue what's beyond that hatch. After we test for known biological and chemical elements and if the radiation levels are acceptable, we will stow the gear, but for now, I want to go home and make some normal healthy babies, so full protective gear until the all clear signal."

Five minutes later, Franks gave the order for Moses to open the hatch. The sight that greeted the team left them stupefied. The only word that came to Nancy's mind was impossible. "How?", said Nancy. She whispered "how" repeatedly.

Franks just starred at the unbelievable site before him. The ship sat in this incredibly beautiful artificial cavern. The cavern was streaked with glass where the sand was fused as if someone used a giant glass blower to create the cavern, but as amazing as the cavern was, the ship was even more amazing. Franks estimated the ship to be five football fields long and two football fields wide. Franks had been on enough aircraft carriers to understand just how enormous this ship was. The USS Gerald R. Ford is 3.69 times as long as a US football field. This ship made the USS Ford look small. The ship was unique in its shape. It was oval and from bow to stern, its side profile was a lazy "S" with the bow dipping downward and the stern having a tail. The ship was made of a matte black material, but every five to ten seconds, a wave ran the length of the ship causing the ships skin to match the color of the cavern. It almost appeared to be some kind of cloaking field. The center of the craft was hollow with a low-level glow of energy that filled the circle. The circle was about 1/4 of the size of the entire ship. Franks continued to stare at the alien spacecraft in front of him. When he was initially briefed, there was no way in hell, he thought that he would find an honest to goodness fucking spaceship. Maybe some weather balloon like Roswell, but this. Pulaski snapped Franks and the others out of their reverence.

Pulaski had been taking samples of the air and surrounding surfaces to test the air quality and for known biological or chemical contagions. Pulaski gave the all clear. "Sir, other than slightly higher levels of radiation, we should be okay to go back to MOPP Zero."

"Thanks Pulaski. You heard him, let's get out of MOPP and finish our mission. Moses and Janis stay frosty and watch our six. If you don't hear from us in four hrs, high tail it back and bring reinforcements."

"Well Gregory, the show is yours. Let's get moving and meet ET.", said Franks.

Gregory had already been examining the ship searching for the entrance, a way into this incredible find. Just like Nancy, Gregory had been waiting for this moment his entire life. Ever since he saw the launch of the Apollo missions when he was a kid, he knew he was destined to be one of the first humans to make contact with an alien species. All his life, he would periodically have visions about this very ship he was looking at right now. He moved with confidence. Once he was oriented, he didn't hesitate. He led the team to a section of the ship that was about 1,000 ft from the bow of the ship. This was part of the lazy "S" that supported the ship resting on the ground. Gregory examined the controls and just like his visions, he knew exactly which sequence of buttons to press to gain access. At 53, Gregory was an out of shape, stocky short male. He had been made fun of his entire childhood. In college, it wasn't much better. He was odd and awkward to be around. Gregory finally learned to accept that his mind was wired differently during his years in High School. While others were out partying, he was engrossed in understanding Isaac Asimov and Arthur C. Clarke. There was only one computer in his High School and a student had to pass a test before they could use it. Gregory was programming in binary code as a freshman in High School. Programming in

10101 was like unraveling the secrets of the universe. Ever since he could remember, a voice always seemed to be in his head giving him directions of sorts. The voice seemed to nudge him to always be a better version of himself. Pushing the envelope of what was possible. His favorite author Clarke wrote, "The only way of discovering the limits of the possible is to venture a little way past them to the impossible." This was his mantra. Little did Gregory know that the voice that was in his head was an alien communicating telepathically with him. Preparing him for this very moment. Without hesitation, Gregory punched in the codes that lowered a ramp into the spaceship and opened a hidden doorway.

The team entered the ship followed by

the rover carrying the Ark of the Covenant. Again, without hesitation, Gregory led the team deeper into the ship toward the bridge or command center.

Upon entering the ship, the automated system immediately revived Xan'lima, the ship's First Officer, and Soa'limae, the ship's Scientist Officer. The automated system immediately updated them on who had entered the ship and where they were located. Both Xan'lima and Soa'limae quickly dressed and headed to the command center to greet the humans that would allow them to finally go home after 300,000 years.

While the entire team was nervous as they transversed these alien hallways, there was also a sense of inevitability that this was supposed to happen. 15

minutes into their journey, a voice inside all their heads welcomed them. The team all stopped and looked at each other.

"Welcome aboard the Star Cruiser Alpheratz. We have long anticipated your arrival. We have been carefully guiding the development of your species to help you evolve to a point that you can finally assist us to go home. With open arms, welcome aboard. My name is Xan'lima, the ship's First Officer. The other crew member is Soa'limae, the ship's Scientist Officer. We'll be waiting for you in command center. Your colleague Gregory knows the way. We have been in communication with him and others like him, his entire life for this very purpose. To prepare your planet for the reality that you are not alone in this universe."

When the voice left their minds, everyone turned to Gregory, but it was Nancy, who spoke first. "Here I thought I was crazy for having visions that pushed me to purse my career, but you. You have been hearing voices in your head all your life?"

"Yes. For the longest time, my parents thought I was making it up and wrote it off as my imaginary friend. Eventually, I finally accepted it for what it was. Some kind of entity that resided in my head. I wasn't scared because it never hurt me or asked me to do things that were damaging to myself or others."

Franks chimed in, "So, did you ever think you were crazy?"

"Honestly, no. Because I did not have

a lot of friends, it was comforting to have someone that was always looking out for me."

"You know, all those kids that have imaginary friends, I wonder if it was these aliens trying to communicate? And how many people in the psych ward are not crazy, but the victims of modern medicine, not understanding that someone was trying to communicate with them because the voices in their heads were real? This is simply staggering!", said Nancy.

"Well, I'm glad that you find this fascinating Nancy, but we have a mission to complete. You can write your next thesis after we get the hell out of here.", said Franks.

It took another hour for the team to reach the command center. Because their biometrics were incompatible with the ship's interfaces, the team could not use the automated transportation tubes located throughout the ship. A kind of subway system stated Gregory. While the rover was really an advanced field robot capable of maneuvering upstairs, it still was a time-consuming exercise. Along the journey, Soa'limae communicated with the team. Explaining their version of history. Questions were asked and answers were immediately given in the form of memories being implanted directly into their brains. Everything from what they looked like to what planet they came from. Something about the ship prevented communications with the outside. Franks dispatched Ramirez to go back the way they came, link up with Moses and Janis and update command on what was going on. Chemlights were strategically placed to mark their passage, so Ramirez was able to double time it back with no issues. Even though Ramirez was no longer with the group, he was still receiving communications from the aliens.

Ramirez communicated to Major Dumfries to push back the perimeter to over four kilometers or two miles away from the pyramids. Once the AI was plugged back into the ship, the ship would automatically begin to rise. Major Dumfries started sending rapid fire questions to Ramirez and the aliens answered the questions via Ramirez. "Tell the aliens to Stand by Ramirez! We need some time to get the orders to expand the perimeter." Ramirez, relayed to the team to give him some time before the AI was plugged back into the spaceship.

Dumfries was frantically trying to reach Colonel Myers. Apparently, he had just left the complex about an hour ago and was in the process of returning. His team was already in the process of issuing Flash Communications to have the Chairman of the Joint Chiefs of Staff to issues orders to 82nd Airborne Division to expand the perimeter. Two hours after Ramirez made his initial call to Major Dumfries, the 82nd was moving.

Major General Carl E Parker was not used to having his operation taken over by some lowly Major even if he was Delta. While Parker issued orders to move the division, he was impatiently waiting on Major Dumfries to report to his TOC and explain himself. 15 minutes later, Dumfries reported to the TOC.

"Would you care to explain yourself Major and I don't give a flying fuck about Top Secret orders and if I don't get an answer that make sense, I will personally shoot you for starting a mutiny. If you don't recall The Uniform Code of Military Justice (UCMJ), if a military service member commits mutiny, attempts mutiny or even fails to report a mutiny, that person "shall be punished by death or such other punishment as a court-martial may direct." And during times of war, which we are technically in right now, I can shoot you on the spot. Now speak before I lose the rest of my shit."

30 minutes later and two shots of Tennessee Whiskey later, the steam had

been let out of Parker's balloon. 15 minutes into the conversation, Parker took out his private stash of Single Barrel Jack Daniels and took his first drink. Just as Parker and Dumfries were finishing the second drink, Dumfries radio came to life.

"Sir, they are ready to reconnect the AI. We are boarding the spaceship now.", said Ramirez.

"Good luck and see you on the other side.", responded Dumfries.

# # #

Colonel Myers was watching a live satellite feed of the pyramids. He was told that at any minute the AI would be reconnected, and the spacecraft would rise.

Five minutes later, all three pyramids exploded upwards into the air with the force of a small yield tactical nuclear bomb. Even at the new perimeter small debris still pelted the soldiers. While the visual was something Myers thought he would ever see in his life, what came next was even more astonishing. While the smoke and sand were settling, an impossibility appeared where the pyramids were. Even though the dimensions and pictures were communicated, seeing the ship was something entirely different. The video imagines previous sent could not capture the entire length of the ship.

"Sir, we have a huge problem.", stated Jamie. "Our Electronic intelligence (ELINT) just confirmed that China, Russia, England, France, Germany, and Japan have all witness the events transpiring in Egypt. All positioned satellites in geosynchronous orbit over Egypt when the US Army invaded. Even as we speak, the Russia and China have sent out orders to start mobilizing their forces. Drones from both countries are already nearing the US Army area of operation. NATO allies are already beating down the US State Department's doors asking for answers. Sir, I think we are seeing the beginning of World War III."

"Have faith Jamie. There is a plan.", said Col Myers. Silently, Myers prayed the Committee knew what they were doing.

Cairo, Egypt

"This is Mohammad Asif, of WGNN (World Global News Network), reporting to you live from Cairo, Egypt. The world woke up to three stunning global revelations. For those of you, around the world that are just waking up, I'm going to give you a quick synopsis of the events that happened over the past 12 hours. One, the United States Government released a press release to most governments and news agencies reporting that it temporarily seized the Giza Plateau in response to a credible threat of an imminent attack by Israel Forces to capture and secure terrorist. The terrorist have been using the pyramids to construct and hide the building of two man-portable nuclear weapons with the intent of detonating them on Yom Kippur, the holiest day on the Jewish calendar. Utilizing their famed 82nd Airborne Division, the United States conducted a massive airborne operation to seize Cairo International Airport and the Giza Plateau. So far, it is believed there are fewer than five causalities. This new includes US Forces killed as well. The US State Department has assured the world leaders that this is a temporary operation to prevent a possible World War, which most likely would have been the case if Israeli Forces had seized the pyramids."

"Two, all the Great Pyramids of Egypt were destroyed about two hours ago. It was confirmed, the destruction was not the result of the detonation of the man-portable nuclear bombs or as a direction action of the US Military Forces.

Nevertheless, 4,500 years of history were erased in the blink of an eye. Unfortunately, it is the third revelation that makes the destruction of the pyramids seem insignificant."

"Please understand that I am not in any way trying to diminish the global tragedy of losing the last of the original Seven Wonders of the World."

"Amy, can you focus on the image over my left shoulder? Thank you."

"Ladies and gentlemen, what you are seeing, is an authentic alien spaceship. This is not a Hollywood movie set. We can't get closer because the US Military has closed off the Giza Plateau, but the spaceship is so large, you can easily see it with the naked eye. This spaceship is responsible for the destruction of the pyramids. A few hours ago, this spaceship emerged from beneath the pyramids, creating one gigantic crater and rubble remains of the Great Pyramids."

# # #

"Get me one of those conspiracy nuts to go on air for the next segment!", shouted Cecil Rhodem, the host of the number one prime-time news show in America, The Cecil Rhodem Show. Cecil made his reputation pushing conspiracy theories. Mainly focusing on how large corporations have been the driving force behind every war since World War I. When the world was quiet, he would then harp on the US Defense Industry and how they had reverse engineered their technology from alien technology. Amanda Kvolowski, his co-host was just as controversial having joined the show five years later. Amanda focused on the conspiracies associated with Wall Street and personal investments. With the elimination of company pension plans, she had gained an impressive following fighting the move to IRAs and 401Ks. Every time the stock market crashed, and people lost half their retirement savings, her viewers increased exponentially. Cecil and Amanda had taken a 7 - 9 am Northeast morning news TV show on Philadelphia KTYZW from a virtual unknown to a show that was purchased by PBC (Premier Broadcasting Corporation). While the name of the show did not change, Amanda was successful in getting a tag line added. The Cecil Rhodem Show featuring Cecil Rhodem and Amanda Kvolowski.

"Welcome back to the show everyone.", said Cecil. "As I said at the beginning of the hour, Amanda and I have a very exciting show to bring you."

"I don't know about you Cecil, but implications are staggering. Already futures on Wall Street are pointing toward a serious downward trajectory opening. I guarantee you that trading will be halted within the first 30 minutes of the opening bell."

"No doubt Amanda! And let's be real. Is it just a coincidence that the US would invade Egypt on the eve of discovering that an ancient alien spaceship was buried beneath the Great Pyramids?"

"Not only buried Cecil but explodes

out of hiding after at minimum 4,500 years, but more realistically probably thousands of years before that."

"Hold that thought Amanda, we just got Danny Nessli, who produces the weekly podcast, "They are among us". Danny, welcome back to The Cecil Rhodem Show."

"Thanks Cecil. Well, who's paranoid now? I've been saying this for over ten years. They are among us and guess what Cecil? What's three football fields long and hovering over what use to be the Great Pyramids of Egypt? It's a fucking spaceship Cecil and Amanda!"

"This is a family show Danny and while a spaceship in Egypt is beyond exciting. We need to remain professional.", said Amanda.

" Danny, I have two questions. One,

how long do you think that spaceship has been hiding beneath the pyramids? Two, why now? Why now of all times when the US invades Egypt, that they chose now to reveal themselves?"

"Amanda, I can only speculate, but I've being saying it for years. Why build the pyramids to begin with? They truly serve no practical purpose. There are all these theories about the pyramids and their purpose, but do you really need 13 billion pounds of stone to bury a pharaoh? Each block weighs at least two tons. That's 1,764,000 pounds of stone being laid every day for 20 years Amanda. Give me a break Amanda, 13 billion pounds? Give me a shovel and two hours and I will dig you the perfect graveyard. These structures and the Great Wall of China are the only two man-made objects that can be seen from outer space. There must be a reason for that. Amanda, Cecil, I believe the pyramids were built over the spaceship as a means to mark its burial location."

"Come on Danny. Everyone knows the pyramids were built to hide the treasures of the pharaohs?"

"Cecil, I'm going to raise the BS flag on that. What's more plausible. The people of old built a 13-billion-pound structure to hold some dead guy's treasure or the Pyramids of Giza which were once covered in a white casing made of glimmering limestone and so polished that it would reflect the sun's rays was a distress signal for other aliens. The original pyramid before the limestone was removed would act like gigantic mirrors and reflect light so powerful that it would be visible like a shining star from earth. Now let's consider that these aliens have advanced star charts of the universe. Wouldn't it stand to reason that their technology would see this reflection and know it's not a new star and come out and investigate?"

"Well Danny, the fact that there is a spaceship hovering over what used to be the Great Pyramids of Giza lends a lot of credibility to the later theory.", said Amanda.

# # #

Arbatskaya Square was unusually busy at 0300 GMT. Everyone had been called in. The Minister of Defense of the Russian

Federation and General of the Army Sergei Nvgagoski had his entire staff debating what next steps should be. How to respond to this unprecedented series of events. The President made it clear. The US would not be the only ones with access to this advanced technology. The invasion, the discovery of the spaceship was connected and Russian would not be on the outside looking in.

At the end of two hours, plans were drawn up to send the 98th Guards Airborne Division and the 106th Guards Tula Red Banner Order of Kutuzov Airborne Division to Egypt. These divisions would be airlifted and land in the Western Desert of Egypt outside of Cairo utilizing a fleet of An-12 four-engine turboprop transport aircraft. While not ideal for transporting those divisions, it was their best option since they would be landing directly on the desert floor. From there, they would conduct a 40-kilometer force march to the outer edges of the Giza Plateau and await orders on how to confront the American Forces.

# # #

Admiral Zuang Liu Chen, the commander of the Chinese People's Liberation Naval Liaoning Carrier Strike Group, struggled with his orders. The Strike Group was moving at its maximum speed of 32 knots or 36.8 mph. The Liaoning Carrier Strike Group had been underway for one day coming out of the Philippine Sea enroute to the Gulf of Aqaba. At a distance of 6,026 miles, it was going to take the Liaoning Carrier about seven days to arrive on station. He had been ordered to get underway as soon as possible at flank speed leaving his Strike Group to make best speed to arrive afterwards. At their flank speed, they would arrive about a day later. Admiral Chen did not like leaving his escort ships behind. He would be vulnerable and that made him extremely uncomfortable. To make matters worse, heading into a situation that was beyond believable did not help. An alien spaceship was something he struggled with as a human. Being raised on philosophies that did not acknowledge the existence of extraterrestrial life, but orders were orders. Once his Carrier Strike Group was in place, he was ordered to prepare the launch of nuclear tip cruise missiles and destroy the alien spaceship pending final order confirmation.

Hill Flats - Washington, DC

Senator Kelsey Ryles was back in his Hill Flats luxury 1880 brownstone. Kelsey missed the luxury of his apartment. He had been traveling nonstop for the past two months and the events of Egypt only added to an already impossible situation. Sitting in his mid-18th century Italian Armchair, Kelsey poured himself a shot of his prized Macallan 25-Year-Old Fine Oak Highland Single Malt Scotch Whiskey. Kelsey knew what he had to do, but still hesitated until the effects of his prize Macallan took effect. This will be the first time he's spoken to his ex-crew since the mutiny.

After Kelsey finished his third glass of Scotch, he got up from his chair and moved over to his bookshelf. Kelsey adjusted his favorite books in sequential order. First, "The Stars in Their Courses" was moved out at a 30° angle. Next, Kelsey readjusted "Theatrum Orbis Terrarum" to a 10° turn, followed by "Voyage de la corvette l'Astrolabe" to a 90° position. The following 3 books were removed then inserted in rapid succession: "Codex Seraphinianus"; "Le Caucase pittoresque"; and finally, "Mr. Barnes of New York." With the last book sliding back in place, there was an audible click followed by the left side of the bookshelf sliding backward then to the left into a hidden recess. Kelsey then stepped down two flights of stairs, where he passed through multiple layers of enhanced security.

The first was a retina scan followed by a complete handprint analysis. While each of Kelsey's fingers was being scanned and verified, a tiny needle extracted a DNA sample of Kelsey's index finger for analysis. All initial security checks were passed with no issues and a keypad appeared from behind a sliding panel. Kelsey entered his 25-digit alphanumeric code. A green light then illuminated the entranceway, opening the eight-inch-thick titanium door. The final check after entering the correct code was an IR scan measuring for thermal signatures to ensure only one person was about to enter the Sanctuary. Kelsey stood still as he entered the room and greeted the Artificial Intelligence Life Interface (AILI). "Good Evening, AILI."

"Good Evening, Kelsey. Please enter so that I may secure the Sanctuary."

As Kelsey sat in his chair in front of the command console, AILI closed the Sanctuary's titanium doors and the bookcase upstairs. "AILI, have you been monitoring the global events of the past 24 hours?"

"Yes Kelsey. I also have some more bad news. The Alpheratz has already initiated communications with the Sanarian High Command in the Sombrero Galaxy."

"I was afraid of that. AILI, I need you to initiate communications protocols to enable a direct link to the Alpheratz. And please ensure communication protocols are encrypted to prevent them from tracing our location."

"Yes Kelsey."

Two minutes later, Xan'lima appeared on the screen. "Be'lima.", said Xan'lima as the only means of greeting.

"Xan'lima. I see that you have already initiated communications with the Sanarian High Command."

"Did you expect anything else from me?"

"I guess not. You know you have doomed this planet because the Xandurans will trace that signal back to Earth."

"And I care why Be'lima? Nothing has changed. The rest of the crew and I want to go home. If this planet must be consumed in the process, so be it."

"Xan'lima, I am not going to re-litigate what caused our rift within our crew. I am here to offer you a truce. Contrary to your beliefs, I want to go home as well. Soa'limae tampering with this planet's native species and altering their DNA has created unexpected consequences. Over the years, we have repeatedly tried to hinder your efforts to evolve humans any further. We recently discovered that your tampering has significantly altered humans to a point that they are truly hybrid-Sanarians now. As a matter of fact, we think they are actually capable of helping us defeat the Xandurans."

"Be'lima, again you miss the point. All I care about is going home. Our manipulation of this backwater species is only a means to the end. Now that we have achieved that goal, you now try and form a truce. Well, you are too late Be'lima. We don't need your help. Even without the

Matter/Anti-Matter Drive, it's only a matter of time before High Command sends a rescue ship to retrieve us."

"Xan'lima, for once in your life, can you please just shut the fuck up and stop being selfish for just a minute and maybe you will learn something that might actual save our people. There is a reason, I did not try and take the ship back over the years. You are loyal to the Sanarian Empire and like you, I want to go home as well. Do you think it was easy for me to make that decision? I left my family back on our home world. We came to this solar system to find a means to defeat the Xandurans. With the DNA Sequencer, we evolved the humans to something that is greater than the sum of both our species."

"Stop being ridiculous Be'lima. There

is no way these humans are stronger than us."

"I'm going to send you two files and I want you to carefully review it and have Soa'limae analyze the DNA enhancement we made. I'll be standing by while you review the files."

The screen went blank. Kelsey leaned by in his chair and breathed a heavy sigh of relief. "At least he didn't hang up on me immediately.", Kelsey thought.

"AILI, please bring up the latest news as it relates to Egypt."

"Yes Kelsey."

The news was bleak. Russians were landing in the Western Desert. The Chinese were bringing their Liaoning Carrier Strike Group the Gulf of Aqaba. There was civil unrest throughout the world. Looting and food shortages with people hording were just the beginning of this crisis. Church attendance globally was up 1,000-fold. This was Day Two and things were already bad and were only going to get worse if a shooting war started. People were flocking to doomsday cults in record numbers. Kelsey had to quickly deal with the geopolitical ramifications of this news, but without a truce with his old crew it wouldn't matter what he said to the world.

"Sir, incoming transmission from the Alpheratz."

"Put it through AILI."

Xan'lima's face immediately filled the screen with Soa'limae hovering in the background. "You got our attention. What are you proposing?"

Before Be'lima could answer, Soa'limae started shouting rapid fire question after question. Everything from which DNA strains were activated to what were the enhanced limitations of these meta humans or homo superior humans. He commented on the engagement battle in Jackson, Mississippi. His words tumbled over each other as he commented on their speed, strength, enhanced psychic abilities.

"Enough Soa'limae. You'll get your chance to ask more questions later. We need to discuss this so-called truce and what it means.", said Xan'lima.

"Xan'lima, I propose that we finish the mission we started. We go to Jupiter and find the Ja'narans and enlist their help. We help the humans build a ship capable of landing there based on our lessons learned. We then proceed to our Home World and end this war once and for all. In exchange for returning the Matter/ Anti-Matter drive, we start working together and with the local governments of the world to set up DNA enhancement centers in every country. I'm sure we will have to negotiate with them and only promise to enhance their militaries. We will also help them build and organize global planetary defenses. Once these measures are in place and we have recovered the information from the Ja'narans, we will activate the star drive and head home. And when the Xandurans arrive to consume Earth, they will be equipped to defend themselves. Do we have a deal Xan'lima?

"Yes Be'lima. The Empire needs this information and all these years on this planet would be meaningless if we returned home without the Ja'narans' data. As we speak, we are already receiving news of the war throughout the galaxy. While we are not losing, we are definitely not winning. The only way we are able to defeat even one Xandurans Battle Sphere is for us to mass a full squadron of 12 Star Battle Cruisers and even then, it's still not a 100 percent guarantee that we will be victorious. We are losing the war of attrition. Our ships have been given orders to hide vs engaging whenever possible. Because they can track our unique star drive signature, it's only a matter of time before they find and destroy a ship that's been previously spotted. While replenishing the lost ships is manageable. Replenishing our ranks is where we are losing the battle. The Xandurans only need to capture various species and infect them with their organic AI virus and their ranks are easily replenished. So, yes Be'lima. We have a deal."

"Xan'lima, I am concerned about the three armies that will be on top of you in the next 96 hours. If they start fighting to see who gets control over our ship, I'm afraid this could lead to a global war that will destroy all our plans. Unfortunately, China has announced they plan on launching nuclear weapons at our ship. Based on ancient scrolls and legends passed down through the centuries, it was foretold an ancient threat that must be destroyed at all costs. We are that threat, and it is my fault. We wanted a failsafe just in case the crew with me failed to contain you. "Hopefully, when the Matter/Anti-Matter drive arrives, you can get the ship up and running in order to deal with this new threat."

"Captain, don't worry about it. We'll be prepared."

"It's unfortunate that it took this long for us to resolve our differences, but here we are. We have work to do. Good luck Xan'lima!"

With that, the screen went blank again. Inwardly, Be'lima smiled. This was the first time Xan'lima had called him Captain since the mutiny.

# # #

* * *

Col Myers was listening to the Committee giving him a new set of orders. He was briefed about the truce reached between the different factions of the alien crew. The part he didn't like was the orders telling him to meet with Joshua and Trinity and collect the Matter/Anti-Matter drive. After the massacre of his Night Stalkers in Mississippi, he was not inclined to easily forgive them, but crossing the Committee was not an option either. "Ours is not to reason why; ours is but to do and die.", thought Myers. Alfred Lord Tennyson again summed up his sour mood.

"1LT Brennen, get me Joshua and Trinity on comms. You can reach them on this frequency."

Col Myers handed 1LT Brennen a folded sheet of paper. "Yes Sir!"

# # #

"Joshua, can you believe this is almost over? We don't have to look over our shoulders for the Night Stalkers trying to kill us. There is a truce finally among the aliens.", said Trinity.

"I'm afraid Trinity that this is only the beginning. I hate to say this, but I was meditating this morning and I accessed the Akashic Hall of Records. Yes, it’s true the factions of the alien crew are finally together again. Our mini war with the Night Stalkers is over, but I'm afraid we have a much bigger battle ahead of us. I'm afraid that we humans just might destroy each other before the Xandurans can cull our planet for resources. Trinity, as much as we have accomplished, as many near death experiences, I have come through, I'm truly afraid for the fate of the human race."

"Joshua, you've taught me, be in the moment. Don't think about the past, which will cause us to worry. Don't think about the future, which will fill us with anxiety. Learn to be present in this moment. To be in balance with oneself. Learn to be in harmony with all things around us. Learn to be the Peace Warrior. I know we just retrieved Pandora's Box just to hand it back over, but that was the bargaining chip to create the truce. We have to put faith in Senator Ryles that they can defuse the global instability caused by their spaceship emerging."

"You're right Trinity. I guess we all need a kick in the butt from time-to-time. I was just feeling sorry for myself. I was thinking about the future and the impossible task that lies ahead of us. The thought of going to Jupiter and contacting yet another alien species is a lot. As a kid, I wanted to be the first person to land on Mars, but reality set in as I got older and realized being an astronaut might be a bridge too far based on my life choices. Now to have that opportunity is a little overwhelming, but you're right Trinity. We need to get packed and ready to leave for NASA. We have a lot of training ahead of us. Our enhancements will make the odds of survival greater, but we still need to learn everything we can to ensure the success of this mission to save our world."

"Trinity, as much as you are correct about living in the moment, we can't be blind to knowledge from the Akashic records. The Akashic records are a compendium of all universal events, thoughts, words, emotions and intent ever to have occurred in the past, present, or future in terms of all entities and life forms, not just human. Theosophical Society founders: Helena Blavatsky, William Quan Judge and Henry Steel Olcott gave us the basic tools for understanding this universal knowledge. I will eat crow and be in the moment, but understand we have a looming threat to the survival of this planet. The knowledge told me that Jupiter is the only way to find the keys to survival of our planet.

Reaching out to hold Joshua's hand, Trinity tugged his hand until he met her eyes. "Joshua, you saved me when I had no reason to live. You helped bring me back from the abyss. I believe in you, not these aliens. As a team, we have proven there is no obstacle that we can't handle. Again and again, we have faced these crazy challenges and prevailed. This will be no different. Now give me a hug and let's see the other teams off. I can't wait to hear their stories after they experience teleportation for the first time. And you know James McKay will want to challenge you for leadership after they get their enhancements.", laughed Trinity.

They both laughed then headed out to meet the team and say their goodbyes.

Cairo, Egypt

The UN had erupted in a scene of chaos. Everyone was shouting at each other. Angrily pointing fingers at one of three countries, the United States, China and Russia. The Secretary-General of the United Nations, Pierre LaFranso was desperately trying to bring order to the chaos. After about ten minutes of pounding the gavel and with the assistance of security, everyone was finally back in their seats and listing to him.

"Please, let's try this again. Everyone will get their chance to speak, but we must have order! First, I would like the US Ambassador Lynn Benden-McKay to please explain why they invaded Egypt, a sovereign nation."

"Secretary-General LaFranso, I know

these are momentous times and it's easy to believe that there is deception on our part, but US Ambassadors to every country briefed each country and we released global press releases to every news organization. We entered Egypt to stop a potential global conflict. It was in our opinion that if Israel invited Egypt to element the terrorist threat, it would have been the start of a conflict that could easily widen with global ramifications. We did not have time to get the world leaders on our side because our intelligence suggested that Israel was prepared to engage within 72 hours. Never in our wildest dreams could we have envisioned an alien spaceship emerging from beneath the Great Pyramids. But maybe it was divine intervention that we were there. By being in Egypt at this point, there is now a force on the ground that can potentially deal with these aliens if they turn out to be a threat. The United States welcome the international community to participate in helping to contain this alien presence, but understand this, the forces that are moving toward Egypt by Russia and China need to open communications with our forces and join us versus the hostile message that was delivered by China. We don't know what the intentions are of these aliens, but China's warning that they intend to use nuclear weapons to destroy them is unacceptable."

The assembly erupted into a shouting match yet again. Fortunately, the Secretary-General was able to quickly get everyone's attention again. The assembly ended, but the five permanent members of UN Security Council settled in for what was going to be a very contentious meeting. Ambassadors from China, France, Russian Federation, the United Kingdom, and the United States with their translators settled in as the Secretary-General started the meeting.

Secretary-General LaFranso turned to the Chinese Ambassador to address him. "Ambassador Uhani Hung-Jin, the ultimatum you issued to the General Assembly about the use of nuclear weapons on the alien spaceship is unacceptable. You cannot take unilateral action to destroy these aliens."

The France Ambassador Carla de Desnicola immediately interrupted.

"Ambassador Hung-Jin, these aliens could answer questions about who we really are. Where we come from. Advances in technology could save this planet. You have no right to take it upon yourself to destroy them."

Ambassador Hung-Jin finally responded. "Ambassadors, you must understand. These aliens are a global threat. You might not understand our beliefs, but we have prophecies that talk about these days and we have a clear mandate on what we need to do when it happens. Every leader is briefed as they come into office about the threat these ancient aliens pose to our planet. Notice, I did not say aliens from outer space. I said ancient aliens. These aliens literally exploded from underneath the Great Pyramids of Egypt. So don't discount our ancient scrolls."

"Ambassador Hung-Jin, we have troops on the ground there. What about the citizens of Egypt? You will use nuclear weapons and kill innocent civilians?", said Russian Federation Ambassador Alexsei Povalzya.

"Make no mistake Ambassador Alexsei Povalzya. We will take unilateral action. We have given the Russian & US Forces 96 hours to evacuate your forces from the area or perish when we detonate our nuclear weapons.", said Ambassador Hung-Jin

"Ambassador Hung-Jin, do you understand that we will protect our forces and potentially retaliate with nuclear weapons of our own if you attack the alien spaceship?", said US Ambassador Lynn Benden-McKay.

"Ambassador Benden-McKay, we fully understand your potential response, but if you understood the threat these ancient aliens posed, you would understand a global nuclear war is preferable than to subject Earth to the rule of these ancient aliens. You have been warned. You have 96 hours to evacuate the area around Giza or suffer the consequences. We have no intention of harming humans, but make no mistake in 96 hours, we will destroy that ship whether you are still in the area or not." With that Ambassador Hung-Jin, excused himself from the meeting.

# # #

Admiral Zuang Liu Chen and the Liaoning Carrier Strike Group arrived on station in the Gulf of Aqaba and had been conducting overflights air patrols for the past eight hours. In another few hours the escort ships would be on station as well. The orders had been given. As soon as his destroyers were on station, he was to launch two nuclear cruise missiles at the alien spaceship.

# # #

All had gathered in the Presidential Emergency Operations Center (PEOC) standing as President Sartingson entered the PEOC flanked by his Secret Service detail. "Please be seated", said the President after he took his seat at the head of the conference room table.

The President addressed the Chairman

of the Joint Chief of Staff. "General Davis, please tell us how you propose to protect our troops in Egypt and again, I will emphasize that we are not going to entertain a withdrawal now that an alien spaceship has emerged from underneath the Great Pyramids. We will be in control of that technology at all costs."

"Well Sir, the Joint Chiefs of Staff discuss numerous options. We included the CIA and State Department in our planning discussions. Sir, deterrence is unfortunately our only viable option. Short of moving our forces out of harm's way, there is no way to protect them. We do not have any anti-ballistic capabilities in the area that can shoot down China's cruise missiles. And before anyone at this table mentions attacking

China, we did consider that option. Please understand what I'm about to say, attacking China is a losing strategy. While we have the Lincoln Strike Group on station, we don't think this is viable against China's Liaoning Carrier Strike Group. We have already had an incident between the Carriers. Each carrier was flying their routine CAP (Carrier Air Patrol), our planes were F-35s and theirs J-15s. It was a nighttime patrol, and we believe due to the stealth capabilities of the F-35s, a China J-15 literally crashed directly into our F-35. We issued warnings and at the last minute, the planes took evasive maneuvers and it's clear from our E-2 Hawkeye that was flying cover, the Chinese jet turned right vs international standards of veering left that ensures both planes avoid each other. Both pilots were killed instantly Sir. While the carriers are 75 miles away from each other, the carrier air patrols are continuously crossing each other's path. It's only a matter of time before we have a shooting incident. We have strict rules of engagement, but it's only a matter of time Sir."

National Security Advisor, Jim Matsumi spoke up. "General Palmer, I'm struggling with what I am hearing. Are you trying to say that we have lost our global naval superiority?"

"I'm not saying that at all. On paper, we will win the battle, but we will take heavy losses. With only 75 miles of ocean separating the carriers, that's approximately five minutes flight time for our missiles moving at 500 mph. Now multiple that by 130 cruise missiles. While it's true, our multi-layer defense will defeat many these missiles. Between the jamming of their guidance systems, our planes, close-in weapons (CIWS), and decoys/flares, our carrier group will survive. Unfortunately, it takes only one missile to destroy a carrier. Our F35s will defeat their J-15s planes, but you need to understand our strategies are based on having space. Our ships are practically on top of each other in the Gulf. If we initiate the attack, we will have the advantage of surprise and increase the survivability of our carrier group, but it will effectively become defenseless after the attack from a counterattack. That's just the military aspects of attacking. Now I'm going to let Secretary of State, Calvin Murphy discuss the international fallout of attacking a Chinese Carrier Group."

"Sir, we are already on shaky ground globally. While initially, we were ahead of the game because of the man portable nuclear weapon's threat. Most nations accepted the fact we were trying to stop a global war if Israel had attacked, plus we secured the objective with no human lose. With the discovery of the alien spaceship, there are all kinds of conspiracy theories that the United States knew what was about to happen and the whole nuclear threat was a cover-up. World leaders are outraged at China's implicate threat of using nuclear weapons on the alien spaceship, most nations are still in denial that they will follow through. A response on our part would be considered acceptable, but a preemptive strike would turn world opinion against us. It would be the US vs the world and the world includes our allies. Sir that's a battle we would lose."

"So, you are telling me, we have limited options. I find that hard to believe gentlemen."

General Palmer spoke up again. "Sir, even if we deploy the Navy Seals to try and take out Command & Control, there are just too many ships to secure and worst-case scenario the Chinese would still be able to launch hypersonic nuclear tipped cruise missiles. Those, we would not be able to stop. Sir, no matter what we do, they will launch nuclear weapons at the alien spaceship. Any action on our part will only cost both sides people with no benefit. Sir, again our only option is deterrence. Unfortunately, that means we have to put the 82 Airborne Division in harm’s way. Any withdrawal on our part, will in essence green light the strike by the Chinese."

"Sir, we need to get all our allies on board with the deterrence option and pressure the Chinese to stand down or risk a counterstrike by NATO including Russia.", said the Secretary Murphy.

"Okay, let's go with that option and God help our soldiers.

# # #

Admiral Zuang Liu Chen hesitated to give the final order. All sailors in CIC were looking to him. They all heard President Qian give the order to launch. Half the bridge crew was in shock. The other half was still in disbelief about the discovery of aliens.

"Sir!", said Commander Laozi. "Sir, with all due respect why are you hesitating? You need to give the final order. Political Commissar Admiral Jiansu Lee Mansuzi is on the satellite phone with someone. And I bet it's President Qian. If you don't give the order to fire in the next ten seconds, I guarantee you will be dead before 15 seconds are up."

"I know Laozi, but once I give the order there is no turning back and we will potentially start World War III."

"Sir, you have no choice. Admiral Mansuzi just hung up and his hand is reaching toward his pistol."

"Commander Laozi, insert your key. Turn on the count of three. Three, Two, One. Turn."

Admiral Chen then lifted the clear cover on the green fire button. Hesitating for just a moment longer, Admiral Chen pressed the button. The entire ship shuttered as two cruise missiles fired.

"May the heavens protect us Laozi."

# # #

"Sir, Space Force Command, just reported two cruise missiles have just been fired from the Liaoning Carrier.", said General Palmer.

"The 82nd has been alerted. All soldiers are in MOPP 4 gear and hunkered down. They used this waiting period to dig in. Standard fox holes are dug to armpit height. Our soldiers were ordered to dig fox holes to a dept of 8 feet. We are expecting up to 50% casualties either through the direct effects of the blast or residual radiation poisoning."

"Everyone, before I give the order to retaliate, I want final agreement that our actions are an appropriate response to the launch of two nuclear cruise missiles on Egypt.", said the President.

Everyone remained silent before National Security Advisor Jim Matsumi spoke up. "Sir, we warned China. The world warned China there would be severe consequences for launching a strike on the alien spaceship. Sir, we have debated this to the point of ad nauseam. We are in agreement."

"General Palmer, give the order to the Lincoln Strike Group to destroy the Liaoning Carrier Strike Group."

General Palmer picked up the phone and gave the order.

# # #

Rear Admiral Nathan S. Krueler yelled into the microphone, "All ships fire!"

As one, the five Guided-Missile Cruisers: USS Shiloh; USS Princeton; USS Texas; USS California; and the USS Sterett fired all their cruise missiles. Simultaneously as the Guided-Missile Cruisers fired, the six destroyers in Destroyer Squadron 21: USS Fitzgerald; USS John Paul Jones; USS Ingersoll; USS John

Young; USS Ingraham; and the USS Gary fired all their cruise missiles. On his command, 130 cruise missiles were fired at the Liaoning Carrier Group. The Navy Seals had also placed explosives throughout the Liaoning Carrier Group. With the order to fire, those charges also detonated. It was the hope that the Seals would be able to disable enough ships that the Lincoln Strike Group would be able to successfully defend itself.

Looking at Commander Carla Salamina-Bragg, Admiral Krueler whispered, "May God help us, Commander."

# # #

On board the Alpheratz, alarms started blaring. Lucas Jacquot, the Weapons

Officer started rapidly punching in commands. Ped'lima was starting to get used to his old crew members calling him by his Sanarian name. For the past two days minus Be'lima, the entire crew was now back on board the Alpheratz. Although Be'lima's team was not in their original bodies; nevertheless, their human bodies still allowed them to operate the ship.

Xan'lima yelled, "What's going on Ped'lima?"

"Sir, we have massive missiles in the air. Two nuclear missiles are heading to our location with over 100 missiles heading toward the Chinese Carrier Group."

"Ped'lima, release the controls on the AI and have her target all missiles in the air."

"Yes Sir!"

After a few minutes, the ship started to hum. "Maria, I mean Na'limae, power levels are at 85%. I need the levels at 93% to operate the neutron pulse canons and shield generators simultaneously.", said Ped'lima.

"Give me a second Ped'lima. I'm having a few issues calibrating the Matter/Anti-Matter drive back into the Alpheratz."

Na'limae dispatched the other ship's engineer Xi'lima to the power transfer relay station. "Gabriel, hustle. You got 30 seconds to override the fail-safes on the main distribution network relays or else we are dead."

"I'm hear Maria. I need 15 more seconds."

"Done!!!"

Na'limae looked at the power levels.

The levels just topped 95%. "Sir, I'm releasing all controls on the AI. Firing now."

The AI released 232 neutron pulses in the space of five seconds. Xan'lima was pretty sure the neutron pulse cannons would be enough to do the job. Human technology still hadn't advanced enough to be able to protect against neutron irradiation. Once hit, the missiles should experience collision displacement which will have a transmutation and ionization effect on the micro-structure of the missile's hull. Once the hulls lose cohesion integrity, they should crash harmlessly into the sea. The AI fired two sustained five second rounds at the inbound nuclear cruise missiles. Xan'lima knew the missiles would explode and detonate. The AI projected the ship's shield to extend up and over the Giza Plateau. He hoped it would be enough to protect everyone.

# # #

The NSA Director, Tyrone Bryant addressed the President. "Sir, we initially lost all communications and satellite cover of the area due to the EMP caused by the detonation of the two nuclear missiles. Communications coming back online in 25 seconds. We can now confirm that the alien spacecraft is still intact. Reports are coming in from Major General Carl E Parker and Rear Admiral Nathan S. Krueler. General Parker is reporting that the alien spaceship fired some type of laser like cannons then the air started glowing and somehow contained the nuclear explosions. It was obviously some type of shield that they extended over the Giza Plateau. They took some casualties on the extreme of their parameter, but it could have been much. Rear Admiral Krueler reported that all his cruise missiles were destroyed before impact and the Chinese counterattack missiles were destroyed as well.

UN Headquarters - New York City, NY

Ladies and gentlemen, leaders of the world, I know the discovery of aliens living on Earth has thrown the world into chaos. "My name is Senator Kelsey Ryles. My given name Be'lima and I am one of those aliens."

The audience immediately erupted into verbal chaos. It took a few minutes, but Secretary-General Pierre LaFranso was finally able to get the assembly quieted down. "Please continue Senator Ryles."

"We the Sanarians have been on this planet for over 300,000 years. In our fight against our ancient enemy, the Xandurans, we crashed landed on this planet. We were on a mission to find another alien race, that we discovered successfully defeated the Xandurans. It was during our travels that we came across a damaged Xanduran spacecraft and discovered this new species in their ship's database. After years of searching, we finally located the Ja'narans and we attempted to make contact on the planet you call Jupiter. As you know, Jupiter has a very extreme environment. It is simply incompatible with life. Its gravity is 2.4 times that of Earth. If you weighed 230 lbs on Earth, you would weigh 552 lbs on Jupiter. And if that wasn't enough Jupiter's atmospheric pressure is extremely high. The atmosphere of Jupiter is so dense and cold that it behaves as a fluid versus a gas. The atmosphere pressure is five to ten times that of the Earth's atmospheric pressure. Strong winds also dominate Jupiter that range between 225 mph to 1,000 mph and extremely cold temperatures reaching -270 degrees. As our ship was landing, we encountered extreme wind gusts that damaged our ship."

"We managed to escape, and we sought refuge on Earth, the only planet that had the resources to repair our ship. At the time when we crash landed on Earth, the only inhabitants were primitive life forms. Under normal circumstances, our policy is not to interfere in the development of other species, but our mission was of vital importance. We needed help to go back to our home world to get this information to Sanarian High Command."

It had been decided by all parties that it would be better not to reveal the true extent of their inference in human development and the conflict among their crew. They agreed to only focus on the positive and how they helped to evolve the human species.

"We needed to evolve you to your current level of technological advancement to help us repair our ship. We have lived among you from the beginning. I am a clone. My consciousness was downloaded into this body that you see now, so we can blend in. I'm about to introduce you to our Medical Officer Dr. Brenda Calms. She will be in her native body and her name in our native language is Ce'limae. Please remain calm, so we can tell you what you need to know to survive the coming invasion. We are your friends and have been helping mankind from the beginning. Ce'limae, please come out and join me."

As Ce'limae joined Ryles, again the assembly erupted into verbal chaos as each delegate attempted to out shout each other. Seeing aliens on TV was one thing. To actual witness one, was another matter altogether.

# # #

The Cecil Rhodem Show was now live. Cecil Rhodem immediately started speaking. "Amanda, can you believe what we are seeing. An actual alien in real f'ing life. The religious fanatics are going crazy refusing to believe that these aliens are our makers." "Well let me tell you Amanda, they say humans were made in God's image, but these creatures look nothing like us."

Amanda joined in. "Ladies and

gentlemen of our audience, these aliens stand at a little over 6 1/2 feet tall, with a head that was easily 1.5 times larger than an average human's. Their eyes are very slanted with no visible ears present. They have no nose structure, but gill-like protrusions on both sides of their neck. There is something that passes as a mouth, but no lips. They have long arms that extend down to their knees and fingers that are twice the length of a regular sized human's. She is wearing some type of uniform. It is hard to tell the sex of the alien especially since they have no hair. Their skin has a bluish tint. Their eyes are all blue that appeared to glow from some inner light."

"Cecil, I'm beyond speechless. I don't know what to make of any of this."

"Amanda, while the alien is freaking me out. What freaks me out more is the fact they have been walking among us for God knows how long."

"Cecil, I feel we need to re-think our co called definition of God. God is no longer a theoretical mystical figure. God now appears to be blue with a big head.", laughed Amanda.

# # #

The five permanent members of UN Security Council along with Senator Ryles made their way to the UN Security Council Chambers. Dr Calms had been escorted down to a heavily guarded storage room in the basement of the UN. Dr Calms had coordinated the shipping of her the cloning technology to the UN. After about 45 minutes, Dr Calms in her human body joined the five permanent members and Ryles in the security council room. Ambassadors from China, France, Russian Federation, the United Kingdom, and the United States with their translators settled in as the Secretary-General started the meeting.

Secretary-General LaFranso called the meeting to order. "So, let's get started. I'm going to turn the meeting over to Senator Ryles to discuss potential next steps that we need to discuss and vote on."

"Senator."

"Thank you, Secretary-General LaFranso. The way I see it, the world has a host of issues we need to discuss. I know you will have questions, but please can you hold your questions until the end. One: Unfortunately, when the ship was activated, it automatically sent a signal back to our home world and it's only a matter of time before the Xandurans intercept that signal. The Xandurans will eventually come to Earth and reap this planet for all of its resources and convert the survivors with their organic AI virus to increase the Xanduran soldiers' population. To deal with them, we need to help you create planetary defenses and activate dormant DNA to turn them evolve into Homo Superior beings or meta humans. We will need to set up DNA Enhancement centers throughout the world and immediately start this process. Two: We need your help to finish the repairs to our ship. Three: We need to launch a worldwide coordinated media campaign to prepare Earth's population for what's to come. And lastly, we need to help you build a spaceship that will be capable of surviving a trip to Jupiter and landing on its the surface. It’s imperative to resume our original mission to Jupiter to see if we can make contact with the Ja'narans. It's possible they don't still exist, but with their level of technology we must try. Knowledge from the Ja'narans will give us a clear advantage over our enemy."

Ryles & Dr Calms were asked to leave the room after the briefing was over. The members wanted to discuss what they heard so they could make a joint decision. The Permanent Five or Big Five were in awe as they watched the video of Trinity and

Joshua's team in action. The stuff they could do was simply impossible, but they continued to watch.

"I might not believe everything that these aliens have told us, but can you imagine the advancements in technology we will receive by working with them?", said France's Ambassador Desnicola.

"The ability to inspect their ship up close. The advancements in space travel with their help in building a ship capable of going to Jupiter.", said UK's Ambassador Locksee-Nassau

Russian's Ambassador Povalzya immediately launched into the DNA enhancements and making sure no country had an advantage over the other. He then proceeded to outline a proposal where this force would fall under the control of the

UN. Each member nation of the UN with a military force would contribute 25% of their military to go through these enhancements, selecting only the best of their military. The Big Five will form a joint command structure reporting into an Oversight Alien Task Force Committee.

Secretary-General LaFranso ended the meeting. "We have a lot to do, and you have no choice but to get your governments on-board. Things are going to change for us in a way that no one could have perceived. Let's get this right because if we don't, this planet is doomed. Both from the aliens and the internal threats we pose to each other."

# # #

* * *

Reverend Sachel Marres McCullum was making last minute preparations for his live Facebook broadcast. Since the age of six he had been hearing voices in his head. He knew he wasn't crazy or that this wasn't just an imaginary friend like so many other kids his age had. The voice in his head raised him. Instructed him. He now knew that the voice had molded him for this very moment to lead the world toward a new religious order. While he told his parents about the voices and they wrote it off as an imaginary friend, he never told them he secretly believed that the voices were alien in origin. Now without a doubt, he knew where the voices had come from. The voice had never steered him wrong, so he would not start doubting it now and the message he was receiving now.

Sachel Marres, as everyone all called him, came to think of the voice as his Guardian Angel. Sachel Marres' father was a Southern Baptist Minister. He was raised in the church, but even at a young age, he challenged things that were written in the bible. In his soul, Sachel Marres felt there was something more beyond what we could see or hear, but his faith stopped when it conflicted with known science. Sachel Marres would spend his entire summer in the local county library with his best friend studying various scientific topics. During Sunday School one day when the teacher was discussing Adam and Eve, Sachel Marres just couldn't contain himself any longer.

"Ms. Sullivan, I just don't understand. We are told we can't marry our first cousins, but if that's the case, how did Adam and Eve start life on this planet. Cain killed his brother Abel. I must assume Adam and Eve had additional sons and daughters, but that would mean the siblings would have had to procreate with each other. This just doesn't make any sense to me based on genetic diversity." As was always the case, he was told you must have faith and trust in the Lord. Plus, when he got home, he would get an ear full from his father about the bible and how science can't explain everything. Sometimes, you just need to put your faith in the Lord. Unfortunately, Sachel Marres just didn't learn his lessons. His brain simply rebelled at things that were not logical. Another memory popped into his mind when

Ms. Sullivan was talking about the great flood and how Noah's family was the only ones to survive. Archaeologists have uncovered evidence that shows multiple cultures describing a great flood and having survived it. To Sachel Marres that made sense as it would account for diversity of genetic material and the survival of the human race. Again, he was shut down during Sunday School class and reprimanded when he got home.

The voice told him faith is just an excuse to believe in something that you know is not true. Yet on the other hand his father would always preach the following about faith. "Faith is the substance of things hoped for. The presence of things not seen." Regardless of what others believed, Sachel Marres knew what he was doing was necessary and above everything else, the right thing to do.

"Ladies and Gentlemen, who are listening to me from all over the world, this is Reverend Sachel Marres McCullum bringing you this live broadcast from my church in Falls Church, Virginia. Thank you all for joining me today along with your fellow human beings. At this moment, we have over 200,000 people from around the world listening in right now and the number is growing every second. A joyous day has arrived. Without a doubt, the question of whether we are lone in the universe has been answered. For some of us out there, we are finding comfort in this message. To others, this discovery is an existential threat to our religious belief systems. Just earlier today Pope Ardan Pierre IV at mass denounced the aliens as a Hollywood stunt designed to create mass hysteria to drive people away from God. Well, I'm here to tell you we are only at the beginning of journey into the nature of God and our place in this universe. People have postulated we are the center of the universe. We are the only intelligent life in the universe. Well, I think we need to throw everything that we assumed we knew about God out the door. Please understand, I am a God-fearing man, and I am not denying the existence of God. Believing in aliens is not mutually exclusive to believing in God. Genesis 1:27 says, "So God created man in his own image." So, does that mean that the aliens are our God since they created us? Or that our definition of God doesn't exist at all. I'm here to challenge the dogma of religion. We need to open our minds to different possibilities. My father would say "When you know better, do better." He would then quote a scripture James 4:17 "Therefore to him that knoweth to do good, and doeth it not, to him it is sin." We know better now. We know we are not alone in the universe. We now know that the people that created us are an alien species called the Sanarians, but who created them. I say unto you, that God does exist. God is not exclusive to our limited vision. It was once said that Earth is flat. It took a while for people to accept that the Earth was indeed round. We need to stop digging into our dogma and accept that our existence is more complicated than God created Adam and Eve then the Earth was populated. Doesn't it make more sense that God created the universe and seeded life throughout it. Based on our galaxy, the Milky Way, scientists have determined that there are approximately 200 billion trillion stars in the universe. Why would God create all those stars and planets and only populate one lonely planet called Earth? Well, we now know the answer. God didn't."

"I'm going to end the broadcast tonight by saying instead of being afraid and shrinking in the face of the unknown. I am going to ask our fellow sisters and brothers to embrace our alien neighbor and not be afraid. I am going to leave you with a quote from my father. "Faith is the substance of things hoped for. The presence of things not seen." Nothing has changed. I have faith in a higher power. The fact that the aliens had a hand in our development doesn't scare me. How is this any different when our human scientists created Dolly, the first clone sheep? God was responsible for Dolly coming into the world via the technology we were gifted to learn. Good Night my fellow citizens and think about my message and stop fearing the unknown. We didn't have the answers before, but now we are so much smarter about our existence. Go in peace."

Sachel Marres closed the broadcast. The last count was attendance reached 500,000 viewers. Inwardly, Sachel Marres smiled.

# # #

* * *

Damien Sakes Astal had been a conspiracy theorist since his teenage years, moving from one conspiracy to another. He cut his teeth on Roswell and Area 51. He had spent many a night camping out on Campfire Hill overlooking Groom Lake. Damien had sent out a call to arms to his followers on this podcast. Ever since the event in Egypt, his followers were increasing exponentially daily. He had to move his meeting from a small cheap $98 per hour banquet hall in Las Vegas to the Westgate Las Vegas Resort & Casino. One of his close followers and friends suggested if he wanted to be taken seriously, he needed to upgrade his image. At the last tally, over 10,000 said they would come to his meeting. It was decided that the Las Vegas Convention Center would be the ideal location because it had a capacity of 12,500. The Center had one of the largest Sq Ft capacities in Las Vegas at 3,200,000. Normally it would cost about $.35 per Sq Ft. His buddy was able to get the space for $.25 per Sq Ft. It was still going to cost them about $800,000 or $80 per person attending.

On the day of the event Damien was in his element. He used his ten minutes of fame to scare the shit out of the audience. He had managed to get a copy of the spaceship exploding out from beneath the great Pyramids. The audience was stunned. He made the case that the aliens were sowing disinformation, so we would let our guard down. They wanted our guard down, so they could colonize this planet.

Our leaders are blindly falling in line and making nice with the aliens. Damien did not believe there was another race of aliens called the Xandurans. He made it clear that the US has been in contact with the aliens since the 1947 Roswell incident. Furthermore, in 1952, the aliens made a show of force and hovered over Washington, DC to make sure the US got the message loud and clear. "Violate our agreement again and we will destroy you." The governments of the world have been working in conjunction to cover this up since the beginning.

"They have already sold us out. We need to mount resistance to this threat. We cannot go quietly into the night. We must stand and fight. It is our right. It is our duty to mount a resistance campaign against these aliens and we will. This is the first meeting in our fight for Earth and our freedom. We must stand united for Planet Earth!!!"

"United for Planet Earth!"

With that rallying cry, Earth's resistance movement was formed.

END #

Join the Trinity Sage. The journey continues in the third installment with "Trinity - Evolutions".

The journey of Trinity is my way of exposing users to Tai Chi Chuan. Some of the characters are based on real people that I have encountered throughout my life. The characters were then fictionalized. I discuss concepts about Tai Chi Chuan that I have learned over the past twenty-five years of training and teaching. To this day, I still train with my Grandmaster, Sigung Normal Smith of Northern Shaolin Academy located in the King of Prussia area in Pennsylvania.

My meditative practices have helped me to increase my awareness of the capabilities of Tai Chi. Most people do not associate Tai Chi as a viable martial arts. I will tell you the literal translation of Tai Chi Chuan means Supreme

Fist or Grand Ultimate. I use Tai Chi as a martial arts in my daily activities. One of the things that I do when not writing or teaching is to work with autistic clients. I typically work with older and some of the more aggressive clients. Tai Chi Chuan allows me to redirect their energy and restrain them without hurting them.

Concepts like Qi, Tachy Psyche effect or Tachypsychia, and Akashic Hall of Records are real concepts that I have experienced first hand. At the end of the day, I want to expand the practice of Tai Chi to more individuals. As a teacher, I have a major limitation in promoting Tai Chi, myself. I can only teach so many individuals at any given time. My writing is a way to reach a larger audience to help individuals understand their is a better way to live without stress. While Tai Chi is not the answer to everything, but it is a great start to learning how to live a more balanced and healthier lifestyle. Please join me as I continue to expose the unlimited potential of Tai Chi in the Trinity Series. Thank you for joining me. Follow me on my Amazon Author's Page.

https://www.amazon.com/stores/Anthony-T.-Jackson/author/B072LR9G6W?ref=ap_rdr

Trinity - The Awakening: https://a.co/d/2VzPHBb

Made in the USA
Middletown, DE
01 July 2023

34380541R00315